To: Kecki,
I Hope you Enjj
Little Spooy.

Bluebird

By

W.W. Hill

authorHOUSE™

1663 LIBERTY DRIVE, SUITE 200
BLOOMINGTON, INDIANA 47403
(800) 839-8640
WWW.AUTHORHOUSE.COM

© 2005 W.W. Hill. All Rights Reserved.

No part of this book may be reproduced, stored in a retrieval system, or transmitted by any means without the written permission of the author.

First published by AuthorHouse 03/18/05

ISBN: 1-4208-2220-9 (sc)

Library of Congress Control Number: 2005900353

Printed in the United States of America
Bloomington, Indiana

This book is printed on acid-free paper.

Chapter 1

The jolt of the landing gear announcing the arrival of his jet to the Duluth Airport woke him up. The ground was covered with a nine inch coating of snow and when he opened the port window the glare of the sun hurt his eyes.

He had boarded an early flight from Dallas-Fort Worth Airport so that he might make the most of the day with his daughter and her family, he had slept the entire trip and felt sore from the cramped seats in coach. He was in desperate need of a cup of coffee and his first stop when he cleared the gate would be the welcome Starbucks sign.

As he sipped the hot black liquid he glanced up and down the concourse. The Southwest area was fairly empty at 8:20 on a Saturday morning. He located the arrow for baggage claim and started in that direction.

As he moved down the wide walkway he noticed the armed National Guard people that seemed to be ever present.

As he traveled since the 9/11 disaster. It was a real pain in the ass the way the travel habits of normal people had been effected after that attack.

He turned to follow the change in the direction of the baggage claim arrows and stepped onto the down escalator to the ground level area.

As he passed the security check section he saw the lines were getting longer as people were arriving for the flights.

The bag claim area was nearly empty, like the flight north this morning. He tossed the empty cup in a receptacle and turned his attention to the conveyer that had just started moving.

"Good Morning Grandpa." The voice said from behind him.

He turned to see his daughter, her husband and a bundle of blanket, snow sun hat and finally a very small baby girl. His first grandchild, her name was Amy and she came into the world one year ago today. Six pounds two ounces and screaming like a hyena. She was presently getting some sleep having been wrapped warmly by her mother to protect her from the 22-degree weather outside.

He hugged his daughter and Grandchild tightly. "Hello Baby" He kissed his daughters frozen face and pinched her cheeks. "Is it cold outside?"

She smiled brightly "You'd better be ready for it. Did you bring some warm clothes?"

"What you see is what I brought." He turned to shake hands and give his son in law a big hug. "How have you been Kevin?"

"Great Bob, we're running a little late. We got a pretty good snowfall last night and the freeways are still a mess. "Did you have a good flight?"

He turned his attention back to his daughter and dropped his carry on to reach out for Amy. "I don't remember ever leaving DFW, I fell asleep as soon as I sat down." She was light as a feather and was a little longer than the last time he had seen her. His last visit about six months before. "She is really growing."

"We have some teeth, Grandpa" His daughter kidded. "Two on top, and three on the bottom."

The buzzer goes off on the luggage conveyer announcing the arrival of the bags from his flight and he hands the baby back to his daughter. "How many bags did you bring, Dad?" She asked as the conveyor started to fill.

"Just the one and a carry on. If I had anymore I probably would have missed the flight, DFW Security is ridiculous." She could hear the aggravation in his voice. "175, 000 new Federal employees and not one with any manners."

He grinned at her and started towards the belt when he saw his bag. "He looks pretty good." Kevin said to Kathy when his father in law was out of earshot.

"He looks tired." She replied, watching her father reach for his suitcase. "At least he can get two days rest while he's here."

Bob turned to look at his little family, and thought how perfect they looked. They had been married three years and the move to Minnesota had made it hard for him to visit as often as he wanted to. He really missed his daughter and now that Amy was here he felt guilty about not being able to spend more time with her.

"Let me get that." Kevin said, grabbing the bag from his hand and leading the way toward the exit.

"I really missed you." He said leaning over to give his daughter another peck on the cheek. As they moved towards the doors he could feel the air get colder and when they walked out into the sunshine the blast of Minnesota winter hit him in the lungs. "Damn it's cold!"

Kathy laughed and covered the baby's head from the crisp morning air. "The news said it was fifty degrees in Dallas today."

"I carried my coat on, it felt great at home when I left." The air made his nose hurt, he didn't like winter in the Northern states. When he was younger, living in Pennsylvania he didn't seem to mind the long winters, but after moving south in the seventies he did everything he could to stay warm in winter.

The walk to the parking garage was a short one and soon they were in the car heading for town.

"How do you like Duluth?" He asked Kathy, the baby was waking up and starting to fuss.

She glanced at Kevin and he grinned as she started to answer. "I like it a lot more since we moved into the new apartment. No more steps. We have an elevator, and security." She uncovered the baby as the heater in Kevin's Toyota had started to work. "Say hi to Grandpa." She said to the baby as she shifted the covers enough for Bob to see Amy clearly in the car seat behind him.

The child's eyes were bright and she was smiling widely as they turned into the entrance of the gated community the kids called home. The security guard at the gate gave them a careful look and waved them on.

"The place looks nice." Bob said, noticing all the trees and shrubs that had obviously been transplanted to the area.

"This all used to be slums. The city tore down everything and it sat empty for a while. They opened these new homes about three months after we moved up here, but the waiting list was so long for a three bedroom that we just got in two months ago." He turned into the parking garage and used his pass card to open the gate. "Everyone wants to live downtown these days. I think everybody is tired of spending an hour a day in the car."

"Make that close to two hours in Dallas and the Metro Plex." Bob answered. Kevin guided the car to his spot marked 221. "It seems like every city is spending a lot trying to get some life downtown. Downtown Dallas is coming back again and the town houses they're building there are going for high prices."

"Kevin is only ten minutes from the office and he gets to come home for lunch when it's not busy." Kathy was wrapping the baby up again and she was starting to fuss. "Hold on Amy, we'll be home in a minute." Kathy led the way to the elevator room and they started up to the second floor.

Bob was impressed with the kid's choice for an apartment. The place was, of course, new and everything was spotless. The halls and entrance were beautiful and when Kevin opened the door to their apartment the soft beige of the walls gave a warm, welcome home, feel to him as he walked in.

"Give him the tour while I change Amy." Kathy called to Kevin as she started down the hall.

"Right this way to your room" Kevin started in the opposite direction with Bob's bags. The guestroom was off the living room and was a comfortable large room with a private bath. "I hope you like the room. She has been fixing it up for your visit this month."

Bob glanced around the room and saw a small caption of his life in the pictures on the walls and shelves. There were a lot of pictures of his late wife and she looked more beautiful in each one as he looked them over carefully. Kathy was their only child and was very close to her mother. His job or jobs as he came up through the ranks as a reporter had kept him away from home quite a bit and a lot of pictures were of Kathy and her Mom. He wondered what part of the world or the country he might have been in when some of the pictures were taken.

"Do you like the room?" Bob returned to the present and smiled at his son in law.

"It feels better than home!" He put his arm around Kevin's shoulder and held him tight." Show me the rest of the mansion."

They returned to the living room. The room had large windows and the courtyard outside was obviously a beautiful sight during the summer, but it was presently covered with the fresh snow and gave Bob a chill. The dining room connected to the kitchen with a serving counter and he could smell something on the stove that perked his senses.

As he lifted the lid on the large pot on the stove the aroma of homemade spaghetti sauce filled the air of the room and he was suddenly reminded of how hungry he was. "My God that smells good." He rattled the lid and called out to his daughter. "Do I have to wait for the pasta or can I eat this the way it is?"

"You better get out of there, I'll have lunch ready in a half an hour. Don't spoil my surprise." She appeared in the doorway with the baby. She was in a set of pink pajamas and smelled of baby powder as he held his arms out to her.

She seemed to hesitate for a minute, but when she heard his voice, soft and low, she held her arms out to his. As he brought her close to him she went right for his nose. She seemed to really enjoy grabbing him by the schnoz. Down through the years the Budweiser had turned it a bright red and made it quite a centerpiece of his ruddy complected face.

Amy laughed as he tried to get her to turn loose, so he could follow Kevin through the rest of the apartment.

"This is the nursery," Kevin said as he opened the door to a brilliant yellow room with all kinds of Sesame St. characters on the walls. The baby shifted her attention from his nose to point to the faces and make noises that were probably names for the ones she liked.

His daughter's bedroom was a light gray and he recognized the bedroom set he and his wife had given them for a wedding present.

"Your home is beautiful!" He told Kathy when they returned to the kitchen. She was busy getting ready for their meal and the rooms were full of smells that were making his mouth water.

"Thanks Dad" She said taking a second from her work to give him a big hug and a kiss. "It's great to have you here. What do you think of the nursery? I did the faces myself."

"Good job, she was trying to name them for me."

"She watches them in the morning when I am busy and she never makes a sound." She dropped the spaghetti in the pot of boiling water. Did Kevin show you his office?"

"I was saving the mess for last." Kevin laughed as he guided Bob to what looked like a closet door in the hallway. The door opened to a very cramped room that looked more like a storage closet than an office. He wasn't kidding when he called it a mess. Every corner was full of equipment. The workbench in the center was piled high with circuit boards of every size and the shelves that went from ceiling to floor were jammed to overflowing. "What do you think?"

"I admire your sense of neatness and organization" Bob said and they both had a good laugh. "How can you find anything?"

"Sometimes it's hard but things have gotten cramped at the office and I keep bringing things home." He picked up a piece of equipment and looked at it carefully. "It's not like the software racket. You could put your whole life in a briefcase, hardware takes up more space." He shook his head and put the piece back down on the counter making sure it didn't fall on the floor. "You want something to drink?"

"I'm on vacation" Bob started back towards the kitchen. "I'll take a beer."

"Do you miss Microsoft?" Bob saw his daughter glance at Kevin as he thought before answering.

"I miss the stability. I miss being in Dallas and being able to go out without bundling up like an Eskimo during nine months of the year." He opened the bottle, poured and handed Bob the glass of cold beer. "I don't miss the way the office was when things began to slow down in 2000."

Kevin pulled out a chair at the dining table for his father in law and got a bottle of juice from the fridge. He took Amy and put her in her high chair so Bob could drink his beer. "These people have given me a unique opportunity and with my background in software the sky is the limit."

"You sound like you are happy in your work! What are you working on now?"

"You know how everyone is security minded since 9/11 and how more and more people are getting involved with passenger protection."

"Do I ever" Bob complained sipping his beer. "They turned my bags inside out in Dallas and it took an extra hour to get through the checks. They really seem to be overdoing it."

"I know what you mean but they are at a loss for any other options. People are demanding security. The airlines are facing monstrous lawsuits. The government's face is red for being caught with its pants down. The terrorists are holding all the cards." Kevin paused and took a sip of juice. "Holding all the cards up until now. I am working on a project that will have multiple applications, but will be a major set back for any established individual or organization who has been using our free and open society against us."

"Are you talking shop?" Kathy called from the kitchen.

"Sounds interesting, tell me more." Bob leaned forward, tickled Amy on the neck and continued listening to Kevin.

"Have you heard of computerized Facial Recognition?"

"A little bit." Bob thought, "They tried to use it in Tampa, Florida and Atlanta, Georgia and the ACLU had a field day with it, calling it a violation of our first amendment rights."

"Correct. The police departments there decided to discontinue the programs rather than get into drawn out battles about its legality." Kevin seemed to get very serious. "My company is being given an opportunity to demonstrate our systems in Canada. This is all pretty hush, hush now."

"Why is Canada so interested in this type of system?" Bob's curiosity was beginning to show. He had been with the Dallas Evening News for the last ten years, making a good living as an investigative reporter. He had a good reputation in the field for being honest and tenacious. People didn't mind talking to him because they knew that, off the record, still meant something to him and he respected the privacy of individuals. "They don't have an overwhelming crime problem up there."

"They took a lot of flak after 9/11 about how easy it is for anyone to cross from Europe or Asia through Canada into the U.S. Our 3500 mile border is one of the easiest to cross undetected. They have an increasing drug and gang problem developing and they plan to take steps to nip it in the bud."

Kathy began to serve the meal. Bob was starving and the first bite of homemade garlic bread seemed to melt in his mouth. "Great Baby. This hits the spot." He took a bite of the homemade sauce and asked. "I know they don't have the ACLU up there, but they have organizations that can be almost as big a pain in the ass for the authorities if they want to.

"The general sentiment up there is one of solidarity on the offensive front against terrorist organizations whether they be foreign or internal." Kevin took a bite of salad. "The food is great." He complemented Kathy as she sat to begin feeding Amy and start on her own meal.

"Thank you Mr. Security expert. Can't we talk about something else at the table? You can e-mail Dad from Canada about this next week."

"You're going to Canada?" Bob asked surprised.

"I start to set up our first demonstration next week. I'll be up there for two weeks." He looked over at Kathy and she glanced back at him with an odd look. "Maybe less than two weeks if everything goes okay."

Bob felt the awkwardness at the table. "At least your family will be safe in the new apartment while you're gone." He patted Kathy's hand. "This place seems pretty secure."

"I'll be okay, Dad, I just wish he didn't have to go." She smiled at Kevin.

"It should only take a day or two to set up and get all our links together. The actual demo will take a day and the screening and result presentation should take two days at tops." Making an attempt to put Kathy at ease.

"Where are you going to do all this?" Bob asked trying to keep the conversation going.

"A little town called Dauphin."

"Is that near Toronto?" I don't remember that name." Bob had done a lot of work in Toronto and Ottawa on some political stories during Mulrooney's Administration.

"No, it's in Manitoba." Kevin replied.

"Manitoba," Bob could not help but grin. "Where the hell is Manitoba?"

"It's a little town in the Western part of the Province. The town has two major parks and game reserves surrounding it, which creates part of the main reason for the demo."

"How does that create a need for a Facial Recognition System?" Bob's curiosity was peaking and his daughter began to smile.

"Looks like the blood hound is trying to pick up the scent."

He smiled at his daughter. "Old habits are hard to break."

"This area has a lot of problems with poachers. It is a fairly secluded area. Not really backwards, but the people live pretty simply and the people in Ottawa thought it might be a good place to start."

"They're going to spend all this money to catch a few poachers?" The idea didn't seem practical to Bob."

"Not really." Kevin put his napkin down and took a breath to start to get his point across. "Canada is a lot tougher on criminals than we are. They prosecute at the drop of a hat and in a number of instances they have found that criminals will leave one Province and move on to another to avoid being caught by the same authorities. It is easy to go from Province to Province up there, just like it's easy to go from State to State down here."

"There are a lot of private cabins and summer homes near the State Parks and Preserves and the number of break-ins, burglary and property thefts are beginning to rise. They feel if they can catch the poachers they might also be arresting the people who are doing the other crimes in the same general area." Kevin took another bite of spaghetti.

"How will you identify those people in order to apprehend them?" Bob asked, now finishing eating and intensely listening to Kevin.

"In a lot of instances people have pawned articles or sold items that have been later proven to be stolen. A lot of the shops or stores have video cameras and surveillance tapes. Pictures of possible offenders have been recovered from those tapes and we will be able to match those to anyone who might come into view of our cameras."

"That seems like a stretch, in a town that small in Manitoba."

"True, but when you take into consideration these facts, Canada has its version of our FBI and CIA. The Royal Canadian Mounted Police do most of the major crime investigation. Add to this all local, city and Provincial Police, Department of Transportation and Immigration offices and you have one of the most thoroughly informed law enforcement organizations in the world." Kevin leaned back, completely pleased with his presentation.

"Why do you say they are that well organized?"

"One computer system. One major information bank. All agencies from the intelligence community to the local Constable on the beat are linked to the same system with a complete and now restricted sharing of information.

"No top secret files?" Bob queried "No hidden juvenile records?"

"None!" Kevin stepped up his pitch. "In order to access and utilize the Canadian system any and all law enforcement or investigative agencies must agree and comply with a complete free and open exchange of data. No secrets."

"What about National Security issues? Surely the CIA isn't going to open its books to the world! What would happen to our people overseas?"

"This just pertains to criminals. People, who have been booked, charged, interrogated, tried, convicted, incarcerated or punished for crimes. Be they big or small. Misdemeanor or felony. Corporate or civil. State County, State Federal, Provincial, they will all be there." Kevin was pleased and smiled at his wife who smiled back knowing how involved her husband was and how much he believed in his system.

"Are any other countries involved?" Bob was trying to digest how important this system could be as a tool in world wide crime fighting.

"Nearly every country in the world. With our links through Interpol-Scotland Yard- the U.S. NCIC and Canadian RCMP and the Soviet Unions up and coming technology, if a person was photographed in the Ukraine trying to buy plutonium and is later scanned by one of our cameras in Seattle trying to clear customs with a French passport we will be able to know and have a definite match in a matter of minutes."

"That is a long way from Dauphin, Manitoba my boy. I can see how phenomenal this system could be but what has this got to do with poachers in Dauphin?"

"We have to start somewhere." Kevin started. "We have to show a practical application in an area in a Province in a Country that wants to take a strong stand against crime and criminals. Canada has seen a fifteen-percent increase in violent crimes in the last two years. They want to stop it before it starts to become the monetary stone around the neck of every Law Enforcement Agency in the Country. They see what a cash problem it has become in the U.S. and don't want to follow in our footsteps."

"Law enforcement, security, criminal courts, prisons and rehabilitation consumes sixteen percent of the budget. That's a number you won't get from the house, the senate or the Whitehouse, but that is what crime costs the people in the USA. I didn't add the money we are spending to try and fight a loosing battle on drugs through Mexico, Central and South America. No one knows how much money is spent there. There is no way to add it up." He took a breath and leaned back in his chair.

"Ready to get down off the soap box?" Kathy asked with a glance first at Kevin and then to her Dad. "Let's go into the living room."

Kevin was in a hurry to continue. "If we can show results in a rural fairly unprotected area the Government feels it will be able to slowly activate the system in more populous areas without serious repercussions due to the success in the early tests."

"This thing works like a scanner?"

"Basically, only the applications are enhanced by the software. In the past, mug shots or security cameras were on film or tape, but since 1998 anyone who has been booked has their picture taken with digital cameras. Most have a much higher definition and the clarity is what makes this system so special. In addition to facial recognition our software zeros in on the eyes."

"Your eyes are like a fingerprint, the cornea is never the same in two people. It changes a little bit with age but the software even allows for a little alteration, because of retinal or cornea deterioration or damage and is still capable of a ninety nine percent accurate identification in the case where digital cameras were used in the original booking photo or surveillance observations."

"You feel that the system is accurate enough to hold up in a court of law if it is put to the test?" Bob was getting interested in the application that could be available for such a system.

"We have been quietly testing this system with up grades in software for the last six months. I have a ninety seven percent rating on the system, if it even suspects it might be wrong my system goes back, double and triple checks itself before giving a decision."

"This will give law enforcement quite an effective weapon against career criminals." Bob nodded his approval to his Son in Law. He knew this young man was smart but this was a system that could change the way law enforcement spent valuable time investigating crime.

"Not only career criminals but first time offenders. If a young man robs a convenience store and he has a driver's license his picture is on file and a simple scan of the security camera tape will be enough for a positive identification."

"Sounds a little like big brother is watching a little too closely." Bob tried to inject a little reality.

"I know what you mean but if he had been watching or had been able to watch a little more closely we might still have the World Trade Center Towers standing."

"I sure can't argue with that concept." Bob had seen so much corruption throughout the system in his twenty-four years as a reporter that he knew what too much power or information could do if it was in the wrong hands. "Everyone's lives changed when those four planes were hijacked and I guess things will never be like they were before."

"All the information in the world is as good as the person or organizations that acquire or control it. I feel that Canada, with their wish to secure their coastal and international borders in this state of siege from the outside will be a great place to start." Kevin got up and headed for the kitchen. "Can I get you another beer Bob?"

"Sure, I'll take one." Bob replied, now rocking Amy in an overstuffed chair, he looked at his daughter. "He really knows his stuff!"

"Thank you, Dad. Is she asleep yet?"

"She sure is, but let her be for a while, this feels really good." He continued to rock and she continued to smile at him.

As Kevin walked back into the living room, Kathy spoke up, "No more business talk." Then to her Dad. "How's the house, Dad?"

He laughed softly. "The backyard looks like it's barren."

"You never were much of an outdoor person, Dad." Her thoughts went back to her time at home.

"Your mother had the green thumb. I can't get interested in the yard. My schedule is so bad I never know when I'm going to be home."

"I thought you were staying home more now, Bob?" Kevin asked.

"I thought I was too. They put me on a desk where I take care of more local stuff, but it seems like all the local stuff has connections somewhere else that needs looking into."

"I just finished a series of articles on zoning irregularities. Several council members seemed to be involved. Seems a large development corporation was spreading money around, a lot of money. The corporation was based in Phoenix, Arizona and seemed to have an unlimited source of cash. I spent a week in Arizona digging around and found that most of the business was transacted over the phone from Columbia and Brazil. They wanted me to go down there for a month to see how deep I could get into the story, but I have a feeling I would have ended up about six feet deep in the ground."

"The story still had a good ending. We saved a few older homes and the eminent domain boys were kept in check for a while, but you can't keep progress in check forever."

That evening they laughed, played with Amy and talked about old times. Bob was interested in Kevin's work and planned to find out more about his system, but tomorrow was another day.

He fell asleep looking at his wife's picture on the wall, thinking of her working in the garden and how beautiful his home used to be before she died.

After a quick breakfast and about an hour of playing on the living room rug with Amy, Kathy announced they were taking Bob for a ride so that Kevin could show off his office.

The snow had melted a bit and the streets were still a mess, but the traffic was light and the office was only a short drive away. The building was an unimpressive three-story brick structure with very few windows. There was only a narrow door in front. Kevin used his pass card to get in the first door and once everyone was in, the door closed. He used his card and a code number on the keypad to gain access to the lobby.

"Good Morning, Mr. Bennett." The guard said glancing at Bob and recognizing Kathy and Amy.

"Good Morning Ed." Kevin replied signing in on the register. "I'm showing my father in law my office. Ed, this is Bob Shroud." Bob and Ed shook hands. "Anyone else coming in today?"

"Nice to meet you, Mr. Shroud. Mr. Lyons gave me a heads up to look for two technicians coming in from Minneapolis, but no one has showed up yet." Ed logged in some numbers and checked his watch. "Go ahead up."

Kevin had to use the keypad to enter the elevator, and his pass card to get the elevator to move.

"This seems to be a pretty secure location." Bob observed as the elevator started to move and Amy started to laugh.

"We control a lot of data and the information in this building could be dangerous if it got into the wrong hands." The door opened on the third floor and in front of them was a glass room with a very impressive computer system.

Bob had seen a few computer rooms in his travels and this was one of the most elaborate. There were cameras everywhere. It consumed the entire third floor. There were no windows just computers. "Quite a set up." He said as Kevin beamed.

"Bob, this is one of the fastest super computers in the world. Our main office in Minneapolis draws from this unit. From this desk," He said, pointing to a counter full of screens and keyboards. "I can access information on anyone who has ever had or applied for credit. Ever purchased a car, home, washer, dryer, or lawn mower. Basically any purchase in the last eight to ten years, that was over three hundred dollars. All the major and minor retailers keep records on purchases and use that information for marketing."

"Their marketing departments report and sometimes sell that information to the four major credit reporting agencies and we are linked directly to their computer system."

"This computer breaks down the information from regional to an individual basis. It combines any information on a single person, credit, drivers license, IRS, NCIC, FBI, you name it and it puts it all together, assigns the individual a number when you access that person by scan, name, number, picture, alias and bingo, a complete history and profile."

"Through gasoline credit card purchase, we can normally pin point a person's location within three or four minutes.

"This is really scary." Bob didn't want to burst Kevin's bubble, but he was wary of the implications that the system could have. "I thought you said you would be able to hook up with the American Law Enforcement computer system in the future, but you say you are linked up now."

"Sort of." Kevin sensed the tone in Bob's voice and toned down his presentation. "We are linked to the Canadian Immigration and Criminal Systems and they have separate operational agreements with all the American counterparts."

"The problem in the States is that every agency has a different system. No one shares information. No two computer systems talk the same language to each other. There is so much duplication, but no cooperation. Even with the solidification of the people, since 9/11 the law enforcement organizations still don't interface their information. If one requests specific info on a suspect it still takes a lot of hassle and red tape to get the job done."

"In our system even tips or suspected covert or suspicious activity would be added to the individual's profile. When the computer detects a pattern that seems odd or illegal it kicks out that individuals name and the authorities can cut down on wasted time chasing leads and go directly to the source."

Bob could see the logic and practical application, but he still had the nagging feeling of the government looking over his shoulder. He had had that feeling before and didn't like it.

Amy was fascinated by the lights and the noise from the computer and was having a time glancing from machine to machine as they blinked and clicked doing their job.

"We just used the back door to get in the house." Kevin paused and felt better when he saw Bob start to smile a little. "They are all so worried about someone breaking into their systems that they spend all their security applications keeping people out. Once you are inside there is nothing to keep you from free and easy access to everything. That's where my software background and applications go to work."

"Very impressive, but still scary." Bob realized he had Kevin nervous and wanted to change the subject a bit. "When are you headed to Canada?"

"The day after you go back. I'll be taking the company van up. It's a full days drive and I figure I'll loose three or four hours at customs because of the equipment I'm taking up. Some of the pieces I use are foreign made so the paperwork will be a pain. I plan on spending all day tomorrow getting paperwork ready and talking with the broker in Canada."

"Well, I hope you have a safe, productive trip and that everything works well up there." The baby had grown tired of the lights she couldn't play with and was getting grouchy. "We better go, she sounds like it's dinner time."

"Do you want anything from Canada, Bob, Cuban cigars, anything?" Kevin was kidding as they went down on the elevator.

"You better be careful or you'll end up as an entry on your own computer as a smuggler." Bob joked and then thought. "If the deal goes through, I'll take a bottle of good Canadian whiskey and we'll crack it open when I get up here next time." He patted Kevin on the back.

"I still don't drink, but I'll match you ounce for ounce with orange juice." The elevator passed the lobby level and went down another floor, as it thumped to a halt, Kevin picked up the intercom phone and called Ed. "Ed this is Kevin, we're going out through the garage."

"Yes, Sir, I'll log you out." The speaker squawked out loudly. "Have a good day and I'll see you tomorrow."

The garage area was well lit and had about twenty-five spaces and lots of wire fence around the security pass points, Kevin had to use his card and pass code twice before they reached the door. "I'll be taking that one up to Dauphin." He said pointing to a large Ford Econoline Van. "It has four wheel drive and it may come in handy." The van looked large and the oversized tires made it sit high.

"Looks like you'll have plenty of cargo space." Bob said as Kevin used his pass code to open the oversized door and let the sunlight flood the area.

The door opened to a wide alley with more fencing on both sides and they walked down to the street where they had parked. "That place looks like Fort Knox." Bob observed more cameras on the roof and sidewalls that seemed to cover every foot of the surrounding area.

"Well covered." Kevin said as he strapped Amy into the car seat and closed the door. "The other security guard can probably tell you what you had for breakfast by the smell of your breath." He laughed a bit as he got in and closed the door.

"The other guard?" Bob quizzed.

"There is a secure room on the second floor that handles all surveillance, Ed is just window dressing."

Kevin winked at Bob as he started the car back to the street leading home.

Back at the apartment Kathy put Amy down for a nap and started dinner. Bob walked into the kitchen and hugged his daughter from behind. "I love you." He said into her ear. "We can go out for dinner, my treat, you don't have to cook."

"I wouldn't think of it." She turned to give him a hug and a kiss. "I love cooking for you. I put a roast in before we left and it should be done in a little while."

Bob sat down at the counter and watched his daughter putting the meal together. She knew her way around the kitchen. Her mother taught her well. He tried to think of meals they had shared and realized it had not been enough. "Kevin really likes his work, doesn't he?"

"He sure does." She answered over her shoulder. "He's in his hole now doing something. He'll be out in a minute."

"The stuff he's working on is pretty important. Do you two get a lot of time?" Bob wasn't trying to pry but he couldn't help it.

"Yes, Dad, we do." She said. "He brings a lot of stuff home and gets to do quite a bit from here. He had a special line installed and has a link right from his workshop. He can access that electronic marvel from my coat closet." She seemed to find that quite funny.

Bob noticed the computer on the kitchen counter, complete with camera. "Does he use that to work on?"

"No that's just for me to talk to him and let the baby see him during the day. We talk ten or twenty times a day. He's always checking in with us when he's gone."

She looked at the computer for a few seconds. "That is my link to the world. I'm pretty much a home body."

"Are you happy Baby?" Bob thought he heard a not of despair in her voice.

"I'm doing okay, Dad. This project has a lot of our future riding on it and Kevin has really been busy." She moved things around on the stove. "Once this presentation is through we will get some time off and the pressure will be lifted off his shoulders a bit."

"He's really wrapped up in it, isn't he?"

"His software designs will be worth a fortune if this goes through. All the hard work will finally pay off." She smiled at her Dad. "I think I will be able to handle being rich quite well."

"What's this about being rich?" Kevin entered the room and got Bob a beer from the fridge.

"She's already spending your next years salary." Bob joked as Kevin gave her a kiss and took a bite of whatever she had on the stove. "I like the idea of the computer and the camera."

"We see each other all day long. I even have a laptop set up with a special cord so that we can gab when I'm traveling."

"What did we do before we had computers?" Bob had a bit of joking sarcasm in his voice and the kids laughed.

Dinner tasted like one of his wife's meals. He ate too much and halfway through the meal Kathy started telling stories that had them laughing, Amy didn't know what was going on but her belly was full and she joined in.

Bob didn't want to go to bed but he finally excused himself, kissed the girls and headed for his room. He was going to take the early flight back and had to change planes in Minneapolis.

Chapter 2

The morning came too soon and he didn't feel like leaving. Kathy had coffee ready and he sipped the cup as he headed for the nursery to kiss Amy goodbye. She was cuddled up in a ball but her face was pointed towards him and he kissed her softly on the cheek. "I love you," he told her and turned to see his daughter smiling at him from the doorway. "I love you too and I promise I'll make the time between this visit and the next much shorter," they hugged tightly.

"I'll miss you dad!" She said with a few tears starting to gather in the corner of her eyes. "I hope to see you soon." She kissed him and held him tight.

"You can bet on it" he was choking up, "take care of my granddaughter" he kissed her forehead as Kevin entered the hallway.

"I have the car warmed-up," he said grabbing Bob's bag.

"Bless you my son for taking care of my warm blooded body." Bob chuckled never letting go of Kathy as they walked down the hall.

He stopped in the hallway and opened the door to the workshop but was a little surprised to see it full of coats. He pulled his jacket off the hanger and put it on as Kevin came around the corner with a small brown bag, "Kathy made a roast beef sandwich for later. She said you really liked them."

"This will be greatly appreciated somewhere over Iowa," he said tucking it in his jacket pocket.

They hugged again, "take care dad and call me when you land in Dallas, I love you."

"Thanks for the hospitality. You have a great house, and I really liked the room. Be safe." With a final kiss he turned to follow Kevin down the hall to the elevator.

The ride to the airport was a quick one and there was a lot of traffic. "A lot of people going to work," Kevin volunteered as they neared the airport exit. "I'll be in the thick of it when I start back into town."

"Kevin, I really had a good time. You kids seem to be doing pretty well," bob said as they took the departing flight lane. "I hope things go well in Canada. Be careful on the trip and good luck with the presentation." As they stopped at the curbside, Kevin started to get out. "Sit tight Kevin I can get the bags and they look pretty busy." He got out and grabbed the bags from the back seat. He set them on the curb and reached in to shake Kevin's hand. "Take care son, if you need anything call."

"I will Bob. Thanks for coming and I promise I'll have more free time when this thing goes thru." He shook Bob's hand tightly.

As he pulled away from the curb he watched Bob start into the airport and hoped he knew how much he admired him. He was the father he never had. Kevin's father died in an accident when he was six and his mother was both mom and dad until he met Kathy in high school. He and Bob had become quite close when he and Kathy went to college together and decided to tie the knot. He really wanted to show him that he could be a great success and if this system took hold he could basically write his own ticket. There was a lot riding on the next few weeks. He pulled his recorder from his pocket and hit the record button. "Be sure to buy Bob a bottle of the best Canadian whiskey."

The rest of the day was spent inventorying the items and packing them in the van before the trip.

Kevin didn't know much about customs and the requirements. He had contacted a broker in Winnipeg, Manitoba and they had sent him the forms to fill out and the instructions for making out his commercial invoice. Since there actually was no sale involved it was pretty simple. The hard part was making out all the U.S. export declarations so he could get everything back across to the U.S. when he was through. The point of origin papers for item's manufactured outside of the U.S. were the biggest pain in the ass but Kevin had a secretary to do all the typing and that helped on the time involved.

They were through with all the hardware and were listing all the loose miscellaneous pieces when Alan came down to the garage area. "Are you taking the whole building?" He asked with a grin.

"Just about. I hope they don't charge me by the pound." Kevin was counting the boxes of blank disks he was taking, "I think I have everything I need. I don't know if there is a computer store in Dauphin."

"I'm sure there is something up there. If not call and I'll overnight it to you," Alan volunteered. "Mary, when you finish with Kevin I could use your help up stairs, have a good trip Kevin and good luck. We're all counting on you!"

"Cross your fingers for me and make sure you keep my dedicated line open. If I have any problems I'll use our satellite link but I would really rather not count on that." He smiled, "too many ears!"

Alan was starting to the door, "be careful and scream if you need us, we'll be waiting for your feed."

Kevin went back to the final pieces and turned to Mary, "you can split if you want. I'll finish this up then you can type up all the inventory and make a pile of copies. The broker said four of each. We'll keep them happy. Make sure I have five or six copies of that introduction and clearance letter we got from immigration dept. I think that will make it easier on the trip across the border when they know we're working for them." He thought for a minute, "I'm going home and drop off my car. I'll get Kathy to bring me back and I'll leave at about six tonight."

"Are you going to drive all night?" She asked concerned.

"I want to cross the border first thing in the morning. I don't know how long it will take and it's a full days drive from there to Dauphin, I'm not too comfortable with all this stuff in the van."

"The alarm works," she said kiddingly.

He counted the extra cables and listed them on the inventory. "That's the last of it. I'm outta here. E-mail me copies of everything and I'll fax it to the broker later today."

"Okay" she said placing the last carton in the van and locking the back door. "See you later."

Kevin headed home thinking about any loose ends he needed to tie-up before he left. He had covered all the bases. He stopped at a small flower shop and bought Kathy some fresh cut flowers and picked up a small teddy bear for Amy.

She met him at the door with the baby in her arms. Both the bear and the flowers were a hit. "I packed every warm piece of clothes I could find." She told him as she put the flowers in a vase with fresh water. Amy was trying to eat the ears off the bear. "I hope you don't catch cold."

"Don't worry honey," he reassured her tickling Amy. "I'll have two or three people up there to help me with the outside installation and I can stick to the inside stuff. What can I bring you back?"

"Just you," she said placing the vase on the table and hugging him around the neck. "Just you" she kissed his head.

"I have a little faxing to do, I'll be out in a few minutes," he said starting down the hall. He opened the closest doors exposing all the coats hanging and touched the switch behind the door frame. "Did you get a look at your dads face when he saw the closet?" He smiled over his shoulder at her.

"That was mean. You should have explained that room to him." She wondered what her father thought when he looked in and saw no workroom.

"I'm sure he figured it out. With his background and training he probably put two and two together when he was in here on Saturday."

He downloaded and printed the papers from Mary and faxed copies to his broker in Winnipeg. They e-mailed him back that they would have documents at Canadian Customs for him in the morning and to be safe on the trip.

He loaded his bags in the trunk of the car and went back up stairs to get the girls. "I'll get you all the important numbers as soon as I get checked in, in Dauphin."

"Call me every couple of hours while you're on the road. Are you sure your cell phone will work up there?" Her voice was getting more concerned as she knew it was getting closer to his leaving.

"I'm going to Canada, not the North Pole." He hugged her and zipped the jacket up close to Amy's neck and picked her up. "Come on girl, send your daddy off to the cold, cold north." They started down the hall and he glanced around to make sure he had everything, "Let's go!"

The trip to the office was a quiet one. She was used to him having to travel but usually it was only for a day or two and never by car for nearly two weeks. "Please be careful" she reached over and squeezed his hand.

"I intend to. Don't worry. Just say a prayer the system works and maybe I won't have to go out like this again." He thought about how important this was for their future. "Think positive and pick out a nice white Mercedes."

They laughed as he pulled up to the garage entrance and removed his bags. He opened the over head doors and took the bags inside. She was standing by the car when he returned. He leaned in the back seat and kissed Amy who had fallen asleep as soon as they left. She was still holding the bear. "I love you both" He held her tight and she pulled at his hair. "Ow!"

"You better hurry back" she kissed him and brushed away a few tears. "We'll miss you. Be careful and call," with that she got in the car and headed down the alley waving back at Kevin who was standing in the alley hoping everything would go well.

It took him about an hour to make sure he had all his paper work and say his good-byes at work. They all wished him well and he was off. It felt good to finally be headed out. The evening sun was going down as he drove Northwest from Duluth on what he knew was going to be the most important trip of his life.

He drove most of the night and arrived at Noyes as the sun was coming up. He had slept a few hours in Crankston leaning over the wheel. The sleep helped but he was so excited about the trip that he could have done without it.

He had called Kathy a couple times early in the morning but choose not to wake her up during the night. She was glad to hear his voice in the morning and they hung up just as he pulled up to U.S. Customs.

He dropped off a few papers and his export declaration. They stamped and signed his copies and sent him over to the Canadian side.

Canadian Customs looked at his papers and sent him to Canadian immigration. He presented his letters to the agent and they went back in the office. In a couple of minutes a man came out, not in a normal uniform but in a suit and tie. He presented his card and extended his hand. "Mr. Bennett, it is a pleasure to meet you." His smile was broad. "My name is Michael Witham and my superiors said I should help you in any way I can."

The man had huge hands and a grip like a bear. "Happy to meet you Mr. Witham. I appreciate the offer of help. I'm just passing through here but if you'd like to come with me to Dauphin there'll be plenty to do."

They both laughed. "Can't leave my post but you'll be close to some of the best ice fishing in Canada and I hope you get to take a day to enjoy some of it." He had Kevin by the arm and was leading him back to Customs with a brown large envelope in his arm. "I'm going to get you passed through Customs as quick as possible and you can be on your way."

The Customs people who were very pleasant before snapped to attention when they walked into the office. Michael told Kevin to wait and went into an office behind the desk. He returned with another man in Customs Blues and what looked like oak leaves on his shoulders. Kevin thought he was an officer.

"This is Mr. Kevin Bennett," he said introducing Kevin first. The officer extended his hand. "Mr. Bennett is doing some work for the ministry of immigration and would appreciate your help getting him on his way."

"Nice to meet you Mr. Bennett, my name is Philip Chiles. I manage the post. I received a packet from your broker. And I believe everything is in order. If I might have your paperwork I will only take a few minutes of your time."

"Thank you," Kevin said extending the large packet of papers he had brought with him.

"I'm leaving you in capable hands Mr. Bennett," Michael said as he shook Kevin's hand. "If I can be of help in any way please don't hesitate to call and good luck in Dauphin. I wasn't kidding about that ice fishing," he said as he walked out the door.

"Thank you," Kevin said as he thought about how cold it probably was on the lake in Manitoba in the middle of March.

It was only a few minutes before Mr. Chiles returned with his papers. "Everything is in order Mr. Bennett." He handed Kevin a larger pile than Kevin had given him. "You may proceed. Be sure to check in with your broker to let him know you have cleared and please be sure to check in with us as you leave the country so we can cancel these bonds."

"Thank you for your help."

"You're welcome, have a safe trip." The Customs man turned and was back in his office in a matter of seconds.

As Kevin walked back to his car he noticed the long line at the U.S. Customs entrance. The security had really been increased since 9/11 and it took a lot longer to cross into the U.S. He was surprised how easy it was and knew the letters from Ottawa had a lot to do with it.

The air was cold and a wind from the North was making it seem colder. Kevin was glad to be headed away from the port of entry and into Manitoba. He called the broker and let him know he was cleared. The broker requested that he get the bond papers to him as soon as possible and that he would return his exit documents so that Kevin would not have a problem when he returned to the U.S. He suggested a motel in Portage La Prairie and said he would send over a messenger to pick the papers up from the desk, to save Kevin a stop at the office.

The motel and a hot shower sounded pretty good and he headed north.

When he arrived in Port La Prairie, he checked in with Kathy and made sure that she and Amy were okay. His next step was to call Mr. Brett Leeland, who was his contact in Dauphin. He let him know he would be arriving at noon the next day and Brett gave him directions to his office in Dauphin.

"See you tomorrow." Kevin said at the close of the conversation. He had talked to Brett several times and he seemed like a nice person. He set up his laptop and relaxed on the bed. He fell asleep with out signing off. It had been a long day.

Chapter 3

After a good breakfast Kevin hit the road. The weather was clear and crisp. As he traveled north he passed through a few short snow flurries. He was surprised that it was not colder. The trip from Portage La Prairie was a quick one, about two hours. He arrived in Dauphin at about eleven and decided to drive around town and look for some good places to set up his cameras.

The town had a fairly little downtown area and everyone seemed to be on foot. He spotted at least three high travel spots that would probably be good at around lunchtime. The town looked like tourism was a big part of its business and he imagined how crowded it would be during the summer. Just north of the town he found a sports auditorium that announced ice hockey games for Friday and Saturday. "That would be a perfect place," he said into the recorder. "Check out clearance on hockey arena" If it was a public venue it would probably be a cinch.

He found a large grocery store that looked fairly busy and the local, Home Depot type, building supply store. He made notes of the names on his recorder as he parked outside the city hall building and jotted down the location on his note pad. At 12:30 he locked the van and entered the building.

Brett didn't look anything like he imagined him. He was a very small man with a deep voice. He was using a desk in the City Councils Chambers and a very helpful receptionist led Kevin in through the stained glass door. "Mr. Bennett is here to see you Mr. Leeland."

Brett stood up and looked up at Kevin, who was still a full head over him, "Welcome to Dauphin Mr. Bennett!" His voice really sounded like it belonged to someone else.

"We finally meet, and Kevin will do just fine." He smiled and shook Brett's hand as the young women headed for the door. "Thank you," he called after her.

"Your welcome," she replied, never looking back.

"She'll be on the phone in two minutes and you'll be the subject of gossip at ten dinner tables by tonight. They don't get many strangers here during the winter. It is good to finally put a face with a voice. Please call me Brett," he motioned for Kevin to take a seat.

"We are all very excited about this project." He opened the file that was on the corner of the desk. "There are a lot of people in our government who are anxious to see if all you speak about is possible."

"Very possible and very accurate," Kevin pulled his note pad from his pocket. "I took the liberty of selecting a few locations. I hope they will be acceptable. If you need to make any substitutions or if you have anymore suggestions, I have plenty of cameras."

"I have two adjoining rooms with plenty of space for you at Dauphin Inn. My people emptied one and set up several tables. I have extra power and phone lines run to the room. I have three people ready to start for you whenever you are ready for them. They work for our private security contractor and are well-trained in installation of security cameras or surveillance equipment. I have a Pick-up and a Sedan at your disposal and if you need anything else please let me know."

"You seem to have gone over my wish list pretty well. I can't think of anything right now, but if I do I'll sure call."

I have to leave and get back to Winnipeg this evening but here is my card with my twenty-four hour number and my cell. I have arranged for my people to meet you at 2:00 P.M. in the lobby of the motel."

He scanned the list Kevin had given him. "These locations are among the ones I suggested and here is an additional list of places we would like you to try to cover."

"Consider it done!" Kevin liked the way this man worked. Not like working with most of the bureaucrats in the states. He looked at the list as Brett packed up his papers.

"I wish I could be here longer but I'm needed at the office. Please call me when you are ready for the demonstration or if you need me before that," he held out his hand to Kevin. "Let me know if you have any problems. This is very important to both of us!"

"Okay Brett, thank you." Kevin thought as he shook the man's hand. "Brett, if I need to test the system, what do I need to do?"

"The lines I have had installed in your extra room are direct link lines. You have the codes and the system is directed to allow you access." He turned to leave and then paused, "please be careful, both of our governments stand too loose, a lot of cooperation if anything goes wrong. Good luck!" With that he walked out the door leaving Kevin alone in the room sweating profusely. He hoped it didn't show.

He gathered up the papers Brett had left on the desk and returned to the reception area. "Can you direct me to Dauphin Inn?" He asked the lady at the desk.

She seemed a little more relaxed since Brett was gone. "When you walk out the front door and look to the left you can see the sign about two kilometers north on Main St." She said. "It's a nice place and the food is rather good."

"Thank you," Kevin said with a smile and started out the door.

"Will you be in Dauphin long?" she asked.

"About a week." He answered as he walked out the door.

"See ya around," she called after him and he could imagine her going for the phone.

He drove to Dauphin Inn and was surprised with how large it was. He noticed the three-bucket trucks in the parking lot that most probably belonged to the three people Brett had waiting for him. The place was probably bustling in the summer season but was pretty empty right now.

The sign out front said Go Hawks Go. Kevin thought that was the high school team or maybe the local hockey team. He parked near the office and walked through the large doors in front. They must have been eight inches thick. The place was all logs and was really beautiful. The green metal roof looked a little out of place, but gave the building a nice clean look.

The lobby was large and he could see the restaurant and lounge were fairly empty. The 'Please seat yourself sign' seemed appropriate. There was a young woman waiting to help him as he approached the desk.

"May I help you?" She asked with a big smile.

"My name is Kevin Bennett and I believe you have some rooms for me."

She came alive, "Yes Sir Mr. Bennett" she grabbed a registration card and slipped it across to him. As he started to fill it out she handed him two keys. "Number 105 is your residence room and they prepared 106 as your utility room" she beamed. "All you have to do is sign the bottom, we have all your information."

"Thank you," he looked at her name tag, "Barbara, have you heard from the people who are to meet me here?"

"Yes Sir, they are in 109, 110 and 111 and will call you at 2:00 P.M."

"Thank you again. Is the restaurant open all day?"

"From seven A.M. to midnight Sir and the lounge stays open until two A.M." She thought a moment as he headed to the door. "If you need anything else just dial 0 on your phone."

"Thank you," he said pushing open the thick doors. He was thinking of what a busy afternoon he had ahead of him and hoped the people chosen to help him like to work.

He carried his personal stuff into the room that looked like a hunting lodge that had a bed in it. the ceiling was high and there was wood everywhere. Even the chairs were made of logs with large overstuffed cushions. He tried one and it was surprisingly comfortable.

He set up his laptop and adjusted his camera. There were three additional phone lines leading to the desk in the corner and he decided to make one of them his link to Kathy. It only took a second and he was looking at his wife. "Good afternoon!"

"I checked in at the Dauphin Inn and all this wood makes me want to go out and catch a grizzly bear," he joked.

"Is it nice?" She was looking at him doing something else with her hands. "I'm unpacking groceries."

"It'll do. I have to meet my helpers in a few minutes. We'll make this a short one and talk a good while this evening. I love you."

"I love you too. Talk to you, later, Amy's asleep now but I'll have her up when you call." She blew him a kiss and disconnected.

He walked to the connecting door to the other room and walked through. They had placed four eight-foot long tables and several folding chairs in a large u shape in the empty room. He walked around the outside of the configuration and was happy to see plenty of power strips and phone line hook-ups. Brett had been thorough.

He heard the phone ring in the other room and hurried to pick it up. It was Mike Byron, the lead man of his crew. He told him to meet him out front of 106.

Kevin went back to 106 and opened the front door propping it with a folding chair. The three men were walking down the porch toward him and he was glad to see they were all young.

"Mike Byron," the first man said holding his hand out to shake Kevin's. He turned to introduce the others "Philip Byron, no relation and Chad Philips."

"Nice to meet you all. This will be the utility room and I think the first thing to do will be to get all my gear from the van. The three moved quickly and started unloading the equipment."

"Have we got it wired okay for you?" Mike asked. "I got the print from Brett. You have eight station locations with six lines at each station. The lines are all junctioned over there on the wall but work independently. I have a UPS in the bathroom and about sixty minutes of back-up power in case we lose the local source." He was all business. He figured Brett had sent him three good people. Kevin was feeling better already.

Mike went on as the others kept carrying equipment. "I ran extra power to your room and put three clear lines behind your desk. You will be able to monitor everything that happens in here over there."

"This is great Mike," Kevin said heading out the door. "That unit goes in the other room by the desk" he told Philip on his way in with another load.

"What kind of reach do your bucket trucks have?"

"We brought two twenty-fours and one thirty-six. Mike grabbed more boxes. "We have plenty of all types of fixtures and mounts and many miles of video cable both exterior and interior. How many video feeds will we be installing?"

Probably about fifty." Mike's eyebrows went up. "Can you do that many in two days?"

"Mr. Leeland told us to do whatever you needed, so if you need it, you got it. How many locations?" Kevin liked his attitude.

"Four major locations and a few simple installations." Kevin answered.

"They roll up the streets at seven o'clock here so we'll be able to work late without being bothered. We brought enclosure boxes. The weather changes up here pretty quick in the winter."

"Good idea," Kevin was glad they had thought of just about everything. "I have the list and I'll leave the installations up to you and your crew. We want maximum coverage in high volume areas. We need to keep the cameras as low as possible without being to obvious."

"We do a lot of mall work and think you will be happy with our coverage capabilities." Mike sounded reassuring and Kevin could feel the pressure in his shoulders start to relax.

The unloading was done, Mike let Kevin know they were going to start on some locations immediately and they left. He closed the door to 106 and started setting up equipment.

Set up went rather quickly and by six o'clock he was sitting back, double checking configurations and was ready to go on line with Duluth for some tests.

"Hello there!" He heard a woman's voice in the other room. He walked in to see Kathy on the laptop screen smiling at him. "Where are you?" She said kiddingly. "Hello daddy." She held Amy up to the screen and the baby made a grab for the camera.

"Hi baby," Kevin said as he slid into camera view. "How's daddy's girl?" The baby laughed when she saw him.

"She's been waiting and I figured I better get you before she got mad." Kathy held the baby against her chest and backed up so Kevin could see them both. "How's it going?"

"Great, the guys are really good and I feel better already." He paused, "It's coming together honey."

"I'm glad. Dad called. He made it home safe and asked how you were doing?"

"Tell him I'm fine. I'll e-mail him tomorrow."

"Are you eating?" She asked knowing he would get so busy and wrapped up in his work that she sometimes had to insist that he take time to have a meal.

"I'm about to go over and see what kind of steak I can put on the company American Express Card," Kevin joked. "I'm starving and I'm almost set up here. I was just about to get online with my girlfriend in Duluth."

"Watch it buddy," she snapped jokingly, knowing he referred to the computer system as his girlfriend. "Show me your room."

"Okay," Kevin got up and picked up the camera making sure he had plenty of cable and started giving her a video tour of the room.

"I love it, all the wood is beautiful," he moved to the utility room "It looks big."

"They emptied the room so all my equipment fits pretty well." He paused to turn back to the other room. "It'll get a little messy when we get all the video wiring in here but I'm real happy with the set up."

"Get something to eat." She smiled and waved the baby's arm. "Say bye bye to Daddy. Thanks for the tour. I love you."

"I'm headed for the buffet." He laughed. "Love you both," he blew Amy a kiss as she said bye-bye. I'll leave the line open."

He decided to eat and then run the tests. Everyone will have gone home in Duluth by then and he would have no distractions.

There were only three other tables occupied when he entered the restaurant. They looked like local people. He chose a table by the window and smiled as the waitress brought him a menu and a glass of water. "Hello," she said. "May I get you a drink or something from the bar?"

"I'll take a coke," he answered as she headed towards the kitchen. He decided on a sirloin and a baked potato.

He plugged the earphone cord in his recorder and put it in his ear to recap his messages and make some notes. "Buy Dad a good bottle of whiskey and get present for the girls."

The meal was great and very peaceful. The waitress kept checking on him and kept his glass full. He thought about how it would be to bring the family up here for vacation. The area was beautiful and he could just imagine how great it would be during the summer.

When he got up to pay the bill he looked behind the register at the shelves on the wall. They had several rows of Canadian cigarettes. One brand caught his eye "Kathy Cigarettes?" He asked the girl as she ran the card.

"They pronounce them Kathay" she handed him a box. "I think their French."

"Give me a pack" he smiled "That's my wife's name." He walked down the steps of the lodge. He looked at the tall trees and made his mind up to bring Kathy and Amy for a vacation one day.

When he walked back in his room he saw his laptop blinking and checked his e-mail. A message from Allen making sure everything was okay and a note from Bob thanking him for a great weekend. He put his cigarettes on the nightstand as the desk was already a mess and answered both the e-mails and sent Kathy and Amy a little love note.

He turned his attention to the other room to make sure all was well with the phone lines and his hook up with Duluth was secure and clear.

He hammered away at his main keyboard for a few seconds and his girlfriend in Duluth acknowledged his call. He typed in his code word, "Alchemy" and ID number code and the machine came alive.

"Hello Kevin!" The artificial female voice said. "How may I help you?"

"I need to run some online tests to ensure integrity of outside links," He said into the mike.

"Please furnish visual identification for clearance," the machine answered. Kevin adjusted the camera for a close frontal picture of his face and hit the enter key. "Visual identification confirmed Kevin. What shall we do?"

"I need to lock in some direct telephone line numbers for the Dauphin project and I need you to run integrity and security checks on them."

"Please enter the numbers."

Kevin began to enter the numbers on the keyboard. It took only a few seconds for the computer to respond. "All lines are secure and are linked directly to your equipment in Canada. One line is linked to your laptop."

"Thank you, I will be keeping that line on that constant link until the test is through."

"Yes Kevin, anything else?"

"I want a complete record of all of all actions and entries up here to be down loaded to my home station as it progresses."

"You will need to give me additional security information to permit me to do that." The computer waited a couple of seconds. "Please enter secondary security code."

He entered another series of numbers. "Thank you Kevin. It will be done on an entry to entry basis. Anything else?"

"No thank you." He hit several keys. "I'll talk to you in the morning."

He turned off the lights and left room 106 illuminated by all the running lights on the work stations and the power strips on the floor. As he settled into bed and looked into the other room it looked like a small city lit up at night. A very powerful city. Sleep comes quickly. Tomorrow was going to be a long day.

Chapter 4

"Good morning!" The cheerful voice said and the room was illuminated with his wife's face on his laptop. "Time to get up and make my coffee."

"I wish I could," he answered sitting up in the bed and moving closer to the camera.

"Ooo," she laughed, "a bad hair day."

He looked in the mirror and smiled at the way his hair was sticking straight up, "one more like that and I'll turn off the camera."

"Okay I just thought I'd say hello. Amy and I are headed out to the doctor for her check-up today and I will be gone for a while."

"Okay, take care, how's the weather?" He was rubbing his eyes.

"Cold and snowing. How about there?" She asked.

"I don't know yet, ask me later."

"Bye, have a good day. Love ya."

"Okay baby. I love you. Be careful driving. Bye." He headed for the shower. The hot water felt good and he thought of the things to do today while he rinsed off. As he was drying the phone rang.

It was Mike. "Good morning Kevin. Would you like to join us for breakfast?"

"I'll be there in five minutes, thank you," Kevin replied glancing at the clock satisfied with their 6:30 start. He hurried and dressed and opened the door to a cold but brilliant day.

The waitress was pouring coffee as he approached the table. There were "good mornings" all around and he settled into a chair. The men were all looking pretty bright and he wondered how late they had worked. "Long night?" He asked of Mike. The other two snickered.

"We finished nearly all of downtown at two this morning." He looked at the menu. "Thought it would be better to get it out of the way. This morning we'll do the rink and the post office and tonight should finish up most of it."

"Wow!" Kevin was impressed. "You guys are good."

The men smiled at his compliment and Chad asked, "I can run some video links into your work room this afternoon if you want to start checking camera angles and operation."

"That would be great." Kevin stopped to order from the waitress. "I should be ready by then." He looked around the dining room and was surprised at how many people were there. "This must be the place for breakfast, huh?"

"I think so. Do you want to put a camera in here?" Mike asked sipping his coffee.

"No but I would like to put one in the parking lot facing the entrance so we can get some shots as they walk out."

"Done. We'll do that late tonight. Philip park your truck by the power pole in front when we come back tonight and you can slip one up real quick. We'll blend the link with the cable lead to the motel rooms."

Their breakfast came and they all dove into their food. Kevin was thinking about how much Kathy liked breakfast and noticed how beautiful the view out the big glass window was. He was definitely going to bring them back here for a vacation one day. "This place is really great." He remarked to the men.

"During the summer it's full of tourists. The fishing is great and during the fall the hunters take over. Some big Elk up here," Mike was talking. "A sportsman's paradise."

"I thought there were a lot of protected lands here?" Kevin asked.

"For sure, but Manitoba is a big place," Philip said between bites. "Half an hour in any direction and your in some of the best hunting in the Province."

They finished their meal without a lot of talk and the men got up to leave. "I've got breakfast," Kevin said as the waitress approached with the check.

"Thank you," Mike sounded appreciative, "we'll see you later."

"Wait a minute," Kevin said digging a card from his wallet and handing it to Mike, "my cell number is on there and I'm going out for a few things. If you need me just holler."

Mike said "okay," and they were out the door. Kevin had another cup of coffee and continued looking out the window as the place started to empty out.

Chapter 5

After running a few tests on his systems he decided to go out and do some shopping. He drove past the rink and saw the trucks clustered near the building. He saw a sign for Dauphin Lake and decided to take the short drive to take a look.

The lake was frozen solid and he was surprised to see dozens of ice-fishing cabins across the ice. There were quite a few cars and pick-up trucks parked besides some of them. The lake was large and there were cabins all over the hills surrounding it. "What a beautiful spot." Kevin thought.

He pulled his camera out and stopped to snap a couple of shots of some cabins that were really large. "It must be nice," He mused thinking of how much money it must take to have a summer home like these.

One the way back to Dauphin he saw a small liquor store and stopped to buy Bob his Canadian whiskey. The place had a sign on one end of the building Hawkins Bait and Lures. Inside was a mix of convenience store and liquor mart. A little of everything you would need to spend a couple of days at the lake.

"May I help you?" The voice came from behind the counter covered with lottery tickets.

It was an old lady who couldn't have been over 4'11" tall. Kevin had to smile but quickly asked, "What is your best bottle of Canadian whiskey?"

"Well lets see," she said stepping out into the crowded isle and selecting two to show him. "This one is most expensive," she held one up, "but most of the drunks I know up here say this one is the best." She presented the other for his examination.

Rather than chose the wrong one he decided to be sure, "I'll take them both," he said taking them from her hands and walking back to the cash register.

"You planning a party?" She asked with a grin.

"No, I don't drink. They're a gift for my father-in-law in Texas." He dug out his wallet and handed her his AMEX card, "I told him I'd bring him a good bottle back." He took a bag of nuts off the shelf to his left and put it on the counter as she began to ring up the transaction.

"I hope he enjoys it," she scanned the nuts. "We get a lot of hunters and fishermen up here from Texas. Anything else?" She waited.

"No that should do it." He continued to look around at the conglomeration of the goods jammed into her small store. "You have everything here don't you?"

"Yep. I save people a lot of trips into town." She said handing him a card and pen so he could sign the transaction slip. "I've been here for twenty-six years and I can probably name everyone that lives in Dauphin." She gave him his copy and put the bottles in a bag.

"Well thank you for your suggestions and maybe I'll see you if get back up here in the summer." He started for the door but a small carousel with small hanging ceramics caught his eye. They were five-inch wall diameter plaques that said Lake Dauphin, Manitoba and had names on them. The one that said Amy stood out and caught his eye. He picked it up and looked it over, it was hand painted and he looked for one that said Kathy with no luck.

"Find something else?" She asked as he returned to the counter.

"I'd like one of these for my daughter," he handed her the piece.

"You'll need one of these." She moved out into the isle and to the carousel. Behind the plaques were heavy cardboard mailers that he had not noticed. "Put it in one of these and you won't have to worry about it getting home broken."

"Thank you," he said as he paid for the piece and could just imagine his daughter trying to unwrap it. He returned to his van and when he put the bag with the bottles on the seat they clanked together. He made a mental note to re-pack bottles for the trip home.

As he drove through Dauphin he saw the post office and decided to mail the plaque to Amy. He parked and filled out the mailer using the motel address and sealed the flap.

Inside he waited his turn in line looking at the Canadian stamp issues. "Next," the man behind the counter said.

"I'd like to mail this back to the states," Kevin said handing the postman the mailer.

"You need to fill this out," he said handing Kevin a small form. As he was filling out the address and content's information he could feel the postman looking at him. "Any insurance?" He asked never taking his eyes off Kevin.

"How about $25.00?" Kevin answered.

"$25.00 U.S. or Canadian?"

"$25.00 Canadian." Kevin smiled remembering the ever changing rate of exchange.

"That'll be $3.25 Canadian." The postman said with a smile.

"How much are stamps to send a letter to the states?"

".49 cents Canadian." They were both laughing now. Kevin liked this person.

"May I have ten please?"

"Ten Canadian or U.S.?" The postman asked. They both laughed and the people in line who overheard their exchange also joined in on the joke. "How long are you up for?"

"About a week," Kevin replied handing the man a twenty.

"Enjoy yourself," the man said with a wide smile, "Here is your change, receipt and insurance certificate. I hope it makes it okay."

"Thank you." He smiled at the people in line as he headed for the door. He could feel their curious eyes on his back.

By the time he returned to the motel, Chad was waiting for him. "How's it going?" Kevin asked.

"Very well." Chad answered. "I'm ready to run some lines to your hardware. I drilled a hole for a port behind 106 and pushed a few lines through already."

"Fantastic," Kevin said opening his door. He passed through to 106 and opened the front door for Chad. He went back to his van and carefully picked up the bag with the clanking bottles. As he started back to 106, he saw Chad busy behind the main table.

"Where do you want me to start?" He said looking up from the floor noticing the tops for the liquor bottles. "Planning a good drunk?" He asked with a grin.

"Yeah right," Kevin answered with a laugh. He pulled the bottles out and put them down separately on his dresser. "Let's start with this work station and work our way back to the left. That way we won't have to trip over cables unless we have a bad one." He turned on all the lights he had clamped to the back of the tables so Chad could see.

'Things were coming together' he thought as he watched Chad plug in the video leads. "Where are these lines coming from?"

"Downtown and the shops in the strip mall south of here. The next ones will come from the building Supply Ctr. and the Rink and we'll finish up with the motel tonight." Chad had finished plugging in the cables. "She's all yours, try it out." He moved around to the front of the tables to check the results of the first hook-ups.

Kevin brought the video presentation screen alive and the ten boxes on the first monitor seemed nice and clear. "They look pretty good," Kevin said as he changed the zoom on one camera and turned another a bit to get a better shot.

"I opened the vent ports on all the boxes so you shouldn't have any fogging or condensation problems." Chad volunteered.

"I repeat, you guys are good." Kevin smiled, happy with Chad's work and the way the cameras were performing. "I should be ready to start testing tomorrow by noon."

"Good news," Chad sounded proud. "I'm going back to the rink to help the guys. If you need anything call us on the radio." He handed Kevin a Motorola hand set. "It's on. Just hold down the large button and give us a call. See you later." He left, closing the door behind him.

Kevin kept adjusting cameras and changing the focus on others. The technicians had placed them perfectly and he had high hopes of a great test. "Now if I can just catch some crooks," he smiled.

There was a knock at the door. The maid wanted to clean the room and by the way she was looking around he figured he'd better retreat to 106 and close the door. "I don't need anything in 106," he told her closing the door.

He had just started back to work when he heard Kathy call, "hello," and the startled maid screamed. He rushed into 105 to find the maid against the wall and Kathy holding the baby with a curious look on her face.

"It's okay," he told the maid. Trying to calm her down. "It's my wife, hi honey. You scared the maid."

"Sorry," Kathy said as Amy started to jabber and the maid came off the wall to stare at the laptop screen. "Hello," she told the maid. The startled women stared back at the computer. "I'm Kathy and this is Amy." The baby was laughing now.

"I'm Edna." The maid said not believing she was talking to the computer. She glanced at Kevin with a smile.

"Nice to meet you Edna. I'll call you later honey, I just wanted to let you know we were back." She paused for a minute. "Bye, Edna. See you tomorrow." That drew a laugh from the women.

"Good-bye," she said waving her dust cloths at the camera. She looked at Kevin oddly and went back to work.

Kevin smiled and went back to 106 to finish what he had started. He logged on to Duluth and the computer responded, "Hello Kevin, how can I help you?"

"I am passing some video input through to you and I want to make sure you are getting a clear feed."

"Everything seems okay," the computer replied. "Are we scanning?"

"Not at this point, I'm just checking for feed and clarity," Kevin responded.

"A-okay Kevin." The machine went on stand by and it was quiet in the room as Kevin watched the few people passing in front of the online cameras. "So far so good," he thought. Things were going well.

"When we start scanning I want any positive Id's to be printed out complete, with picture and information pertaining to subject. Is that clear?"

"Yes Kevin. Should I pass that information on to your home station?" the computer queried.

"Yes, but don't bother to print. We will begin testing tomorrow at 1200 hours. I'll talk to you in the morning to check all additional feeds."

"Yes Kevin, anything else?"

"Yes, please pass me through to Alan." In a matter of seconds Alan appeared on the main workstation.

"Everything okay?" His voice was full of concern.

"100 percent so far," Kevin could see his face relax. "The guys they gave me are fantastic and everything is ready for a go tomorrow at noon for testing."

"Great, I can take a breath." Alan smiled. "I'm going to minimum personnel tomorrow. Just essential people. I don't want anyone to try and access the computer and screw things up while you are getting up to speed."

"I appreciate that. I plan to start testing tomorrow at noon and scan all weekend. Monday at ten A.M. will be the demo unless something goes wrong."

"I'm not going to be two feet from my phone all weekend and if you need anything please call." Alan's voice was concerned.

"Don't worry, if it starts to unravel I'll be calling for help. Take care." Kevin signed off.

"Thanks, good luck. Talk to you Monday morning."

Kevin pushed away from the table and decided to take a quick nap to try and stave off a headache that seemed to be starting. He went back to 105 and emptied his pockets. He noticed the insurance receipt for his mail and he flattened it out and put a bottle of whiskey on top of it to press it out. He was asleep as quickly as he put his head on the pillow.

The knocking on the door awakened him. As he opened it, he saw his three installers looking in. "Nap time?" Mike said with a smile.

"Headache time." Kevin replied as he opened up 106. "How'd it go?"

"All done except the motel, we'll do that later." Philip went around back to push the cables and Chad positioned himself behind the tables to pull them through and plug them in. "Is everything working all right?"

"It seems to be." Kevin sat down and rubbed his temples. "We'll know for sure tomorrow."

Chad was busy plugging in video leads and the boxes on the monitor were filling up with the sights and views and people of Dauphin.

"Is there anything else you need us to do for now?" Mike asked. "I mean after we set the motel camera."

"Not a thing just as long as I can get in touch with you," Kevin answered.

Mike was plugging in a charger for the radio Chad had left him. "We may take in a bit of ice-fishing but if you need us you need only call. These units reach out about fifty miles and we won't be that far away. Just be sure to charge it up at night. You can leave it on and just put it in the cradle like so." He placed the handset in the charger so Kevin could see. "Okay?"

"Okay. All you need to do is run the motel cable in the wall and I'll take it from there. I really appreciate your good work. Are you going fishing on Dauphin Lake?"

"Yes sir. Chad met a girl who's father has a shack out there and we're gonna try our luck."

"If things go well I might join you on Sunday for a little while. I was by the lake today and it looked beautiful."

"You'll be welcome. Are you through Chad?" He waited for an answer and Philip came through the front door.

"Looks like you're in business Kevin," Philip said looking at the monitors. We put the rink cameras in locations where you get them coming in and going out. You even have one at the entrances of the men's rooms so you can tell who is drinking the most beer," Everyone laughed. Chad finished behind the tables and headed for the door with Philip.

"Thank you again guys," Kevin said shaking their hands. "I really appreciate it."

"Good luck Kevin," Philip said. "I'll have the last line in the wall by midnight." With that they walked down the long porch to their rooms.

Kevin locked the front door and returned to move and focus the cameras that had just been connected. With the exception of the one at the motel everything was good to go. He was quite anxious and was tempted to try it out but he had set the time for 1200 hours tomorrow and he didn't want to confuse anyone.

He took out his manual and made a few final entries before turning off the lights and returning to 105 for the night. He wasn't hungry and planned on a good early breakfast to start the day off.

"Hello there!" He called to the laptop. "Lucy, I'm home!" His Cuban accent was bad.

"Hello Ricky." She answered with a laugh as the screen lit up. "How is your evening?"

"Great! We're all hooked up and everything looks good. We start at noon tomorrow. I'll be up early and test each camera individually but I think everything is a okay."

"Congratulations, I knew it was going to be a snap for you." Her voice made him feel very proud.

"Tomorrow will go even better. Get it done and come on home to your girls."

"Speaking of girls, where's my little cutie?"

"She's been asleep all afternoon. The doctor gave her a shot and after we got home and talked to you she knocked out. She'll probably want to play all night."

"Hang in their momma. I wish I was home." He really missed his girls. "It won't be long."

"I know. I love you." She replied blowing him a kiss, "sleep tight!"

"Good night baby, I love you." He got undressed and crawled into bed thinking about tomorrow and fell asleep.

Chapter 6

Kevin woke up several times during the night and walked into 106 to stare at the camera shots in the dark. The guys were right about them rolling up the sidewalks at night. The town was deserted. Every few minutes a car's lights would pass by but no one was out.

Everything was working correctly. He was just anxious about the test the next day. He had a case of nerves. He went back to bed and closed his eyes. He had to be at his best on Friday.

Chapter 7

He bought the local newspaper on his way into the dining room for breakfast. The thing was only about eight pages but had a weather section. He read as he sipped his coffee. It called for clear, cold weather for the entire week. Good news for his cameras. He looked around for the guys but figured they were sleeping in or fishing. He wondered what time of day ice fishing was the best.

His breakfast was delicious. The place was pretty crowded when he walked out still glancing over the skimpy paper. The paper had almost a full page talking about the hockey game tonight and the rivalry between the two local teams that would be playing. They were predicting a sell out.

He felt good about the possibility of being able to scan a couple of thousand of people under the bright neon lights of a stadium type situation. He entered his room and left the paper on his bed. The last video lead was sticking through the wall and he pushed in into it's port. The last remaining square came to life on his monitor. Everything looks correct.

He called to Kathy and she came on the screen. "Good morning!" She had Amy in her arms. "Say hi to daddy."

"Hi baby." He said as she started to reach for his face on the CPU at home. "Did she sleep last night?"

"She surprised me. She woke up for about an hour and then went out for the night."

"I just finished the last checks," he told her. "I'm about ready to fire things up."

"Good luck baby." She smiled and Amy laughed. "Call me and let me know how you're doing. We love you."

He gave her a thumbs-up sign. "Do me a favor and make sure my computer is online in the workshop. I love you."

"Okay baby," she said and put the baby in her high chair. She went down the hall and opened the closet door. She hit the switch and workshop door opened up. A quick touch of the test button on his control panel gave her all green lights. She hit the open button to make sure there was a disk in the tray and closed everything up. "He's ready to go," she said to herself.

Kevin sat down at his main workstation at 11:40 and began a final check of all systems, he typed in his code again.

"Hello, Kevin," the computer responded.

He complied with the visual ID clearance and began the final set of instructions before beginning the test. His heart was pounding. There were quite a few people showing up on the downtown cameras and a few showing up at the rink getting ready for the night game. The busiest cameras were at the building materials site.

"Are all feeds correct and clear?" He asked as a final preparation.

"Yes Kevin," the computer replied.

"Are we online with all the cooperating agencies?"

"Yes Kevin all systems have permitted access and our links are secure and open." The computer did some final checks. "The test in ready to proceed."

"You may start the test and scanning at 1200 hours. Central time."

"Yes, Kevin's tests and scanning starts in eight minutes seventeen seconds." The computer started the count to start.

Kevin had to get up and pace around. He hurried to 105 to use the bathroom and drain out the coffee from breakfast. He knew that once things got started he couldn't get up for a long time.

Back at 106 he sat down and watched the monitors. He typed a few things on the main station and watched the results on the monitors. Everything was okay. He got up and checked the printer and made sure if had plenty of paper. It was full but he had torn open another ream just to be ready. He returned to the control station to wait for the system to start.

Watching the people, most of them didn't even seem to notice the cameras. He was getting good clear shots of a lot of people and they didn't even seem to know he was there. The computer beeped to announce the beginning of the test and it made him jump. He had been locked on the faces in the monitor.

His main station was set up as a scoreboard. If he had a hit or identification it would register. In addition to that, it would register facial or corneal and the type of registration. The column registers R for police record or booking identification and S for surveillance, as in the event of the subject having been identified as a theft suspect, as a drug suspect or having sold or tried to sell or move stolen goods.

This area also would cover people suspected of terrorism or acting in a way that local authorities felt their actions were worth looking into because of the possibility of a problem. This was the broadest gray area in the system. The last column gave the percentage of accuracy 0 to 100 to show how sure the computer was of its match.

The machine was blinking signifying it was testing but it had to be over 65% before the system would kick out any results on a scanned suspect. Kevin could have lowered the percentage but he felt the higher the positive ID percentage the more acceptable the system results would be.

Kevin was fidgeting in the chair looking all over the connections to make sure everything was all right

He felt he was back in school hoping an experiment in biology would work. He got up and walked around a minute or two, scratching his head when the main station registered a 97% hit and printer started.

"Yes!" He said jumping into the air and swinging his arms around. He stood over by the printer and waited for it to kick out his first match.

As he stood there he realized he had forgotten to program in the locations of the cameras. That was not an important factor but it would be good to have for an apprehension point of view if he scanned an important individual. He made a note on his pad to check with Mike and register camera locations in the morning. Before he finished the main registered another hit.

The first confirmed ID was a local who was arrested on a domestic violence charge in 1997. The charges were dropped and he was released the next morning. This was a good confirmation but not he kind of thing Kevin was hoping for. He sat back in the chair and put the printout in the basket at the end of the tables.

The next printout was a juvenile with an unauthorized use of vehicle charge dropped by his parents after he spent a night in jail. Kevin read the sheet and then sat down. Happy that it was working correctly but disappointed with the kind of fish he was catching. The machine kept on humming, but no hits. Kevin relaxed into the chair realizing it was going to be a long afternoon and night.

Kevin glanced at his watch. Four P.M. The minutes seemed to drag by. He was so bored. The machine had kicked out another domestic violence ID and a couple of traffic offenders who for some reason or another, had been photographed and printed. He decided to talk to Kathy.

"Hello." He yelled as he started through the door to 105. "Is anybody there?"

"We're here," Kathy answered she came into view. "How's it going?" The baby was wrapped in a towel. "I just grabbed her out of the tub." Amy was waving both hands around.

"Okay, I guess." He slumped on the bed. "I uncovered two wife beaters and a kid who took his dads car for a ride."

"Come on, the system is working isn't it?" She tried to perk him up.

"It's working but I don't feel right reading domestic relations reports." He realized he was whining and tried to sound better. "How are you two?"

"We're fine. Don't be discouraged. You didn't expect to uncover Ma Barker making cookies in Dauphin did you?" She smiled and she made sure he could see Amy jumping around.

"Not really." He smiled at them. The machine started beeping and printing in the other room. "There it goes again. Probably a kid who shoplifted cookies from the local bakery."

"Cheer up!" She waved Amy's arms. "We love you!"

"Bye honey." He felt better. "I'll talk to you in the morning."

As he got up to walk back to 106, the machine started beeping several times and the printer seemed to kick into high gear. He walked to the main screen. He was surprised to see ten new hits. He turned to the screen to see nearly all the last ones full of people. That would probably be the Rink and the Building Supply Center. "Makes sense." He said to himself. "Everybody just got off work and tonight's payday."

The first one off the printer was a Mark Lebec. He had out standing warrant's for DUI in Saskatchewan. His record was three pages long. Kevin felt the blood start to flow in his veins. This was the kind of thing Canada was looking for before they would commit to buy his system. He was jumping around again but the printer kept on printing and the main station kept on beeping.

He checked the camera monitors to make sure everything was clear. The rink cameras were starting to fill up with people. He made a couple of focus adjustments and then walked back to the printer.

The next positive scan was a 98% on an Indian immigrant who had an expired visa and a number of warrants in Quebec for traffic offenses, including a failure to stop at the scene of an accident. Kevin was starting to feel as though his future was getting brighter. He heard the computer beep again and filed the last print out he read in the basket.

The printer was buzzing as Kevin watched the main station. The last five were 100% matches and two were corneal. He wasn't expecting that.

The next off the printer was a Richard Attleman. He was an American citizen in Canada for approximately two years. He was wanted in an armed robbery in Nebraska, in which a clerk was shot. He was photographed walking out of the Building Supply Center with a bag of supplies. The system was working.

Kevin was on a cloud thinking about how well things were working. He was using a marking pen to put bright colored marks on the corner of the files he wanted to present to Brett when he arrived on Monday.

The next print out was a citizen of the Dominican Republic, who had applied for entry to Canada as a political refugee but before his papers had been processed in St. John's, Newfoundland he disappeared and was in violation of a number of immigration laws. He had also showed up as a 97% positive ID in a shoplifting at a sporting goods store in Toronto, Ontario. Kevin was feeling better by the minute.

The next print out was eight pages long. 100% corneal ID. Kevin turned the pages over to look at the picture. The man had dark hair, a thin mustache and a beard. His eyes dropped down to the name. TIMOTHY ALLEN McVEY.

Kevin's heart seemed to stop. He read the name again and then turned to the second page and was starring at the arresting picture of one of the most hated men in America. He started to shake his head and looked at the third page that confirmed the charges and booking information in Oklahoma.

Kevin slumped back in his chair, oblivious to the sounds of the computer and the printer. He held the two pictures up side by side and could see the similarities. His first thought was to disregard this as a glitch but he knew how reliable his system was.

He moved to the computer and hammered out some numbers.

"Yes Kevin, what do you need?" The computer responded.

"I need you to re-scan # 406." He hesitated. "Possible mistaken identity."

In a matter of seconds the computer spoke up. "Kevin there is no mistake. The subject scanned at 1705 hours on camera 31, was Timothy Allen McVey. Do you want me to reprint the subject's information and picture comparisons?"

"No, that will be all. Continue scanning as you were earlier directed." Kevin's body was cold. He looked at the bottom of the fourth sheet and saw that the information had been retrieved from the NCIC and the FBI computers.

Kevin got up and walked around the room as the printer continued to buzz. "What the hell have I done?" He wondered as he looked at the pictures. "What in the hell have I found?"

He thought abut calling Kathy but decided against it. What could he tell her? He found a dead man in Manitoba. He could remember what he was doing at the exact moment he heard about the bombing in Oklahoma City. He remembered staring, in disbelief at the TV coverage of the devastation.

He remembered the hatred he felt for anyone who could have perpetrated the horrible attack. "What in the hell had he stumbled onto?"

He paid no attention to the numerous hits that were being printed out. He walked over to the door and opened it to get a breath of air. The cold night was brutal on his uncovered body. he started to shiver and went back inside locking and bolting the door.

Kevin realized it was doing no good to go into shock. He gathered the papers on McVey and put them in the other room. He forced himself to go back to 106 and start sifting through the print outs but his mind was still in 105 with the two haunting pictures.

As the hockey rink started to fill up the printer got even busier. As he read through the ID sheets he came across another eight-page printout on McVey, "the bastard went shopping and then took in a hockey game." The new sheet showed him passing through the entrance of the rink with a program.

Kevin tried to keep his mind on the system but he was totally overwhelmed by what he might have uncovered. He felt quite helpless in this situation.

Here he was with all the major law enforcement computer data banks at his disposal and he had information that a lot of them would want to have. But what in the hell would they do with it and what in the hell was the guy doing alive. He had watched TV the night they executed him. How in the hell could he be in Dauphin, Manitoba attending a hockey game? He was starting to sweat.

He decided to call Bob. He found his cell phone in the other room and dialed his number. It rang five times and Bob's voice came on. "Please leave a message and I'll get back to you." Kevin kicked the wall. The phone machine beeped.

"Bob," Kevin started. "I've got a problem. I'm sending you some information for you to check out. It's six P.M. Friday in Manitoba. Thanks for your help. Please keep this under your hat. Bye."

Kevin walked to 105 and opened the drawer of the desk. He removed an envelope with the Dauphin Inn logo on the corner and folded the second printout and placed it inside. Kevin went to the dresser and put two of the Canadian stamps on the envelope and walked out to the lodge lobby. He decided to mail it to Bob at home.

When he entered the lobby he saw the red mailbox near the desk and dropped the letter inside. As he turned to leave Chad stumbled out of the men's room.

"Kevin," he said in a voice that sounded like he spent the day at the bar. "How about a drink?"

Kevin tried to make a quick exit but Chad cut him off. "No thank you Chad. I just came out to get a coke. I'm in the middle of a test."

"I'll buy you a coke them." Chad stumbled over to him and called out to the waitress. "A coke for my boss." He was flying hi.

"Did you catch any fish?" Kevin tried to make small talk.

"A few but I left early and came back here. I've been in the bar since three o'clock and I'm having a hell of a day." He started to laugh as the girl brought Kevin's coke.

"Thanks for the soda Chad but I have to get back." He headed for the door.

"If you need me just call." Chad joked and headed back to the bar telling the waitress, "put that soda on my bill." He ricocheted off the wall and continued on his way.

Kevin was shaking from the nerves and the cold by the time he got back in the room. The machine was still buzzing and printing out papers. Most of the downtown cameras were blank as the area emptied out. It seemed like everyone was at the hockey game.

The game lasted until 8:30 and the place started to clear out. The computer continued registering hits and printing as the fans thinned out. Kevin watched the monitors to see if he could see McVey leave but didn't see him in the crowd.

Kevin continued sorting and marking the printed reports. He had obtained a great deal of information since he started the test. Enough, he felt, to sell the system. It was obviously a sound success but it was overshadowed by the McVey identification.

He began to worry about the information getting into Bob's hands and decided to e-mail the four sheets to him at the newspaper office. On the top of the current photo he wrote, "Bob, positive ID, hockey game. Dauphin, Manitoba Friday night. Please help me out. Kevin." He scanned the pages into the main workstation and e-mailed it to his father in law.

He felt for sure that Bob would get the information one way or the other. He decided not to tell Kathy about what he had uncovered. He felt she had enough to worry about and didn't want to put more on her plate.

He decided to let the test run continuously through the weekend so that he would have the full amount of available material to present to Brett when he arrived on Monday.

He stayed up late separating the printouts. First by category. Immigration, criminal, local and his final was pile for civil misdemeanors, like the drunk driving and disorderly conduct offenses.

He didn't take his clothes off when he laid down on the bed. He left the lights on but it didn't matter. He was asleep in seconds.

"Wake up sleepy head!" He heard his wife say. He opened his eyes to see her smiling at him. "How did it go?"

"It went well," he said stretching. "We have a winner. There's a lot of sneaky people up here in the woods."

"Do you think they'll be impressed?" She asked sipping her coffee.

"Yes."

"Really impressed?"

"Yes, really impressed." He answered her.

"All right!" She smiled with joy. "I'll go out and pick out the Mercedes." That was getting to be the family joke.

"I'm going to continue the test all weekend so I will have as large a stack of paperwork to give them as possible." He stopped to stretch again. "I'll give you a million dollars for a cup of that coffee." He remembered his call to Bob. "Have you talked with your dad?"

"He's in Orlando at a convention of some sorts, he'll be back on Monday." She looked puzzled. "What do you want dad for?"

"I ran across something up here that I wanted to ask him a couple of questions about."

"Something I can help with?" She asked noting his tone. "Is everything okay?"

"Everything is fine. If you talk to him tell him I sent him some e-mail to look over." He looked at his watch. "Hey, I have to go."

"You're sure your okay?" She said concerned.

"I'm fine, I have to go out for a while. I'll call you later. I love you."

"Love you too." She said knowing something must be wrong. He never asked about Amy. He was really pre-occupied.

He showered and changed in a hurry. He took the recent pictures of McVey and trimmed off all the information leaving just the picture. He slid it into a file and headed out the door. He took the keys to the dark blue Sedan that was in front of his room. The van drew to much attention with its size and US tags.

He stopped at the convenience store down the road and got a cup of coffee and a roll to eat for breakfast. He decided that a good place to start would be the post office.

Chapter 8
Edmond, Oklahoma
Saturday- 7:35 A.M.

The phone was ringing loudly as the older man emerged from the bathroom in his robe.

"Hello," he said roughly, clearly upset at being bothered in the middle of a shower.

"Mr. Fitzsimmons, this is Ed Mott, in your security branch." The man's voice was nervous. "We have had a serious breach."

"What kind of breach?" The older man demanded.

"One of our projects has been compromised. Compromised badly." The younger mans voice had changed to a sound of urgency.

"What project exactly?" Fitzsimmons asked sensing the security's mans state of mind.

"Bluebird sir." The young man said.

Fitzsimmon's face turned pale. "I'll be there in fifteen minutes." He slammed down the phone and headed back to the bathroom.

"Is something wrong?" A woman's voice said as she entered the room with a tray of coffee.

His voice called out from the bathroom. "Have Mark meet me out front with the car in five minutes?"

She hurriedly put the tray down and moved to the intercom on the wall. She depressed one button on the console. "Mark."

"Yes mam?" The voice came back from the speaker.

"Mr. Fitzsimmons wants you out front in five minutes with the car."

"Yes, mam." Mark's voice snapped back.

Her husband emerged from the dressing room in a pair of slacks and a sweater. He looked like he was ready for the golf course but his manner was one of serious concern.

"Do you have time for a cup of coffee?" She asked.

"Pour me one and I'll have it on the way." He said as he slipped on his shoes. He took the coffee from her hands and moved over to the closet. The closet was like another room. He grabbed a security tag from the dresser on the wall and put a ring of keys in his pocket. He took another sip of the coffee and put the cup down on the dresser. "Damn." He said under his breath. He grabbed a jacket off the hanger and threw it over his arm.

"Call Frank at the club and tell them I won't be there for my nine A.M. t-time," he never slowed down as he kissed her cheek and was out the bedroom door.

His house was enormous. As he walked down the hall the paintings and wall decorations seemed to scream of money. He entered the small elevator and hit the one button. The doors were glass and the view as the elevator settled down to the main floor was breath taking. The front of the house was all glass and over looked a hillside and valley that was, despite the winter-cover overwhelming as views go.

He headed for the door and out into the crisp Oklahoma morning air. Mark was standing out front waiting to open the limo door. The car was already warm as he slid into the back seat. "Where to sir?" Mark asked as he put the limo in gear.

"Security," Fitzsimmons barked. "Hurry up." Mark started down the long drive and hit the button on the visor to open the electric gates below.

The Mercedes engine roared as Mark left the drive and started down the two lane highway towards his directed destination.

In the back seat Fitzsimmons was busy dialing on the car phone. "Brady." He said in a gruff voice. "We have problems with bluebird."

"What kind of problems?" The voice asked.

"I have no idea but my people say they are serious, meet me at security as quick as you can."

"I'll be there in twenty minutes, I'm about 100 miles south of you."

Fitzsimmons hung up the phone obviously nervous about bluebird. He spent the rest of the trip watching the countryside pass his windows at 80 miles an hour.

The security building sat alone. It was a one-story structure in the middle of a half of mile square and twelve feet high, chain link fence with razor wire across the top. The guard at the one and only gate recognized the limo but did not open up until he had checked Mark's ID and looked in the back to make sure Fitzsimmons was the only one inside. "Good morning

Mr. Fitzsimmons!" He said as he scanned the badge that was held up to the window. Fitzsimmons didn't answer as Mark hit the gas petal and the car raced towards the brick building in the center of the fence.

Mark parked by the only door to the building and hurried around to open the door for Fitzsimmons. He never said a word as he exited the car and started to the entrance. A security guard in gray pants and a crisp white shirt opened the door and held it for him to enter. Inside there were two people behind the desk. "Good morning." One said obviously used to not having the greeting returned. He scanned Fitzsimmons badge and the guard that opened the door moved down the hallway to open the elevator for Fitzsimmons. He followed the guard into the elevator and leaned against the back wall starring forward as the elevator started its trip down under the small brick building. "He's on his way." The guard at the desk said after he heard the elevator door shut. As he released the button on the intercom and closed the circuit he looked over at his counterpart at the desk and added, "and he's pissed about something."

The elevator dropped about three hundred feet before jarring to a halt. The doors opened and Fitzsimmons walked out and offered his badge to the guard at the desk directly ahead of him. Once scanned Fitzsimmons turned left and used his card to open the electronic door that let him into a brightly-lit room full of office cubicles.

He walked down the hallway about fifty feet and a young man dressed in a military looking jumpsuit approached him. "What the hell is going on Ed?" Fitzsimmons growled at him.

"I'm not to sure sir. We're still putting it together." He turned on his heel and he was walking side by side with Fitzsimmons towards a large glass office in the back of the room.

Fitzsimmons looked at him angrily, "what do we know at this point?" He took off his coat and dropped it on a chair turning to Ed and sitting behind a large desk.

"Some time yesterday." He looked at the tablet he was carrying. "Approximately 1700 hours. It looks like someone made a positive visual scan of Bluebird at his present location."

"That is impossible." Fitzsimmons was shaking his head. "That file can't be accessed by anyone in the country."

"The information was accessed from Canada. Are you familiar with the net link system?"

"Damn it!" Fitzsimmons said pounding the desk. "I knew that plan was going to be a pain in the ass. How much did they access?"

"Everything about Bluebird. It seems they got not one but two perfect visual corneal scans on him last night and the FBI and NCIC computers spilled their guts." Ed stopped, knowing Fitzsimmons was going to blow his top.

"Does Bluebird know this yet?" He demanded.

"Not unless he found out on his own. We haven't had any contact with him since he's become permanent at his present location. He's been on a blackout list."

"Where is this scanning being done and who in the hell is doing it?" Fitzsimmons was getting madder.

"It looks like Canadian Immigrations computer made the verification request.

"What in the hell is Canada doing with that type of scanning capability? I thought our people had that technology tied up. What else did you find out?"

"The scan was done within eight miles of Bluebirds permanent location, so the remote units have to be there somewhere with a hard line link with immigration in one of their larger cities."

Fitzsimmons thought for a minute. "Get a team in there and let Bluebird know we're coming to extract him. Tell him to pack his underwear and be ready to move tonight. I only hope it's not already too late."

"What about the remote station that's doing the scanning?" Ed asked.

"I want it shut down. Gone from the face of the earth. Tell the team to recover any information that the station may have collected and make sure anyone connected with this operation has a total memory loss." Fitzsimmons folded his hands on the desk. "Find out where this shit started. The Canadians didn't come up with this."

"Where should I send the team from, sir?" Ed asked wanting to make sure he covered his own ass.

"Send them out of Manhattan. They know what I need. Tell them I don't want any, I repeat, any loose ends." Fitzsimmons picked up the desk phone and began dialing.

"Is that all sir?" Ed asked.

"For now." He snapped and listened to the rings, "Brady will be here soon. I want him to take over at that time, and I want him to lead that team."

Ed was glad to hear that. He knew the shit had hit the fan and didn't want his neck in the middle. He started for the door, "Ed," his boss called after him. "Why didn't I find out about this for twelve hours?"

"I have no idea sir. I was handed the information of the breach when I walked into my office this morning and I called you." He reached for the door. "Sir, what about Canadian customs?"

"Fuck Canadian customs! Get the team in touch with our people in Winnipeg and have them sweep the area clean. Have them coordinate with Minot and go in low. I don't want Canada to even see their shadow until we can get this secure and get Bluebird out of sight."

"Yes sir," he started out the door as Brady was approaching. "Good morning, Mr. Brady." Brady nodded his head glancing over Ed's shoulder at a very agitated Fitzsimmons. He went into the office making sure the door closed behind him.

"What in the hell is going on?" Brady asked.

Fitzsimmons filled him in on the details. He was shaking his head when the boss finished. "What the hell do we do with Bluebird?"

"We'll stash him in Minot for a while so that we can tie up all the loose ends. We have too many other things to worry about now." Fitzsimmons thought a minute. "I want you on that team leaving from Manhattan. I want to make sure everything is done right up there."

Brady was already moving for the door. "Tell them I'll be there in less than two hours."

Ed was busy on the computer when Brady leaned over his cubical wall. "I'm headed for Manhattan. Tell them I want eight men to have my gear ready." He looked at his watch. "Tell Minot we'll be there at 1600 hours and to have our bird ready."

"Yes sir." Said Ed feeling better to know Brady was taking responsibility for the task Fitzsimmons had laid out. All hell was about to break loose up north.

Brady exited the front door of the brick building and passed Fitzsimmons car. Mark tried not to look at him as he jumped in the idling helicopter that lifted off almost as soon as he closed the door. Something big was up.

Chapter 9

Kevin parked in front of the post office and drank the last sip of his coffee. He saw there was no line inside and hurriedly put the folder under his coat. It was misting a light rain and it was freezing when it hit the ground.

"Good morning!" He said as he approached the desk. The old clerk looked up and smiled.

"If it isn't our American visitor." He eyed the file as Kevin pulled it out of his coat.

I'm trying to find where this person lives and I figure you might be able to help me." He handed the picture to the clerk.

"Grady," the clerk said. "Matthew Grady, Box 1158. He only comes in once a week to pick up his mail. Don't remember seeing him in a few days unless he came in last night. He lives on the north end of the lake somewhere."

Kevin's heart started beating rapidly. "Thank you." He returned the picture and started for the door. He stopped and looked for box 1158. He found it and peaked through the little glass window. "Empty.

He probably picked it up last night." Kevin said to himself.

He steered the Sedan towards the lake and remembered the old lady at the liquor store. As he slowed for an icy curve he thought 'if anyone knows where he lives, she does!'

The trip to the store took a few minutes. The rain was getting harder and was turning into sleet. The road was really getting slippery.

He parked in front of the store and struggled to keep his footing as he headed for the door. it was warm inside and there were a couple of older men leaning on the drink cooler drinking a beer. "Kind of early," Kevin thought as he approached the counter with the old woman leaning on it. "Hello again."

"Hi there. You out for a morning slide?"

"Really," Kevin concurred. "I need some help."

"I'll try," she said curiously as he pulled out the file from under his coat.

Kevin showed her the picture, "the postman says this is Matthew Grady and that he lives on the lake, would you know where?"

"Albert," she called to one of the beer drinkers. "How are your eyes," she chuckled.

"Crossed," he laughed heading to the counter.

"Do you know where Mr. Grady lives?" She showed him the picture. "I've seen him in here but he doesn't talk much. He buys Molson Canadian in a can."

"Oh yeah," Albert said. He's from Saskatchewan and he bought the old Brubaker place. As you go up the lake road his place is on the right side. Right on the lake. Got a shake roof, and the siding is painted red like a barn. I think he drives a white pick-up. Don't go down his driveway in this weather unless you have four wheel drive or you'll never get back up the road."

Kevin was getting more excited. "Thank you," he smiled at the old lady behind the counter and handed her a ten dollar bill. "Let me get them a couple more." He headed out the door waving to the two old men who were leaning on the cooler again.

He nearly fell trying to get back in the car and had to rock the vehicle to get it started back towards the road. This was a good day to be sitting in the room. As he started up the lake road he reached down to check his camera, the window said he had sixteen more shots.

The road was narrow and the sleet was making it dangerous as he drove on looking for the house. As he followed the curve to the right he saw the house ahead. It was fairly small but there was the white pick-up and the red siding. He stopped on the road and pulled over as far as he could without going off the black top. There was nothing moving when he got out and started towards the driveway. Albert was right, it was terribly steep and Kevin was having a hard time maintaining his balance. The pick-up had a Saskatchewan license plate and Kevin took a picture of it. The house was facing the lake with no windows towards the road. As Kevin started around the corner, he noticed the small boathouse down on the lake. Kevin took a few more pictures and then put the camera in his pocket. He walked to the front door of the cabin and took a big breath as he knocked on the glass. No answer.

He knocked again and looked through the glass windows on the front of the place. It was a neat scene inside. He could see a living room and kitchen down stairs and a loft with what looked like the bedroom upstairs. Still no answer. He heard a motor of some kind. The noise was coming from the boathouse.

He moved slowly down the steep stairs to the side of the boathouse. He could hear the hum of some kind of gasoline engine. As he moved along the side of the structure he noticed the front doors were ajar. He held the door in one hand and started to look around to see what was inside. At that moment the idling motor roared and a large snow mobile literally flew out the front doors scaring Kevin so badly that he fell over backwards. The man on the machine didn't notice Kevin as he flew out on to the frozen lake but when he glanced back over his shoulder he saw Kevin struggle to his feet. He slowed the machine and made a slow turn. He saw Kevin dusting himself and waving at him. The man slowly directed the snow mobile back towards the boathouse. He drove to about fifteen feet from Kevin and stopped. "Can I help you?" He asked staring at Kevin.

"Mr. Grady?" Kevin asked of the man. He was wearing a scarf and pulled it down from his face.

"Yes." The man answered. "Who are you?"

Kevin looked at the man and when their eyes met he knew, despite the mustache and beard, he was looking into the cold hard eyes of one of the most hated men in America. "You are McVey." He said seriously.

The man's eyes opened widely and all the color drained from his face. "Who in the fuck are you!" He demanded.

"I'm with the Canadian immigration." Kevin lied realizing what a dangerous position he was in. "I need to ask you a few questions."

He barely finished the words when McVey gunned the motor on the machine and cut the handles hard to the left. The snow-mobile spun around in a tight turn knocking Kevin over and he never let off the gas as he sped away at an unbelievable rate of speed. In a matter of seconds he had disappeared across the ice into a mist of snow and sleet that was falling. Kevin could barely hear the hum of the machine as he turned and tried to hurry back towards the shore.

He slipped and slid, falling a couple of times trying to get up the steps to the house. As he started around the side of the house he heard the phone start to ring. He made his way around the side of the house and fell again. As he started up the steep driveway it stopped ringing. By the time he opened the door to the car he heard it start ringing again.

He turned the car around and started back down the lake road breathing rapidly. Suddenly he realized what a stupid thing he had done. He looked back at the lake to see if he could see the man on the snow mobile but the mist and sleet had swallowed everything up.

When he opened the door to 105 he heard the printer working. He walked through the adjoining door and saw a small stack of reports on the rack. None of the things in the room seemed very important after the events of the last hour.

He checked to be sure that all the locks and chains were on the doors. He pulled the curtain back and stared at the empty parking lot. Only his vehicles and the three installation trucks were in the motel lot. There were a couple of cars at the lodge but things were pretty quiet. He really hoped they would stay that way.

He went back to the main station and punched in his code. "Yes Kevin, what can I help you with?" The computer responded.

"I'm just making sure everything is up and running."

"All systems are currently correct. I have been unable to access the NCIC and FBI systems since 1100 hours today. It seems they have stopped responding to my request."

Kevin felt the hair stand up on the back of his neck. "Have you checked all links?"

"Yes, Kevin all connections are correct." They have simply stopped responding!"

Chapter 10

Brady touched down at the secure airstrip outside of Manhattan, Kansas at 1:30 P.M. and never missed a step. A tall man in a black outfit met him on the way to the sleek jet that was waiting on the Tarmac 200 feet away, "Brady," he announced to the man who fell in beside him.

"Lewis Sir. The others are on the jet ready to go." He handed Brady a clipboard of information.

"Equipment," Brady asked scanning the paperwork.

"On board sir and more is waiting in Minot with our bird. They have two light weight four wheelers on board and will be tracking us on our approach."

The boarded the jet and the door closed behind them. Brady could hear the engines accelerate and the jet start to move. He fell into a seat and pulled out a cell phone. He fastened his seat belt and hit the dial code. It rang once. "Fitzsimmons here." The voice cracked. "Where are you?"

"Just leaving Manhattan, any updates?"

"Yes, the mobile scan is set up at a hotel outside of Dauphin, Manitoba about eight miles from Bluebird's location, coordinates will be on your positioning computer when you arrive there. We have been trying to raise bluebird but have had no response. I'm programming his numbers into your phone as we speak. Code 116 is that clear?"

"Yes sir." Brady answered. "Any idea how many players we are talking about up there?"

"I have no idea but clean the whole mess up neatly. Good luck." And he hung up.

"Yes sir," Brady said into the quiet phone as the jet lifted off from the deserted field. He was in the rear of the jet and he looked at the back of the heads of his team.

Chapter 11

Kevin called out to Kathy. "Hello there." The scan lit up.

"I'm right here. How's it going?" She moved the camera to where she was working, "I'm making dinner." He could see Amy hammering on her high chair. "Say hi to Daddy."

He smiled, "Hi Baby. What's for supper?"

"Tell Daddy hamburger and French fries," Kathy kidded. "Did you have a busy day?"

"Quite busy. I drove around a bit but the weather is getting pretty bad. It's sleeting and the roads are treacherous."

"Stay inside where it's warm. You don't need to be out do you?" She was worried about him. "The weather is bad here too. I'm planning a popcorn and movie evening."

"I wish I was there." He said watching her turn the patties in the frying pan. "I'll talk to you in the morning."

He decided to order some food to go and called the lodge. They said it would be ready in a few minutes and he put his coat on. When he opened the door the wet wind hit him full force. "What a night." He said as he tried to walk down the icy steps.

As he walked in the front door, the waitress was coming out of the kitchen with his order. He handed her his AMEX card and waited for her to run the bill. He could hear Chad's voice in the bar and when she handed him the pen he signed quickly and headed back to the room. As he passed the Sedan he remembered his camera under the front seat but decided it would be okay overnight in the car. He knew everyone in the place.

He locked the door against the cold air and put the chain across the gap. He ate the warm sandwich and washed it down with the cold soda. The food really hit the spot. He dumped the styro-foam containers in the wastebasket and went into 106 to sort the remaining folders.

Chapter 12

The jet touched down and taxied to a remote section of the airfield near a huge double prop helicopter. The team moved from one vehicle to the other quickly and soon the chopper was lifting off.

Brady moved to a console set up near the front of the machine. "Lewis," he said to the young man standing at his side, "you are going to extract Bluebird." He handed him a printed map that was in a packet on the console. "We don't have time to clean the area. So destroy the building. It looks like there is only one way in and out so give yourself time to get back before all hell breaks loose."

"Yes sir," Lewis said. He moved to the others of the team and separated them into two groups.

"I don't want any shooting unless it's unavoidable. I want everyone back in the air before they know we were there." He listened to the difference in the volume of the engines. They were going to silent running for the low quiet trip across the Canadian border.

Chapter 13

The food had made Kevin sleepy. He thought about calling Bob again but knew that he was probably entertaining in Orlando. Tomorrow is another day. He moved over to 105 and stretched out on the bed. He was asleep in moments and as he drifted off he hoped he wouldn't dream about McVey. Sleep was a peaceful relief after the events of the day and the apprehension he had about what might happen tomorrow. He was snoring in a few minutes and he never heard the muffled motors of the twin props as the big helicopter passed over the motel in a wide slow circle.

The large machine touched down in the dark in a farm field about one mile from the motel. The large ramp started to lower and the motors stopped. The two Hummer type vehicles started as Brady approached Lewis. "We're going to give you a head start. You have further to go. Radio me as soon as you have Bluebird. I want you back here before 2400 hours."

"Yes sir." Lewis climbed into the vehicle and it started down the ramp and across the frozen field. They had to cut a fence to access the road and one of the men sprayed a substance in the road to mark where the gap in the fence was for the return trip.

There was no traffic on the road but it was very slippery. The heavy vehicle held the road pretty well. "Turn left here," Lewis said looking at the small computer screen in his lap. "Onto Lake Rd," he said. "About five kliks on the right." No one said a word.

They approached the cabin and he tapped the driver on the shoulder. When the vehicle had stopped he told the driver, "turn around and wait here for us." The other members of the team followed Lewis out of the vehicle.

When they crept past the pick-up he signaled for one man to go around the other side of the cabin and the other followed him. "Bluebird!" Lewis called quietly. There was no answer. Lewis forced the door and the sound of the cracking of the doorframe broke the silence of the night air.

They advanced to the center of the room and suddenly the lights came on and McVey was behind them pointing a large handgun at them. "Who the fuck are you?" He demanded in the glaring light.

"We're friendlies here to take you home," Lewis started but McVey never heard a word. The thud of the blow from behind him rendered him unconscious as the other team member took him out. "Not very hospitable is he?" He joked as he picked up the handgun. "Get him back to the truck and tape him." He looked around and was glad to see a gas stove in the kitchen. "I'll be out in two minutes. I'll set the charges." The other team members handed him a couple of cardboard containers about the size of small milk cartons. As they dragged McVey out the door he moved around the house planting the charges and turning on the small receivers imbedded in them. His last action was to go to the kitchen and turn all the burners on full after extinguishing the pilot light. He hurried out the door and headed to the others up in the waiting Hummer.

"Run that pickup up the road and find a place to roll it into the Lake." He paused. "Make sure it sinks!"

Chapter 14

Brady's group followed Lewis' trail to the road and followed the computer instructions to the motel. They drove in the entrance and saw the lights on in the lodge. There were only two cars parked out front. "Park behind the main building and make sure we don't have any surprises." He and the others exited the vehicle and crept up the stairs. The hand held screen pointed him directly to 106. He kicked the door and it gave then the chain stopped it. He cursed and kicked it again tearing away wood and hardware. All the blinking lights temporarily screwed up the night vision glasses he was wearing, so he took them off and put them on the table. Suddenly the door beside him burst open.

Chapter 15

Kevin had been in a deep sleep when the first noise startled him. He opened his eyes in the dark room. He thought he had imagined the noises and then the second crash. He sat up in the bed and looked for the nearest thing to pick up for a weapon. All was quiet and he thought it might have been something outside. He moved over to the door connecting 105 and 106 and jerked it open.

In a flash a large body hit Kevin and followed him onto the bed. Brady was larger and heavier and as he fell on top of Kevin, Kevin shouted as the air was pushed out of his lungs.

Kevin was smaller but not weak by any means. He kicked and hit at Brady with all his might and was starting to scream for help when Brady pushed a pillow over his face to shut him up. About that time the laptop screen lit up and Kathy said, "Are you calling me honey?" The phrase was barely finished when one of Brady's team fired two 9mm slugs from a silent Beretta through the screen and Kathy went silent. "Damn!" He said realizing what he had done.

"Kill the camera," Brady gasped who was still trying to control Kevin who was fighting for his life, it was to no avail. It took less than a minute for Kevin to quit kicking and punching the larger man. Brady held the pillow down a little longer to make sure Kevin was dead and then got up off the bed.

He looked around the darkened room. Get that laptop. He saw the cigarettes on the nightstand. "Make it look like at accident." He went into the other room. He looked at all the monitors with their empty scenes. He tried to get the main station to respond.

"How can I help you," the computer asked. The voice startled Brady and he moved full attention to the keyboard. He typed in a few letters.

"I don't understand your entry, please try again."

He tried a few more keys. "Is that you Kevin?" The machine asked. "Please supply visual clearance."

The men in the other room were busy. One picked up Kevin's lifeless head and put the pillow behind it and arranged his arms and legs like he was asleep. He tore open the pack of cigarettes and took one out leaving the open pack on the nightstand. He put the ashtray by Kevin's leg. The other man was busy putting the laptop with the shattered screen in his bag. He moved around the room picking up anything that looked important. His partner picked up one of the bottles and started to open it. He saw the insurance receipt and the other papers Kevin had put under the bottles for pressing. "Here," he said handing the papers to the other man who put them in the bag.

He opened the bottle and put it in Kevin's lifeless mouth. He poured a small amount into Kevin's mouth, and put some in a glass in his right hand and tightened the fingers around it. He heard the computers voice in the other room and was spooked by the feeling someone was watching them.

"Are we ready?" He asked Brady. "Zebra I come in," Brady's radio cracked.

"Go ahead," Brady, said thumbing the small transmitter.

"We have Bluebird and we're almost back to the bird. Do you want me to light things up?" Lewis asked.

"Better wait till we get out of here, I'll give you the word." He paused and put the radio down.

"We might be too far away Zebra." Lewis suggested.

Brady was already mad at the computer. He snapped at Lewis. "Don't worry get back to the bird and if needed we'll fly by."

One of the men walked into the room and continued picking up papers and the completed reports. "Is that another camera?" He asked pointing to the small lens taped to the side of the main station monitor.

"Shit!" Brady exclaimed. He hit the eject buttons on the two disc trays and pulled out the discs. "Let's get out of here," he said as he looked at Kevin on the bed. "Are you set?" He was talking to the last man.

"Go ahead," the man said. "I'll be right behind you," he removed his night vision goggles and put them in his bag. He turned on a light in the room to make it a bit brighter. He moved over to Kevin's body and sprayed a small can of something all over the bed. He stood back and lit the cigarette. When he threw the cigarette on the bed by Kevin's hand it ignited the spray and the bed was in full flames. He started out the door when

Kevin's cell phone rang. He picked it up off the top of the TV and put in it his bag. The bed-clothes were in full flames now. He sprayed the can from the bed down across the floor to 106 closing the door behind him. He sprayed all the computer stations and monitors as the fire tried to creep under the door. He looked around and, satisfied with his work, he turned on the lights and exited the room pulling the door shut behind him. He smiled as he heard the computer saying, "Is that you Kevin?"

He hurried to the Hummer and jumped in as the driver gunned the engine. He looked back at the room curtains that were getting brighter but actually looked like someone was up late.

"Why did you turn on the lights?" The driver asked.

"I wanted the fire to get going pretty well before they noticed it." He turned back around in his seat. "I wonder how old Kevin is doing?" He said joking.

Brady didn't laugh. He knew that mistakes had been made and his boss didn't like mistakes. They sped to the helicopter and drove up the ramp that closed as they slid to a stop inside. The big bird lifted off the ground and tilted forward. Lewis looked at Brady who was removing his ski mask. "Light it up." Lewis pushed the button on the detonator and moved to a window in time to see the frozen lake light up brightly with a series of explosions. The big machine headed south quietly.

Chapter 16

Kathy was frantic. She could not get him to answer on his computer and she thought she had heard him yell. When she made it to the computer from the living room she thought she heard a strange voice and saw a shadow.

She was trembling as she dialed his cell number. "Come on Kevin pick up!" She said as the phone continued to ring. "Come on answer. You always answer." She said hopefully. She hung up and redialed but still got no answer. Running to the kitchen, she looked for the motels' phone number.

As a last resort she dialed on the regular phone. "May I help you," the voice said. Kathy was starting to cry. "I need the number for the Dauphin Inn in Dauphin, Manitoba." Kathy's hands were shaking.

"Let me get international information Mam." The operator said.

"Please hurry," Kathy said, "this is an emergency!" International information came on and they told her they would ring the number for her if it was an emergency. She waited as it started to ring.

"Dauphin Inn," the female clerks' voice said.

"My husband is Kevin Bennett, he is a guest with you. Could you please ring his room, I can't get him to answer his call."

Hearing Kathy's voice the girl said, "Sure. The weather is terrible here tonight and it may be affecting his phone. I'll ring his room."

She put Kathy through to 105. The phone rang about 5 times and the girl picked up. "Mam, he may be asleep but there are a couple of people in the lounge that work with him. I'm going to send one of them back to his room and wake him up and we'll call you right back. Give me your number."

"Thank you. Thank you very much!" Kathy said feeling better because the woman was being so helpful.

Kathy gave the girl the number and she hung up to wait for Kevin to call.

The desk clerk finished writing Kathy's number down and started for the lounge.

Chad and Phillip were at the bar. "Hey Chad!" She said loudly.

"Yea Baby." Chad said with a big grin "are you ready to take me home yet?"

"Not quite." She said, laughing at the bartender who was making faces about Chad. "Your boss's wife is calling from the States. He won't answer the phone. Will you go back and wake him up and tell him to call her?"

"He might be in bed with that computer trying to interface." Chad made a thrusting motion with his hips. "He might not want to be bothered."

"Get going." She said as every one had a laugh.

Chad put on his coat and started for the door. "I'll be back." He said loudly in his best Schwartzenegger accent and blew her a kiss. He walked out the door and waved at the camera he and Phillip had installed.

He was having a hard time walking, between the beer and the ice it was difficult. He looked at the windows of Kevin's rooms, the lights seemed to be flashing normal to bright, the closer he got the more he realized something was wrong. As he stepped up on the porch he could feel the heat and realized the room was on fire. He made a foolish mistake, whether it was the beer or the panic to try and save Kevin no one will ever know.

Chad rushed the door and when it crashed open from his weight the cold air hit the fire and the explosion was enormous.

It shook the Lodge like an earthquake and the people inside ran out to see what was going on. Mike was out in the parking lot when Philip ran up to him. "Where's Chad?" He screamed.

"I thought he was with you," Mike answered.

"He came to get Kevin a couple of minutes ago."

They both started towards Kevin's room as the roof blew off the building. In the shadows behind the lodge they could see Chad's smoking body lying against a dumpster. They ran over to him and turned him over. "God Damn" Philip said falling back.

Mike reached for Chad's burnt neck to check for a pulse or any signs of life. "He's gone Phillip." He turned to his coworker. "What in the hell is going on?"

"I don't know," Phillip said crying looking at his friend as the sound of a siren drew closer. "The girl from the Lodge asked Chad to wake up Kevin and he walked back here. That's all I know. Then all hell broke loose."

Mike walked over to the front of the motel rooms but was unable to see anything in 105 or 106 the rooms were fully engulfed. "I sure hope Kevin was out tonight," He prayed.

He backed away from the flames and grabbed Phillip by the arm, pulling him away to safety as the fire truck and ambulance pulled up.

Chapter 17

The phone was ringing loudly as Bob looked out from under the pillow. The sun was just coming up in Orlando and was shining right in his eyes. He reached out from under the covers for the phone on the table. "Hello" he croaked with a scratchy voice.

"Bob, its Mac." Mac was Bob's boss at the Dallas Evening News but the two had been friends for 20 years. Both were hard-core newsmen and liked what they did, "Have you talked to Kathy?"

Bob sat up "No what's wrong?" His friend didn't say anything. "What the hell is it Mac?" He demanded.

"Kathy called, she didn't know how to get a hold of you. Kevin is dead!" Bob felt his chest constrict as though all the air had been pulled out of him.

"What happened? Where's Kathy, is she okay?" He didn't know what to ask first.

"Kathy is a basket case, you need to call her. I have a friend who lives in Duluth and I took the liberty of sending her over to sit with Kathy until we sort things out."

Mac paused and rattled some papers; "I spoke with a Captain Reynolds, who is the RCMP officer trying to sort out what happened. I'm faxing over a list of contracts and names to your hotel. Talk to Kathy and let me know what you need to do. I have my secretary working with your girl to clear your schedule. Call me back and let me know what you need."

"Thanks Mac." Bob said rubbing his head.

"Call your daughter she needs you. Take care." Mac hung up.

Bob dialed Kathy's number. It rang twice and a strange voice answered. "Bennett residence."

"This is Bob Shroud I need to talk to my daughter, is she there?"

The woman's voice softened, "Yes Mr. Shroud. Let me get her." She put the phone down and he could hear her call Kathy. "It's your father."

"Dad!" Kathy said crying. "I need you" She broke down sobbing. "Kevin is dead and I don't know what to do."

Bob never had such a feeling of helplessness as he tried to console her. "Easy baby. Take it easy." He felt himself starting to choke-up as she cried.

"What can I do?" She continued, out of control.

"Easy Honey. Tell me what I can do. I can be up there this afternoon."

"No dad!" She seemed to settle down. "I need you to find out what happened to Kevin. The police called here but they seem all screwed-up. Did you talk to Kevin over the weekend?"

"No baby, I've been down here on this publishers conference shaking hands and buying drinks. I haven't talked to anyone. I didn't even bring my phone."

"He was trying to get in touch with you. He seemed worried about something." She settled down a little. "Dad, they tried to tell me Kevin fell asleep smoking and his cigarette started a fire, you know that's a crock of crap! Help me dad!" She started to cry again.

"Take it easy baby. I'm gonna call Mac right now and I'll be in Canada this afternoon. Is Amy okay?"

"She's fine dad. Just please find out what happened to Kevin."

"Okay baby lock up tight and I'll call you this afternoon." He hung up and dialed Mac on his direct line, he picked up on the first ring and never got to say hello. "Mac, I need to get to Manitoba right now." Bob sounded cold and definite.

"Take the plane. I'll have the rest of our people come back on Southwest."

"I might need some help. Can I take Paul with me?" Paul was a young, eager man who was fast on his feet and had a way with people.

"Take him. I'm calling legal right now and the airport to get you clearance. Bring my plane back in one piece." He hesitated "Bring Paul back in one piece too."

Bob hung up the phone and called Paul's room. He could hear a woman in the background when Paul answered. "Hello!"

"Get dressed and pack you stuff. Meet me in the lobby in 30 minutes." Bob paused. "Did you hear me?"

"I'll be there," Paul said, knowing something was going on. Bob's attitude and voice spoke for itself. He hung up and headed for the shower.

They met in the lobby and Bob stopped only long enough to pick-up his faxes and sign the bill. "Orlando International, Commercial Terminal," He barked at the cab driver. They rode 5 miles before Paul asked. "You okay Bob?" Where the heck are we going?"

"North" Bob said as the cab hit the interstate and headed for the airport. There was no more conversation.

Chapter 18

The helicopter set down in Minot and the team began to file off. Brady removed the tape from McVey's mouth. "Who in the fuck are you?" It was dark.

"Relax soldier," Brady told him "We're on your side."

McVey stared at him as Brady started talking on the phone. "Bluebird is back in the nest." He told Fitzsimmons. "What do we do now?"

"I have another team there to keep him safe until we evaluate our situation. You get back here and bring anything you recovered so that we might see where we stand."

"Yes sir I'll see you around noon." The call was over and he turned to McVey. "You've been compromised and we pulled you out of a bad situation. You need to be patient until we can relocate you."

"I saw the guy yesterday," McVey started and Brady turned to listen. "He said he was Canadian immigration. But he never flashed a badge or an I.D."

"I don't think he'll be bothering you anymore," Brady said as he walked down the ramp. He motioned to the men at the base of the ramp. "Make him comfortable until I get in touch with you!" With that he boarded the jet and the engines started to whine as the door closed behind him.

Chapter 19

Bob saw the police car waiting for them beside the terminal. As he walked towards the officer he saw the RCMP insignia on his shoulders. "Captain Reynolds?" He asked the officer.

"You must be Mr. Shroud. I'm sorry for your loss." The Captains voice was genuinely apologetic.

"This is Paul Martinez my associate." There were handshakes all around and they got in the car.

"The incident happened around midnight last night." The officer started as they turned onto the highway to the inn. "The fire was pretty devastating and there is not very much to go on."

As they neared the inn he could see all the cars and the police tape. "The wooden structure was nearly destroyed. The building was about 40 years old and dry as a bone. By the time the local fire department arrived it was fully engulfed."

The local policeman waved the Captain's car through the security perimeter and Bob's stomach tightened as he looked at the burnt out shell that used to be Kevin's rooms. "Damn" He said as Paul put his hand on Bob's shoulder.

They got out of the car and walked towards the fire scene. Bob noticed the chalk outline where Chad's body was thrown. "Was that Kevin?" He asked.

"No." The Captain paused. "That was the young fellow who tried to get your son in law out of the building. Witnesses say when he opened the door the air must have hit the fire and the force threw him back here."

The steps were still standing but badly burned. Paul asked the Captain, "May I take some pictures?"

"Certainly, but if you see anything that might help us out please let me know." Paul began to snap shots of the fire scene. "We covered the body with that plastic. All the water and cold weather last night didn't help much."

"The building was built on a concrete pad; you don't see much of that up here. The fire didn't get much air until that young man opened the door."

"Raymond" he called to an officer sifting through the charred debris. The man stood up and approached Bob and Paul. "This is Robert Shroud he is a relative of the deceased. Do you have anything yet?"

Raymond shook Bob's hand after he removed his glove. "Our condolences Sir." He shook Paul's hand. "Mr. Bennett used this room as a residence and the other room for his computer workspace." Bob glanced at the melted monitors on the collapsed tables. "My preliminary examination turned up an ashtray and a glass on the remains of the bed. There were the remains of a pack of cigarettes on or near the nightstand. I found two bottles of alcohol in the room.

One bottle on the floor by the bed and the other bottle by the window. It could have been on the dresser or TV but the blast knocked it to the floor. Funny the bottle didn't break. The rug never did burn completely so it probably cushioned the fall."

"At first glance I would say he may have had a drink and fell asleep with a smoke in the bed." The officer returned to his work.

Bob bit his lip. He knew Kevin didn't drink or smoke, Bob didn't want to speak up and spook the Captain, who was being most cooperative. He looked at Paul and pointed to the other room. Paul followed his lead and began taking another series of shots.

Bob's hands were trembling. The afternoon was clear but the temperature was too cold for his light jacket. "How about a cup of coffee?" The Captain offered, pointing towards the lodge.

They walked into the lodge. It was open for business and there were a lot of people who stopped and cast curious stares in his direction. "Back this way," the Captain pointed towards the lounge. There was an officer seated, talking with Philip and Mike taking their statements. "These gentlemen were working with Kevin on his project."

Bob shook hands with the two and introduced himself. The waitress brought coffee and he warmed his hands on the cup as he listened to the officer asking questions of the men. He wanted to know if Kevin had been in the lounge the night before.

"Not at all." Phillip answered. "The waitress said he got some take out earlier but he was in the room with those computers all the time." Phillip rubbed his head with his palms and leaned over the table.

"Kevin was all business." Mike started "He was running tests for a system that he designed for the Government. He was working day and night to make sure things were right for some kind of show for the big wigs on Monday."

"What kind of test?" The officer asked.

"Some type of visual surveillance linked with computers" Mike answered. This made the Captain lean a bit closer to the table.

"Who were you working for?" The Captain asked Mike.

"We work for Brett Leeland with Canadian Immigration. We were on loan to Kevin for this project. We placed cameras and ran cabling to the motel for this project."

"There are three vehicles in front of Mr. Bennett's room. Can you tell me who drives the two with Manitoba tags?" The interviewer asked.

"They were for Kevin if he needed them. Brett had the rental company drop them off. I think he only used the automobile. I never saw the pickup move." Mike looked at Phillip and he nodded his support.

"How many cameras did you install?" The Captain was curious about the test.

"Fifty." Mike replied.

"Fifty?" The Captain seemed surprised. "Have you talked with Mr. Leeland?"

"No sir, I tried to reach him by phone but his office is closed till tomorrow. I called our office and they are trying to reach him at home, we have had no luck yet."

"Where did you install these cameras?" The Captain asked of Mike.

"Everywhere, in town, at the shopping center, at the ice rink and here."

"What do you mean here?" The Captain snapped.

"We put one right in front to scan people at the lodge." Mike responded.

"Show me." The Captain said and they got up and started to the door with Bob close behind.

They walked onto the front porch of the lodge and Mike pointed to the camera Phillip had placed on the pole by the street. The Captain walked to the pole. He came back and told Bob that the camera probably recorded the whole fire. "It's a shame the fire destroyed the system, we would have had a birds eye view of what happened."

Bob's mind was racing as he excused himself. He walked back to the motel rooms, his eyes following the gray video wire overhead. He motioned to Paul. "What's up?" Paul asked. He was changing a setting on his camera.

Bob asked in a low voice "Did you see that gray video cable running overhead?" Paul looked up and nodded his head. "I want to see what that camera over there is looking at." He pointed towards the road and Paul's eyes followed the cable to the camera enclosure.

"I know the wire is burned by the computers but could you fit a new end on that video lead and hook it up to your laptop to see what we've got.

"Sure" Paul said. I just need to get back to the plane and get my workbag.

"Captain Reynolds" Bob said to the approaching officer. "May we use this car to get some equipment from our plane?" He pointed to the rental sedan with the Manitoba tags.

"I don't see why not, it has nothing to do with the fire." He turned to Mike "Do you have the keys?" Mike was already taking a key off his ring.

"I kept the extra in case we had to take them back." He handed it to Bob who handed it to Paul.

"Paul let me use your cell phone." He requested and Paul gave it to him as he walked towards the car.

"I need to call my daughter" He told the Captain and moved away for some privacy.

As he punched in the numbers of his daughter's phone he knew what he had to say but had no idea how to say it. The machine picked-up and he was glad for a bit more time to plan how he was going to deal with his daughter who he knew had to be frantic. "It's me honey. I hope you're okay. I'm gonna try your cell. Take care, I love you."

He thumped the cell phone against his forehead as he hung up. Taking a deep breath he dialed her cell number. She answered on the second ring. He could tell she was crying. "Hello." She said not recognizing the number on her screen.

"Honey its me." He said in a quiet voice.

"Dad, I'm so glad to hear your voice." She started to sob. "What's going on up there?"

"Are you and the baby okay?" He asked trying to calm her down.

"We're fine." Her voice quivered. "What happened to Kevin, Dad?"

"Honey there was a fire." He squeezed the phone as his daughter started to cry. "Right now we don't know what happened or what caused it but we're working with the Canadian authorities to sort things out." He paused to let her cry. "I wish I was there with you."

"No dad!" She said in a strong voice. "We're okay. I want to know what happened to Kevin."

"I'll get to the bottom of it Honey." He hoped his reassurance would help her pain a little but knew the words probably sounded hollow owing to what she was feeling. "Do you feel like helping out with a few answers?"

Her voice settled a little. "Sure Dad."

"I need to know if Kevin had a direct line feed back to Duluth. If he did where did all the feed go to?"

"He was linked up with his office and the house. That night I thought he called out my name to say goodnight but I lost the feed from his PC."

"You mean you were in contact with him that night late?" Bob asked trying to put things together.

"He had his computer linked to mine and it was voice activated. All we had to do was speak and the unit gave us visual and audio contact."

"What about the main computer he was doing his work with?"

"That was linked direct to the office and his work station in his workshop."

"You mean that everything he did up here is on the machine in your house?"

"I'm sure it is Dad." She stopped sounded hurt and her voice became very steady. "What's going on Dad?"

"I don't know Honey." He paused. "Where are you now?"

"I'm at Margaret's house."

"I need you to go home and get all the information downloaded from Kevin's computer. He paused and thought for a minute. "Be careful just get in, get the information and get out. Okay?"

"I'm on the way." She grabbed her coat and started to pack-up Amy.

"Be careful." He insisted again. "Honey, something is odd about this whole thing and I don't know what might have happened but that machine in your closet will answer a lot of questions."

"I'll call you as soon as I get the discs." She was buttoning Amy's sweater and grabbing her purse. Margaret heard her heading for the door.

"Where are you off to Kathy?" She asked drying her hands on her apron.

"I have to run back to the apartment and pick up a few things. I'll be right back." Kathy closed the door behind her and started down the walk to her car.

Chapter 20

"What the hell happened up there?" Fitzsimmons voice was sarcastic and demanding as he tossed his coat onto a chair in the glass office and turned to confront Brady who had still not changed from his dark clothing and had a bit of grease paint left on his neck and ears.

"We had a casualty sir, one Kevin Bennett." Brady was not through talking but his boss cut him off.

"A casualty?" He snapped putting his hands on the desk and pushing his face close to Brady's. "You killed an American Citizen that worked for some type of security firm aligned with the Canadian Government."

Brady never took his eyes off Fitzsimmons. "I did what I had to do sir. Things went a little haywire."

"You're a professional." Fitzsimmons shouted. The people in the outer offices could not hear but they could see the look on his face and busied themselves at their tasks glad not to be the one receiving the tongue-lashing. "Professionals don't let things go haywire!" Fitzsimmons sat down and took a deep breath. "What about Bluebird?"

"Locked down in Minot." He was glad his boss was through yelling. They had been together a long time and he was used to Fitzsimmons moods. He knew things had gotten out of hand in Canada and he knew the ass chewing was coming. "All the information in the motel has been turned into section six for sifting and documentation. We destroyed the rooms in the motel and Bluebird's home, the place was pretty remote and I'm sure the fire took good care of everything."

"Bluebird's file has been removed so the only link is that house and the information in that motel."

"The motel had a live feed to someone. When we were in the room the laptop went live with a visual and a woman came on live."

"Did the computer have a camera? Did they see you and your people?" Fitzsimmons started to standup again and stopped when a young man knocked on the door. He waved him in and held his hand out for the papers the man extended.

"This is all the information on the man in Canada and his company in Duluth, we're still working on what his purpose and connection with the Canadians was."

"Thank you," Fitzsimmons dismissed him with a wave and paged through the small bundle that was Kevin. He paused on a couple of pages and the silence was like an eternity to Brady.

"We should be able to control all information that went to the business location in Duluth but it seems he had a link to his home." He paused. "Get in there and clean up all the loose ends."

"When do you—-," Brady started.

"Now damn it, yesterday, for Christ sake. If we don't neutralize this in a hurry it's going to bring everything down around our ears." He was fuming again.

Brady got up from the table and started for the door. "No loose ends damn it. Get that computer and all the information that might have passed through it in the last week" He turned his attention to the papers again and as Brady passed through the door he called out to him. "Wait a minute." He picked out the sheet of paper with the Canadian mail receipt stapled to it. "He sent some special mail home. I'll bet this is the back-up." He handed the paper to Brady who had returned. "Got it."

Brady took the paper and left the office. As he moved to the elevator he was talking into his radio and planning the next move to try to contain the information that Fitzsimmons was so worried about. He was mad and embarrassed about the situation in Canada and wanted to make things right. "Yes sir" the voice on the radio cracked.

"Brady here" he paused to look at his watch. "Five man crew. Tinker. In 20 minutes. I need a civie vehicle."

"Yes sir, see you in 20 minutes." The voice responded and Brady disappeared in the elevator.

Chapter 21

Bob was watching the inspector poke around in the burnt rubble when Paul tapped him on his shoulder. "You need to see this." He said quietly, tapping his pocket. He led Bob to the back of the porch of the lodge and pulled a small camera out of his pocket. He handed it to Bob. "I found this on the floor of the car, it has a little space left but it looks like someone might have taken a lot of pictures."

"It looks like Kevin's. Let see what we've got." He handed the camera back to Paul.

Paul pulled the camera slide open and removed the small cassette. He set his laptop up on the old table and pressed the cassette into the port in his laptop. "30 images" He told Bob. And the screen cleared. There were a few pictures of the lodge and downtown Dauphin and then Paul paused on a picture of the bait house.

"Can you download any of those?" Bob asked.

"Sure" Paul said and opened his bag removing a small printer. It took a couple minutes but then Bob was holding a 5 x 7 color print of the bait shop. "Nice picture." Bob said. "What else have we got?" He crowded a bit closer to Paul to see the small screen a little clearer.

The pictures were of the lake and a narrow road but then there were a series of shots of a small house and a pickup truck. "Print all those." Bob told Paul.

As the printer was whining they continued to scan the rest of the pictures. The shots went around the side of the house and then down towards the boathouse. Bob breathed in sharply as he saw the picture of a figure approaching on a snowmobile. The last picture was obviously taken from a lower angle and the figure on the snowmobile was moving away. "From the looks of the snow flying he's in a hurry." Bob said.

"Captain Reynolds," Bob said as he saw the officer approaching. He motioned to Paul to cover the pictures. "How's it going?"

"Not too well Mr. Shroud." The Captain pulled his notebook out of his pocket. "Something is very wrong here." He dropped into a chair and turned to a well-scribbled page. He took a deep breath and let it out slowly. "This is a quiet little town, in the space of a couple of hours last night they suffered 2 major fires. People reported heavy aircraft noises and explosions and there is nothing but a bunch of marks in a farmers field and 2 burnt buildings." He closed his notebook and rubbed his head trying to make the headache he was experiencing go away.

"Where was the other fire?" Paul asked.

"A lake house about 10 miles from here, total loss. By the time the fire department got there all that was left were cinders."

"Would you mind if we went out to that location Captain?" Bob asked. He was aware of the odd look the Mountie gave him when he asked.

"Of course not. I have to go out there now, you can ride with me or follow in the sedan." He got up and started towards the steps. Bob saw him pause and turn around to face him. "Mr. Shroud" He started in a low voice. "I sympathize with you for your loss but if you know anything that could help us in this investigation, I would appreciate your help."

"Captain, I appreciate your caring and I promise you that if I find anything that will help you'll be the first to know." He smiled but Reynolds face remained serious.

As Bob turned away he noted the concern on Paul's face. "Looks like some bad shit." Paul said matter-of-factly. "Do you think we should show him the pictures?"

"Not quite yet." Bob said, "I have to put a few things together." They left the porch and got into the sedan. The heat felt good as they pulled out on the road behind Captain Reynolds. Paul was driving and Bob relaxed and looked at the scenery as they moved down the road.

A couple miles down the road they passed the place where the helicopter had landed and the officers were marking and measuring the tracks of the vehicles that passed through the damaged fence. "Something very weird happened here boss."

Bob acknowledged his statement with a nod. "I think you're right" He scratched his head and thought about how much he wanted to sleep. He needed a drink.

"Hey boss," Paul said, "There's the bait shop."

"We'll stop on the way back." Bob said rubbing his eyes. As they turned onto the lake road he saw the Captain's eyes in the rear view mirror watching him. He knew he didn't believe all he had said.

It took only a few minutes to reach the remains of the building. All that was still there to resemble a home was a part of a fireplace still standing. "Hell of a fire!" Paul said as they followed the Captain down to the house.

Bob looked around the area and saw police markers as far as 2 hundred feet away. "Must have been quite a fire." He said as the Captain stopped to wait for him.

"People across the lake said they heard a number of explosions. Some debris made it all the way across the road and into the woods. Odd because the structure only had a wood fireplace and a small gas stove. There is a type of residue present that is consistent with explosives and the force of the blast had to be tremendous."

Bob's throat tightened as he looked towards the lake and saw the boathouse. "Bingo." He said as he and Paul headed down the steps to the lower building.

Bob's hands stung against the cold metal of the boathouse door hardware. Inside was the snowmobile they had seen in the picture. "Looks like the one Mr. X was driving when Kevin took his picture. Bob looked around the boathouse and saw a small telescope fishing rod with a plastic handle.

He heard footsteps coming from the fire site and quickly pulled a handkerchief from his pocket and carefully wrapped it around the handle of the rod before tucking it under his coat.

Captain Reynolds entered the boathouse and looked around but was focused on Bob and Paul. "Anything interesting?" He asked Bob. His eyes fixed on Bob waiting for an answer and Bob wanted to lay it all out on the table but decided to wait for a few more pieces of the puzzle.

"Not really." He looked past the officer to the frozen lake. "What does your investigator say about the fire?" Captain Reynolds knew Bob was keeping something back but thought honesty was best. "The fire was definitely set, probably in four or five places by some type of explosive devices. The cabin was built of wood and had shake shingles so it went up pretty fast. Not too much left but ashes."

"Makes you think they might have been trying to hide something." Bob mused pulling his coat tight around his neck to keep out the cold wind from the lake. "They seemed to have overlooked the boathouse or maybe they didn't see it in the dark." Bob and Paul started up the steps to the house. "I'll see you back at the lodge Captain, I want to look around a bit before it gets too dark."

The officer didn't answer. He stared after Bob and spoke to his assistant. "Mr. Shroud knows a lot more than he is telling us and I'm beginning to resent that." He looked back into the boathouse. "Check registration and ownership on that mobile and try to get some decent fingerprints off some of the things in here." He started out and spoke over his shoulder "Don't dawdle, I feel time is of the essence and I need some hard information to use to find what the hell we are into here." He went up the steps past the burned house and got in his car. "Reynolds here." He spoke into the radio.

"Yes sir." The radio cracked "The major needs to talk to you." There was a pause "Captain, I'm passing you through now."

"Major Overland here, is that you John?" The voice was clear and demanding.

"Yes sir" Reynolds answered. "How are you?"

"I'm confused and damned concerned." He paused for a few seconds. "Give me 5 minutes and call me back on my cell phone."

"Yes sir," Reynolds answered. Quite surprised at his superior's request. He continued to the main road and turned back toward the lodge. He noticed the sedan Bob and Paul were using at a small bait shop. He thought they might be getting a coffee. The air outside was getting colder as the sun started to set.

Chapter 22

The bait shop was small and crowded and the old woman looked Paul and Bob over pretty well when they walked in the door. After a stop at the coffee urn the pair walked to the register and as Paul was paying for the coffee Bob pulled out the pictures and selected the one showing the house and pickup truck. "Do you know this house?" He asked the old cashier.

"I used to but it's gone now." She handed Paul his change. "Had a bad fire last night?" She looked Bob up and down noticing his unshaven face. "Are you the police?"

"No mam." Bob answered sipping the hot coffee. "My son in law died at the lodge last night in another fire and I think the two might be connected."

The woman's eyes saddened "I met that young man. He stopped in here and spent some money with me. He was inquiring about that house and the fella who lived there. I'm sorry about him dying."

"Thank you." Bob said, "Do you know who lived there?"

"Man from Saskatchewan." A voice piped up at Bob's elbow. Bob turned to see a man as old as the cashier with a half-empty bottle of Molson in his hand. "Moved in about 6 months ago. Didn't mix too much."

"Any one seen him today?" Paul asked.

"Nope." The old man scratched his beard. "Him and his pickup both gone and the house burned to the ground. Something funny there eh?"

"What was his name and where was he from in Saskatchewan?" Bob asked loudly addressing everyone in the store.

"Real estate lady once told me he was from way up North, called him ---Grady." He paused for a minute. "Said that he bought the place for cash."

Bob tipped his coffee cup to the group and started for the door. "Thanks for your help." He said as he continued for the door. "Let's take a look at that field before it gets dark."

Paul drove to the break in the fence and pulled to the side of the road. As they got out Bob recognized one of the officers working as the one who was sifting through Kevin's motel room. "How's it going?" Bob asked.

"Loosing our light but we're about done here." The young man responded.

"May we borrow a light and look around a bit?" Paul asked.

"Sure." The officer handed him a large flashlight. "We've taken plenty of pictures, if you want to view them on your laptop I'll have them at the lodge."

The officers were packing up their gear as Bob and Paul looked at the tracks leading to the large area in the center of the field of fresh frozen snow and ice. "Humvees" Paul said quietly. "At least two or three."

Bob looked at him a little surprised "Military vehicles?" He asked.

"Looks like it to me." They had reached the depressed area in the middle of the field. "Looks like a bobbing heavy chopper. The kind our Special Forces use." Paul searched the ground and marked a straight line perpendicular to the tracks. "Here's where the ramp dropped to unload and load."

"Does the Canadian Military have this kind of helicopter?" Bob asked.

"I'm sure they do. All the Military use these because they are so powerful and fast." Paul continued to search around the marks made by the ramp. He kicked at the snow for a little while as Bob buttoned his coat up. After a few minutes he bent down and moved some snow out of his way. He reached down and with shivering fingers picked up a few small pieces of something he offered for Bob's inspection. "Four cigarette butts. Someone was waiting a while."

Bob picked up one of the filtered remains and looked at it closely. "Marlboro." He paused. "American cigarettes?"

Paul shrugged his shoulders as Bob picked up the other butts from Paul's frozen fingers. "Let's get back to the lodge." He said as he started back to the sedan. He noticed how dark it had gotten in the time since the sun had gone down.

Chapter 23

"What in the hell went on down there, John?" His superior asked with urgency in his voice. "My office has been a madhouse over this. The press has gotten wind of the story and are probably about to descend on you."

"We really don't know sir" He began. "We have two fatalities. One person is missing and there were two bad fires. One was definitely arson and there seem to have been some high explosives used to destroy one structure."

"Explosives." His superior snapped. "What kind of explosives."

"We have no idea." We are running tests but will probably have to get things back to the lab for accurate tests."

"I spoke with the local constable and he says there is an American newsman poking around your investigation."

"That would be Mr. Shroud sir. He is the father in law of the deceased. I extended the courtesy to him at the request of Major Lewellen from the Northern District."

"John I don't like this." He paused. "You work for me not Lewellen and I don't want this person screwing up a Canadian investigation. I don't care who he is or who he knows. We don't need to be the laughing stock of some American newspaper." He thought for a few seconds. "Keep him out of your way and if Mr. Lewellen has anything to say have him say it to me."

"Yes sir." John responded. "I'm sending the evidence collected to your lab. It will be there in the morning. I'll deal with Mr. Shroud as soon as he arrives."

"Let's keep Canadian business in Canada John." His voice was very serious. "Something stinks about this!"

Chapter 24

When Bob and Paul walked into the lodge Bob saw the look on Reynolds face and knew they were probably going to have quite a conversation. As he headed for the restaurant the Mountie cut him off, took him by the arm and guided him to the men's room. As they entered Reynolds slid the bolt locking the door and checked all the stalls to make sure they were alone.

"Mr. Shroud." He started. "I have been ordered by my superiors to keep you away from this investigation."

"Captain" Bob started to interrupt.

"Give me a minute Mr. Shroud." The Captain cut him off. "We might be in the woods up here but please don't sell us short. We're not from the woods." He stepped closer to Bob. "I'm sorry about your son in law but this is a Canadian investigation. I feel you know a lot more than you are telling me. "I've been honest and agreeable with you and I expect the same. I don't want to be made a fool of in front of your American audience or my Canadian superiors. I would appreciate your sharing any information that you feel might shed any light on what happened to your son in law and why all this damage might have been necessary." He stopped and stared at Bob.

Bob thought a minute. He knew that the officer was doing all he could to solve the case and to find out what might have happened to Kevin and he decided to give Reynolds everything he had. He walked over to the sink and sat down on the edge.

"Captain I know my son in law was working with the Canadian Government on a Facial Recognition Identification System. I don't know whom he was working with precisely but he told me it was someone in the immigration sector." Bob paused. "He was up here for a demonstration and he was quite excited about the future if your Government bought his system."

"I have no idea what happened after he arrived here but when you let Paul use that car he found Kevin's digital camera and he had taken quite a few pictures of the building that burnt at the lake." He handed the pictures to Reynolds who started to sort through them. "I stopped at the bait shop and the locals there told me Kevin had been asking about the man who had lived in that house. They also said he and his pickup truck had not been seen since the fire." That license plate should be easily traced and the picture of the man on the snowmobile might be of some help but I think fingerprints off the articles in the boathouse will be your best bet."

"Captain my son in law did not drink or smoke so you can tell your people to quit handling this as an accident and start investigating it as a homicide." Bob stopped.

The Mountie was trying to take in all the information that had just been thrust on him. "Why do you think this man might have wanted to hurt your son in law?"

"I have no idea. He might have had a criminal past or something to hide. It looked like Kevin confronted him at the lake and that might of set him off but I feel this was not the work of that one man."

"Go on." The Captain said sitting on the sink next to Bob and looking at the picture of the man on the snowmobile.

"The marks in the field show that a military helicopter landed there last night, at least two teams left that chopper. I feel one team went to the lake and the other team came here."

"Why would our Military do something like this and why have they not come forward to set things right or explain their actions?" The Captain was beginning to follow.

Bob reached into his pocket and held his hand out to the Mountie. He held his open palm up to catch the cigarette butts as Bob dropped them. "American cigarette butts. Marlboro. Who ever was waiting at that chopper was a smoker. I don't even know if they sell Marlboro up here."

"No one in the military could afford them. They're about $11.00 dollars a pack." The man's face went pale. "Do you think that the American Military could have done this?"

"At this point I have no idea. I think there is only one way to be sure."

"What might that be?" The Captain asked.

"Kevin had a camera mounted on a pole in front of the lodge that might have had a clear view of the parking lot and the motel rooms. If it is okay with you I can have Paul repair that video cable and see what it might have seen."

The officer's voice resounded with a tone of excitement. "By all means." He said as they headed towards the door. "I'll get some lights."

They moved quickly picking up Paul who was standing by the front door looking apprehensive. "Are we in trouble?" He asked as he joined Bob.

"Not at all but I want you to repair that cable and see what that camera might have been able to see."

The three men moved out the door and across the parking lot heading to the motel rooms.

"How will it help to see the viewing area of the camera Mr. Shroud? Everything went up in the fire."

"Kevin had a constant feed into the computer system in the room and it was being transmitted back to his office in the States and his home. That data should still be secure and should tell us what went on here last night." They fell silent as Paul finished fastening an end on the video cable and set his laptop up on a burned portion of the building.

As he plugged the wire into the port the screen cleared and they had a clear view of the parking lot and the front of Kevin's two rooms. Bob could hear the Mountie gasp a bit. "Whoever was here last night didn't know they were on camera. That's in our favor. Now we need to get the information from Kevin's home or business and see who they were. I'm sure the heat of the fire and all the other traffic has destroyed the tracks in front of the motel but you might check in the morning."

"What are you going to do?" Captain Reynolds asked.

Bob extended his hand. "I'm headed for Duluth to take care of my daughter and find out who did this to my son in law. I promise I'll give you everything I find."

The men shook hands and the Captain said "I'll drive you to the airport."

Paul had called the pilot and the jet was warming up as they pulled up at the little building that constituted the Dauphin Airport. The Captain waved as they climbed on board.

Paul and Bob dropped into seats as the pilot closed the door and headed for the cabin. "Yell at me when you're 10 minutes out of Duluth I want to shave." He was so tired he never heard the pilot answer.

Chapter 25

The helicopter landed in a remote corner of the small airport about 16 miles west of Duluth. As the ramp dropped a dark minivan pulled out and moved towards the small gate that led to a two-lane road to the city. The van stopped and a dark clothed figure jumped out with bolt cutters to remove the lock. The van moved out slowly and the figure closed the gate and repositioned the chain so that it looked untouched.

The van moved quickly and only stopped for a couple of minutes to remove a set of Minnesota License plates from a car in a Kmart lot before heading towards down town.

Chapter 26

The baby was restless in her car seat as Kathy pulled into her parking space and got out of the car. She unstrapped Amy and covered her with a blanket. As she started up to her apartment she felt happy to see her door and when she closed and locked the door behind her a feeling of safety came over her. She leaned against the wall and hugged Amy tightly. She noticed Kevin's picture on the wall and started to cry softly. A moment passed and she knew this was not doing any good. She opened the hall closet and hit the trip switch to open the workshop. She turned on the light and moved to the computer, which was still whirring on-line. She propped Amy on her shoulder and started working on the keyboard. She opened the disc tray, pulled out the existing disc and inserted a new one. After sliding the tray in she hit the key to download any and all information that Kevin had sent down to the computer. The screen showed download in progress. Approx. 7 minutes remaining.

"I'll think we'll get you some clothes." She whispered to the sleeping Amy. She went out through the closet to the hallway and down to the nursery. As she was putting diapers and a couple of outfits in the small travel bag she didn't hear the glass breaking in the door of the entrance. The quiet footsteps neared her door as she started down the hall. She was reaching for the door as she heard the frame start to splinter as the force of the man's shoulder started to crash against it. She barely made it into the closet and closed the door tripping the switch to seal her and the baby inside the workshop. She heard the door slam against the hallway wall as the frame gave way and the door flew open. She held Amy tightly as she heard the men moving into her apartment. Her hands were shaking and she hoped the movement would not wake Amy up. She could hear them banging things around in her home. At that moment the computer gave a ping and she jumped. "Download completed." The screen said.

The noise got closer as they moved into the kitchen and something slammed into the wall startling Amy. She started to stir and the pitch-black darkness must have scared the baby and she cried out. The apartment went silent as Kathy heard all movement outside the closet stopped. She kissed Amy and whispered in her ear but the child started to cry. She held Amy tight to her chest trying to quiet the noise but it was clear she was not the only one to hear it. She moved to the door of the workshop and slid the safety latch. She leaned against the door to help the small latch if someone tried to force it. The silence was broken by Amy's muffled cries. "God help us," Kathy prayed. It was then that she heard the hall closet door open and saw the light at the base of the door. She felt the push on the door as they pushed on the other side.

"There's something back here." She heard the man's voice as he started to push harder on the door. He hit the door once and the latch held with her help but the latch started to give way as they hit the door again.

"Leave us alone and get out of here!" She screamed. This scared Amy even more and she started screaming as they hit the door again but still it held.

He was just about to hit the door again when she heard the siren, it was getting closer by the second. "I called the police." She shouted. "They know you're here."

"Let's get out of here." She heard the voice say and the other cursed in disgust. The men left the apartment and she could hear them running down the hall. She slid to the floor holding Amy who was starting to settle down a bit and Kathy didn't move until she heard the police enter the front door.

"Mrs. Bennett are you in here?" They called out as they entered the apartment door.

"Is that the police?" She called out. Not ready to open the door.

"Yes mam." The voice answered. "Your neighbors called."

She released the bent latch on the broken door and walked out through the closet to the hallway. The police were surprised to see her appear behind them. She walked towards the living room and started to cry when she saw the mess that used to be her apartment. "Are you two okay?" The officers asked.

She leaned against the officer and Amy started to cry again. "Do you need a doctor, mam?" The officer asked again. "Jim call E.M.S.!" He told his partner.

"No, no, I don't need an ambulance. I just need to get out of here." She said moving the blanket to cover Amy. "I'm afraid they're going to come back."

"Do you know who they were Mrs. Bennett?" The officer asked. He was looking at the mess down the hall and through the kitchen. "They really made a mess of your home. Can you tell me if they took anything?"

She looked around the kitchen and saw her computer was missing. "They took my PC from the kitchen counter."

The officer was looking around and taking note of some of the expensive furnishings and articles in the apartment. "Hard to believe thieves would do all that damage and only take a PC Mrs. Bennett."

"I don't think they were thieves officer. Is there a way you can seal off my apartment and I'll come down and fill out a report tomorrow. I want to get my baby someplace safe and put her to bed."

"We'll close and seal the door, I'm going to talk with your neighbors. Officer Nelson here will drive you home or follow you home to make sure no one bothers you."

"I appreciate that officer." She said and started for the door. The second officer followed close behind her and when they were downstairs he helped her into the car and started to follow her as they left the lot.

As soon as they left the lot she tried to dial Paul's cell number, but the recording said he was unavailable. She tried her dad's number and got the same recording. The traffic was light when they got on the freeway and they didn't notice the dark van pull out and begin to follow them.

When they exited the freeway and stopped at the ramp light the officer noticed the van behind him, it was full of men.

When the van turned the same way they did he turned on his computer and punched in the plate number for a quick check. It took a few seconds but soon the information appeared. The plates were issued to a 2001 Chevrolet sedan registered to a Blanche Wilson from Grand Marais.

"36 to base." The officer said keeping his radio microphone low so as not to tip off the men in the van behind him.

"Go 36." Came the response.

"I'm traveling West on Monroe. There is a black van following me with incorrect plates. I'm escorting a robbery victim home and need you to have the vehicle stopped and checked." He gave his location on Monroe and the plate number. He only hoped help would arrive before they got to the address Kathy was headed for.

"Help is on the way 36." The radio cracked 214 and 86 are close by.

"Be advised there are four passengers in the van plus the driver." In his rear view he saw the blue lights of the other units closing in on the van. The people in the van saw the lights too and started to accelerate to pass Nelson. He decided he would slow them down so the other cars would deal with them. He didn't plan to let them get beside Kathy.

He cut over in the lane in front of the van and jammed on the brakes. The van never slowed up. They hit the back panel of his patrol car with a force that knocked the microphone out of his hand. He was reaching down on the floor when they tried to pass him on the right. He moved over and they crashed into his cruiser again. This time reaching down for the microphone probably saved his life. He heard the automatic fire and felt the pieces of glass from his shattered back window fly around inside his car.

Kathy heard one of the bullets that hit her car and looked back to see Officer Nelson colliding with the van that had been behind them. She sped up and watched the lights get smaller in her rear view. Her heart was racing as she turned onto the street leading to Margaret's house, but her brain started to work. If the police couldn't stop whoever it was in the van the worst place for her and Amy would be Margaret's house. She made the first turn she could to point her back in the direction of downtown.

Chapter 27

Inside the van the 5 men were a blur of activity the driver was busy trying to get around Nelson's car and one of the passengers was firing his assault weapon at the back of the police car that refused to let them near Kathy.

The man in the last seat kicked the back window out and opened fire on the two police cars racing up on their rear.

The unsuspecting officers never had a chance. The passenger in 214 died as the first barrage of automatic fire hit the windshield. Glass fragments hit the officer driving and he did a good job of not loosing control of his car. The officers in 86 saw the gun flashes and called for help. While returning fire.

"Damn!" Brady shouted realizing things had gone terribly wrong. He was seated behind the driver of the van and he heard the bullets hitting the van and knew they needed to get the hell out of there.

He tapped the driver on the shoulder. "Abort. Get us back to the chopper."

The driver nodded in acknowledgment and without slowing made a left turn through traffic to a side street. Only unit 86 was able to follow the turn through the light traffic. The officer on the passenger side was shouting direction changes and requests for back up while trying to fire at the back of the van.

The residential street had a lot of cars parked at curbside and the street was pretty narrow. One of the men in the van slid the passenger side door open and leaned out to fire at the police car following them but in his haste he failed to notice the vehicles at curbside. He started to fire on unit 86 and the van sideswiped a pickup with a camper shell crushing the gunman and throwing his body into the path of the pursuing police car which simply rolled over the corpse and proceeded on after the van.

"Shit." Brady said realizing how perilous his position had become. "Take that car out!" He shouted to the man in the back seat. "Turn out the lights," he ordered the driver.

The man in the back seat waited until the police car pulled closer and then popped up and emptied a 30 shot clip through their windshield. The officers in 86 had dropped in the front seat when they saw the gunman pop up, only good luck saved their lives but when they ducked their car rear ended an auto parked in the street. The collision took them out of the chase and blocked the street as Nelson came up behind them trying to get back in the pursuit.

He had to jam on the brakes to keep from running into 86, he turned right into someone's driveway and then turned onto the sidewalk running parallel with the van. He was unable to see where they were with the lights off but they slowed to make a right turn and their brake lights gave their location away.

Nelson accelerated down the sidewalk hoping no one was out walking his or her dog. He came to the end of the block and turned to follow the darkened van, his lights picked up the reflectors on the rear of the van but he decided to stay back and follow. He found his microphone. "Suspect's van headed South to intersect with RT.2."

The wind through his broken windshield was blowing little pieces of broken glass all over him he could feel his face bleeding but was determined not to let go of his microphone again.

"Brady to 905!" Brady shouted over the wind blowing through the broken windows and open door of the van. "Come in 905."

"Go Brady." The voice answered.

"We're coming in hot. We have company, warm up, lock and load."

"Affirmative Brady, out."

"Van turning west on Rt. 2." Nelson shouted into his microphone over the noise of his damaged patrol car.

Once on the open highway the driver of the van accelerated and easily pulled away from the badly damaged police car. They were near the airport when another police car pulled out in front of them and the officers jumped out to block the road and take up shooting positions behind their car.

The van sped by the stopped police car but the hail of shotgun fire from the officers struck everyone in the van. Brady was hit in the arm. The man in the passenger seat was motionless, as was the gunman in the rear.

"Are you okay?" Brady asked the driver.

"No, but I'll make it." The driver answered. He was slumping to the left but still maintained speed and control of the van.

Brady leaned over the back of his seat and opened a utility bag on the floor. He pulled out two grenades with his good arm. The police car had joined the chase and there were more blue lights beyond the ones that were bearing down on the van.

"What a night!" He said as he pulled the pin from the grenade and started to count, "one, two, three, four." And he threw it out the back window.

The grenade went off directly in front of the police car and threw the vehicle out of control. It swerved to the right and then started to roll over and over. He pulled the pin on another grenade and threw it out without counting. The other cars were not close but his timing was just as deadly. As they neared the airport he tossed the last grenade and the driver slowed to negotiate the gate opening.

He never stopped and the gate blasted open sending the aluminum and galvanized fence parts all over. As he sped towards the helicopter he could see the rotors spinning and the guards waiting to cover their retreat.

They drove up the ramp and the guards followed them into the belly of the dark machine. They both took position at the gun ports as the police cars reached the fence. Between the huge amount of dust kicked up from the giant rotors and the hail of automatic fire all the police could do was drop down behind the cars.

"What in the hell?" Nelson said as the helicopter moved away and then went dark and silent. "Did you see any markings on that thing?"

"Not a one." Responded the officer.

"This is 36, Nelson to base." He said talking to the mike. "The van just flew away in a large helicopter. We lost Mrs. Bennett, has she called in?" He wiped some of the blood from his forehead and looked towards the direction of the helicopter path.

"Mrs. Bennett is here at the station, you need to get down here and fill us in. Let one of the other cars secure the sight."

Nelson put down the mike and turned to the other officer. "I think I'd better use your car, I don't think this one will make it."

"Go ahead." The other officer said pointing to the numerous sets of blue lights headed towards them. "It looks like I'm gonna have plenty of company."

"Thanks." Nelson said as he slid into the seat and turned the patrol car back towards Duluth. It was only then that he realized how cold it was. He had been so pumped up during the chase. The pain is his face and the cold started to set in. The drive back to Duluth seemed to take a long time.

He couldn't believe all the lights that were on in the police station when he drove up. He started up the steps and past the first set of doors when he saw Kathy and Amy sitting in one of the inner offices. The baby was asleep and Kathy smiled. All of a sudden he didn't mind the pain.

Chapter 28

The company jet jarred as it touched down in Duluth and Bob checked to see if he had cut himself with the disposable razor. "No blood, good," he thought. He had slept soundly for the short flight South. Mike had awakened him about ten minutes out and he had put on a clean shirt and the hot water felt good on his face.

Paul knocked lightly on the door. "Bob we've got problems!"

He was drying his face as he opened the cabin door. "What's wrong?"

"I answered your phone while you were in here. Kathy and Amy are at the Duluth Police Station. An administrator from the police department named Bradley called. They're okay." He reassured Bob. "You need to call."

Bob's temples started to throb as he dialed the number. He slumped into a seat and waited for an answer. "Bradley" The voice on the other end of the line cracked.

"Bob Shroud here Mr. Bradley, is my family okay?" He asked the stranger.

"They're fine, just shaken up, I have them at the main station, where are you?"

"We just landed in Duluth, what's happened?"

"We're not too sure. Things are still being sorted out. I'm sending a couple of cars to bring you downtown, if that's okay?" Bradley waited for an answer.

"I appreciate that, we'll be at the Raytheon Hanger, is my daughter handy?" Bob could not help but wonder why he would send two cars.

"Here she is Mr. Shroud." Bradley passed the phone to Kathy.

"Hi Dad, are you okay?" Kathy sounded shaky.

"I'm fine Honey, what happened? Is Amy okay?" He was trying not to rush.

"We're okay dad, but tonight has been unbelievable. I don't want to talk about it on the phone. Get down here and be safe." She seemed a bit relieved.

"I'll be right there Honey, I love you." He hung up and turned to Paul.

"You look like your gonna be sick." Paul said. "What's up?"

"Something bad must have happened." Bob was looking for the hanger as the small jet taxied across the field. His cell phone beeped and he looked to find he had a missed call. He dialed the number and a sleepy Captain Reynolds answered the phone.

"Hello, Reynolds here." His voice was slurred with exhaustion.

"Captain Reynolds, this is Robert Shroud." He paused to let the Mountie wake up. "I'm sorry to bother you. I missed your call."

"No bother." Said Reynolds sitting up and turning on a light at his bedside and picking up a folder of papers. "How was your flight?"

"We just landed, how can I help you?"

"It seems your son in law had dug into something quite intriguing. There seems to have been quite an event up here and no one wants to claim any knowledge of the operation. The individual at the lake house seems to have been born at the age of thirty in Saskatchewan with a great deal of money. But no one in Saskatchewan Government seems to have any knowledge of him ever being there."

He paused to cough and get a drink of water. "I have made several inquiries and will probably not hear anything back until about lunch time today, something is very wrong about this."

"Evidently the problem has not been contained in Canada, there has been a problem here in Minnesota and we're on our way to the police station to find out what happened." Robert appreciated the officer's honesty. "If I find out anything that might help you I'll call."

"Thank you." He paused. "I might add that if you try to get any help from Canadian Immigration expect them to be less helpful. They seem to have a part in this and find themselves in a situation where they have chosen to assume a defensive position."

"Deny, deny, deny. Typical Government."

"Exactly, we'll talk again, good luck." The Mountie hung up and fell back on the bed with the folder on his chest.

Bob turned to Paul and shook his head as the jet stopped at the service hanger. "It seems the guy at the lake house had no history, he just appeared, no one knows where he came from."

"That little town seemed like the perfect place to retire." Paul paused, "or maybe disappear."

The service people opened the cabin door and held out welcoming hands to Bob and Paul as they started down the steps. "Mr. Shroud," the pilot called to him as they started to the office. "Any instructions?"

Bob turned and smiled. "Get some sleep. Thank you and as soon as I find out what's going on I'll call you." He could see the flashing lights of the police cars turning in the gate as his heart started to beat faster.

"Three squad cars!" Paul looked at Bob incredulously. "What in the hell is going on?"

The lead uniformed officer identified himself and shook their hands. Once in the car the trip to the station was a fast one.

"What happened here?" Bob asked the officer in the passenger seat as the cars blew through a red light.

"Not really too sure sir." The officer started. "It began with a break in and turned into one hell of a chase. We took some casualties." He went silent again as they got closer to downtown.

A light snow had started to fall and Bob could feel the car slide a little as they made some turns continuing to ignore red lights. He was glad there was no traffic on the street. As they neared the police station he saw all the news trucks lined up their remote antennas in the air.

"Not a good sign!" Paul said pointing to the reporters talking to the cameras on the sidewalk.

"Go in through the garage!" The officer told the driver and he turned off the lights and followed the lead car to a lower level side entrance. He was busy on the radio telling the dispatcher they had arrived. They stopped by a set of elevator doors and opened the door for the puzzled passengers. "Thank you." Bob said as the officer got back in the car and the elevator doors opened.

David Bradley was a short man with big hands. "Mr. Shroud, I've heard a lot about you." He shook Bob's hand and moved on to Paul.

"Paul Martinez is my assistant." The introductions were over. It was time to get to business.

"Your daughter and grand daughter are fine." He paused, "I can't say the same for some of the men in my department." The elevator started up to the top floors of the station. "Several men broke into your daughter's apartment and were ransacking the place when we responded to the alarm and the calls from the neighbors." He took a breath.

"My officers were in the process of escorting your family to another location when one of them noticed a suspicious vehicle following them. Evidently they wanted your daughter." The hair stood up on Bob's neck. "A very disastrous confrontation ensued and I lost three men. I also have five more in bad condition and a lot of questions." Bradley stopped as the doors opened. "I hope you can shed some light on what the hell is going on."

Bob thought the man was going to hold him up but he pointed towards an office with a policeman standing by the door. "Go see your daughter and then we'll talk."

"Thank you Mr. Bradley." Bob said motioning to Paul to keep his mouth shut and headed for the office. As he reached the office the policeman opened the door and let him in. He heard the door close behind him. He smiled and relaxed as he saw his grand daughter asleep on the couch and his daughter catching some much-needed sleep at her feet.

As the door latch clicked Kathy looked up and smiled as she saw her father. "Dad!" She said starting to get up from the floor.

He motioned for her to stay put, he sat down on the floor with her and put his arms around her trembling shoulders as she started to cry. He kissed her forehead and held her tight.

He let her cry for a while patting her on the head. "Don't worry, I'm here, we'll be okay."

"What's going on dad?" She asked never taking her head out of the folds of his coat. She started to cry harder. "Why did they kill Kevin?" That sent her into uncontrollable sobs and Bob started to feel the tears rolling down his face.

He let her go on a bit holding her tighter. "I have no idea but I'm going to get to the bottom of it." She started to regain control of her sobbing and he asked, "What happened at the apartment?"

She tried to stop crying and was half-successful. "I had gone to the apartment to get the discs and pick up a few things for Amy when these guys broke in." She blew her nose and looked to see if the noise had disturbed Amy but the baby was sound asleep.

"I made it into the computer room and I thought they would leave but they heard Amy cry and tried to get to us." She started to sob again and he held her tighter trying to assure her it was all over but he knew something was terribly wrong for people to be trying something like this.

"You're okay baby." He paused, "We're going to be okay!"

"They heard the police sirens and ran, thank God, the locks on the door had started to give way and Amy and I were screaming but they left." She seemed to relax a bit and regain a little composure. "I'm glad you're here Dad." She hugged him tightly.

"I wish I had been here earlier and you might not have had to go through all this." He suddenly thought about how useless he might have been had he been there.

"They followed us from the apartment and there was a lot of shooting. A lot of people got hurt. The police saved us but I know that a lot of people were hurt." She wiped her eyes and looked at her father, "I thought we were going to die."

"You're not going to die. I'm here now and you and Amy are coming home with me till this is all over." He took the handkerchief from his pocket and wiped her cheeks. "You're a mess." He said trying to change her mood.

"I know," she said putting her head back on his chest. She seemed to relax knowing he was really there. She remembered and reached into her pocket, her fingers closing on the discs. "I think these are okay. I hope they'll help." She pressed them into her father's hand.

Bob was trying not to shake as he held the discs. He could only imagine what was on them and how important the information might be. What could be worth the problems that had occurred? "Believe me, they'll help find out who was behind this and who was responsible for Kevin's death."

"Get some rest. I need to talk with the police." He started to get up and stopped. "Do they know about these?"

"I didn't tell them about them." She answered.

"Let's keep them our secret for a bit." He got up; "I love ya. Be back in a little while." He left the room and joined Paul in the hall making sure the officer was still on the door watching his family.

"How are the girls?" Paul asked obviously concerned.

"Kathy's pretty rattled." He paused, "The baby's asleep."

"Bob this is weird I was talking to the cop on the door and he said these guys were Commandos or something."

"Mr. Shroud." Bradley spoke up from an office they were passing. "Come in and have a seat."

Bob and Paul entered the office and Bradley closed the door. "Is your daughter okay?" His voice was serious and he seemed genuinely concerned.

"She is. They both are, thanks to your people. Thank you."

Bradley's face changed from that of a concerned individual to that of a serious police administrator. "Mr. Shroud, I need some help. I have break in, a burglary, a fatal pursuit, over one thousand rounds fired, vehicles destroyed, dead officers, wounded and injured officers and I have nothing to go on but your family and one dead perpetrator who was dressed better than my swat team." He stopped and looked at his papers.

"What in the hell is going on?"

"I really wish I knew Mr. Bradley." Bob began. "My son in law died in Canada two nights ago under what I feel were suspicious circumstances and now this."

"Your daughter tells me Kevin was in some kind of security service but she doesn't know much more than that. Can you shed any light on what he might have been doing or who he might have been involved with?"

"He was working in Manitoba at the invitation of the Canadian Government. His company does security checks and specialized in surveillance and protection services." Bob paused.

"Your daughter filled me in on all that. I can't seem to raise anyone but the security guards at your son in laws company. They don't talk much. The place was shut down for the weekend so we'll get some help in this morning." He stopped, "I hope."

"Mr. Bradley, in Canada there were signs of a military type Helicopter being involved in the occurrence. People on the ground heard noises and I saw the marks of its wheels and struts in the snow where it landed."

"Exactly." Bradley exclaimed "The bastards had a large chopper at a small airfield west of here and they just drove in and flew away shooting up my officers along the way." He was quite upset. "Do you know why they would have broken into your daughter's home or what they may have been looking for?"

"Not really. Kevin did most of his work at the office."

"Our people found a computer room hidden in a closet. Do you know anything about that?" Bradley was staring at Bob looking for a reaction as well as an answer.

"Kevin's work was pretty sensitive and entailed a lot of restricted information and protected backgrounds and histories. I can only think that he wanted to keep that work from the eyes of anyone that might have been in his house while he and Kathy were out."

Bradley was staring more than listening to his answer. "It just doesn't add up Mr. Shroud."

"Mr. Bradley, I would like to take what's left of my family home to Texas. I know a lot of people down there and I feel I can protect them a little better while we all try to get over this." Bob hesitated. "Is there any reason why she can't travel?"

"None Mr. Shroud, but remember, she is a material witness to all of the events of last night and if we need here back here I want your assurances she will be cooperative."

"Absolutely." Bob pulled out his notebook. "On another note, you said they left a man here. Have you been able to get an identification on him?"

"Not yet. He was pretty badly mangled but we're waiting for response on his prints from NCIC." He opened his folder. "His uniform and equipment are the same type and style that most police departments use. He was wearing military type boots that you can buy at almost any Army-Navy store." He scanned down the pages. "He was firing a fully automatic modified AR15. We're trying to track serial numbers and ammunition now."

"I want to take Kathy and Amy to a hotel so they can get some rest. Can you give us a couple people to keep an eye on their room?"

"Of course. The Hyatt right down the street has great security and I know the boss. I'll call and get you some rooms on an upper floor; I'll have people downstairs and on your floor. If you need anything let us know."

"I want to take a look at Kathy's apartment and pick up a few things that she might need." Bob was asking as Mr. Bradley picked up his ringing phone.

"I'll have a car and driver at your disposal but please keep me informed if you find anything that will help us open this up. Excuse me" He listened to the voice on the phone.

He got up and Bob and Paul headed to the door. He hung up the phone and seemed excited. "We have an identification on our body."

The three men walked out to the hall and a plain-clothes detective handed Bradley a handful of fax sheets.

Bradley looked the sheets over and gave the detective a puzzled look. "This is ridiculous." He said going over the pages a second time.

"What is it?" Paul asked. He could feel the curiosity in the air.

"It seems the body that was in the altercation with my people last night was serving a 20 year to life sentence at the Federal Penitentiary in Ft. Leavenworth, Kansas. This report reads as if he was safely tucked in at last count. No reports of being missing from the population."

Bradley took the detective be the elbow and walked him down the hall. "I'll be right back." He called over his shoulder.

"Paul looked at Bob. "This is bizarre." He said, "What the hell was Kevin into?"

Bob slid a disc out of his pocket partially and caught Paul's eye. "I hope this will help us out."

"From the apartment?" Paul asked.

"Kathy got to them before they did." She was there when they broke in. As soon as we get her and Amy in a hotel room you and I are going to the apartment to see if there is anything else on the computer."

Bradley came back down the hall with two officers. "These men will stay with you until you get back on your plane." He stopped and stared at Bob. "I don't have a lot of faith or respect for reporters but I'm making an exception in your case because of your reputation and your daughter's situation." He held up a finger. "Be straight with me, I lost some good people last night helping your family. Don't dick us around! Help us out! If you turn up anything I want you on the line to me immediately." He reached in his pocket and gave Bob and Paul each a card. "You can reach me 24 hours a day at these numbers. No questions asked. Keep me informed."

He turned and left Bob and Paul with the informed officers. Bob headed to the office to wake Kathy and gather up Amy for the short trip to the hotel.

Chapter 29

Bob got Kathy and Amy in bed and made sure the officers were outside the door. The rooms were on the 12th floor and the police in the lobby were keeping in touch with their counterparts upstairs.

Bob felt pretty sure whoever had been at the apartment the night before was long gone owing to the chaos they had created. The police gave them a ride to the apartment. The investigators were still dusting the front and security doors for prints and the officer at the apartment door wouldn't move till the driver cleared Paul and Bob.

Once inside Bob went directly to the computer room. He looked at the splintered wood around the latches that had saved his family from coming face to face with the intruders. He said a little prayer of thanks when he thought about how small and weak the metal was. "Lucky!" He said and Paul shook his head in agreement.

"Get on that computer and see if there is anything you can find out about the past few days." He told Paul looking around the small room. The police had left the room untouched because the men had never gained access to the inside. Everything was pretty much the same as when Kevin had showed it to Bob a few days before.

"There's nothing here Bob" Paul said pecking away at the keyboard. "Kathy downloaded and deleted all the information, evidently."

"Can you connect with Kevin's home office?" Bob sat down on a stack of cartons and watched over Paul's shoulder as he continued working his keyboard.

The screen flashed "ACCESS DENIED" Paul started over the "ACCESS DENIED" flashed again. "I don't think we're going anywhere Bob. The connection is there but it won't let us through."

"You need his access code or password?"

"No." Paul was still working. "It won't even let us get that far. This computer's not interfacing or connecting with anyone right now. It's being completely blocked out."

"Kevin said he had a hard wire connection to his office, your saying that's not active?"

"If this was hard wired it would be asking for his ID. Nothing that happened here or Canada would have effected that unless his home office pulled the plug." Paul continued typing away but nothing changed.

"Let it go Paul" Bob started out the door.

"Wait a minute Bob." Paul had hit a key and the screen had come to life. "It seems this unit received an order to delete all stored and on hand information from its hard drive at 5:00 this morning."

"Where did that command come from?" Bob asked.

"No way of telling." It could have been here or the base unit it's hard wired to." Paul continued typing. "Where is the company at?"

"His office isn't far away, its here in Duluth and the main office is in Minneapolis."

"It could have come from anywhere then. I think that it could have come from any terminal or mobile unit linked to their main computer."

"If we get to their main computer here in town can we find out?" Bob asked.

"We can tell where the delete and destroy order came from." Paul pushed away from the terminal and looked around the small room. "She was lucky."

"Very lucky!" Bob concurred as they walked toward the kitchen.

Paul looked at the magnets holding pictures of Kevin, Kathy and Amy on the refrigerator doors. "Damn shame Bob" He said as Bob pulled a few of the pictures off and put them in his pockets.

Bob picked the small bag up from the floor where Kathy had dropped it the night before. He walked past the officer dusting the cabinets in the hallway and was going to go into the den but decided against it and headed out the front door.

Once they were back in the car he directed the officer to the front of Kevin's office. Bob went to the microphone pad and buzzed the guard. "May I help you?" The voice cracked.

"I'm Kevin Bennett's father in law. "I'm trying to reach his boss. Can you help me?" He waited for an answer and glanced at his watch. 9am, the sun was poking out from the clouds.

"I'm sorry. There's no one here but me and this facility has been deactivated." The box went silent.

"Is there someone I can call? I need to talk to someone about Kevin" Bob asked leaning down to the speaker and looking up at the camera.

"You might try the main office in the twin cities." The voice paused. "I'm sorry I can't help you." The box went dead.

Bob went back to the squad car and closed the door. "No luck?" Paul asked.

"Talk to the box." Bob said shaking his head as the officer circled around the building.

"The place is like a fortress." The officer offered. "I was working traffic when they built it. The walls are two feet thick, cameras everywhere. Your son in law worked there?"

"He used to." Bob looked up at the blank brick walls. The police car headed back to the hotel.

Chapter 30

Kathy was in a hotel robe when she answered the door. "Hi Dad. How's my apartment?" She hugged him and headed back to the bathroom.

"It's a mess." He looked out the window at the covered roof and remembered how glad he was to live in Texas and away from the damn cold weather. "Are you ready to get the hell out of here and come home with me?"

"I had Margaret send our stuff over in a cab." She had Amy wrapped up in a towel fresh from the tub. "We need some sunshine Grandpa." She said holding the baby out to Bob.

He held her tightly as she started babbling. "Hi precious." He said rubbing his face in her wet hair.

"I stopped by Kevin's company on the way back but the guard said no one was there and the place was shut down."

Kathy looked oddly at her father. "That can't be, I just talked with Alan on Friday morning. Mary sent me papers to sign before noon. Let me call Alan at home."

She walked to the phone by the bed and dialed Alan's office number.

Bob watched as Kathy's facial expression turned to a frown. He said nothing as she hung up the phone and dialed another number. Her frown turned to a scowl as she dialed a third number. "What in the hell is going on?" She said as she put the phone back on the cradle.

"I can't find anyone." Alan's office and home numbers are disconnected. Mary's home number is disconnected." She sat down on the foot of the bed and looked like she was going to cry.

Amy was laughing and pulling at his face. "Don't cry honey." He tickled Amy to keep her busy. "We'll get to the bottom of this. Get the baby dressed and order some breakfast while Paul and I start to check out these discs." He handed her the baby, kissed her cheek and headed to the door. "Kathy, did you delete all the material and the hard drive memory on Kevin's computer?"

"No Dad." She answered. "I downloaded to a second disc because the first was full but I never deleted anything." She was pulling a shirt over Amy's head. "Dad, was my computer on the kitchen counter?"

Bob had to think back to when he and Paul were at the apartment earlier. "I didn't see it Honey." He reached in his pocket and handed her the snapshots "I brought these for you."

She sat Amy on the bed and looked at the photos. She smiled as she looked at them. "You should have brought the clear ones, I blurred these when I set the camera."

"I brought all the ones on the door." He turned to go again.

"There were about three more that came out nice and clear. "I'm sure they were on the door too."

Bob turned back. "Your computer was on the counter by the refrigerator, right?"

"Yes. Kevin had it on a voice activated line so we could talk back and forth from Canada."

"It seems whoever broke in, took your computer and didn't realize that there was another direct hook up in the house. They probably think they have all the information that was out there." He paused, thinking. "We probably have a little breathing room."

"I'm going over with Paul and I'll call you in a couple of hours. Let me know when you finish breakfast." He kissed the girls and headed to the door again. "We'll be in Texas tonight and we'll try to get things back to normal."

"Thanks Dad." She said hugging Amy as he closed the door and made sure the officer was close at hand.

Chapter 31

Paul was all set up on the desk when Bob walked in. "All set Boss." He said holding out his hand for the first disc.

Bob handed him the disc. "I don't know if this is the first or second." It took a minute for Paul to get the computer to start playing the information he had sent from Manitoba. Bob's throat tightened as he looked at his son in law's face talking to the computer and adjusting the different camera settings. "It looks like he was getting set up here." Paul said as he tapped a key making the information and pictures fast forward.

"He's checking camera angles and focus. He must have had a shitload of cameras deployed."

"They were setting up for nearly a week." Bob explained. He saw Paul go back to regular speed and moved in to get a better look at the screen.

"Damn." Paul said in an astonished voice as he watched the screen. "Kevin was wired into the world." Bob's mouth was hanging open.

"Interpol-CBI-FBI-CIA-Scotland Yard, the KGB, look at all these, I thought the KGB was out of business."

He continued to scan the different organizations and agencies that Kevin's computer had been locked onto. "What in the hell was he working on Bob?"

"It was some kind of visual scanning identification system that he had designed and was trying to sell. Canada had given him an opportunity to demonstrate it to them and he seemed to think that the acceptance was a sure thing. He planned on getting rich selling the software system." Paul was still scanning through the lists of law enforcement and investigative computers that the computer had access to. "I can't believe he had been allowed this kind of freedom to this much information."

"I guess this is what that kind of system would be applied to after the 911 problems. If all these people worked together and shared information there's no way criminals could get a leg up on the system."

"He was going to be able to look at a face in a crowd and by checking the cornea or the retina and comparing it to digital mug shots, identify criminals or fugitives." Bob stopped and stared at the screen as Kevin was talking to the computer. "He must have pissed someone off awfully bad."

Bob studied the screen, he noticed that the positioning of the computer camera gave a clear view into the adjoining room. "Stop it right there, Paul." His voice made Paul jump as he reached for the keyboard. Bob could see through the open door to the next room and the two bottles of Canadian whiskey were sitting on the dresser. "I told him to bring me a bottle of Canadian whiskey when he came home."

Paul looked up at Bob's strained face. "Sorry Bob." He said. "You want to keep going?"

"Of course. I want to get to the thick of this. I saw the bottles sitting there and I know why he had them in his room." He scratched his head "Go ahead Paul."

Paul began to scan ahead skipping the minutes and hours of no activity. Each time Kevin would begin to speak they would go to regular time and listen to his words. It was rather haunting to hear him speaking from beyond the grave.

Bob had gone to the phone to order some food from room service when Paul called him, "Bob." He's starting the test!"

Bob finished ordering and hung up. He emerged to see Paul scanning through the different camera shots. "The computer is scanning all the cameras. This software is really something, it looks as if it will key on one if he has a positive ID."

He had barely finished saying his last word when the screen went to the first positive identification of a fugitive. "This is really something." Paul said shaking his head. "This could really be a boom for police departments and national security all over the country."

"Kevin said the computer guaranteed 75% accuracy so it would save a lot of time and wasted resources. Its application at airports alone could save billions of labor costs."

"He's got another hit." Paul said getting wrapped up with the results of the tests. "This is fantastic." He read the information on the screen. "They have the same kind of crime problems in Canada. This guy gets drunk and beats his wife." They both laughed as room service knocked on the door. Bob got up to let the waiter in. He let the boy roll the cart in and set up the side panels.

"Sign here sir" He said handing Bob the bill and a pen, Bob signed it and let the man out the door picking a piece of fruit off the tray. Bob took a bite of the pear and turned back to Paul and the computer. Paul was looking up at him with a scared look. He had stopped the computer and was motioning to the face and information on the screen.

Bob looked at Paul and back at the screen. "That's impossible. Go back to the camera scan."

Paul typed the command on the keyboard and the camera scan of the hockey venue came up. "It's the guy in the picture at the cabin. What the hell?" He looked at the screen again. "Go back to the test." Paul responded and the McVey mug shot and information and the 98% positive match came back.

They were both taking in the gravity of the information they had just seen when the phone rang and they both jumped. "Shut it down, shut it down!" Bob whispered.

"Dad!" It was Kathy on the phone. "Everything okay?"

"Yeah honey. Did you eat?" He tried to sound normal.

"Not much, but Amy was famished." She paused. "What time do you want to leave?"

"We just got a wagon of food. Give us twenty minutes" He motioned to Paul to cut the machine off and wrap things up. "Get your stuff ready and I'll call you." He hung up and slumped into the seat beside Paul.

He looked at Paul pulling wires out stuffing them into his bags. "Do you think this could be correct?" He asked the young man.

"It can't be. But," Paul hesitated. "It has to be. The computer can't be wrong…At least I don't think it could be wrong." He put his hands on his head. "Bob, it stands to reason if all this has happened it may be because this is true." He started packing again. He opened up the disc tray and handed the disc to Bob. "This is explosive."

Bob reached into the desk drawer and pulled out the envelopes. He put each disc in one and put them in his inside coat pocket. Bob's stomach was churning. "Pack up and put some of those rolls in a napkin. Let's get the hell out of here and get back to Texas." He said pulling out his cell phone. "I'm calling the pilot. I want to be in the air as soon as possible."

Paul kept packing. He handed Bob three sheets of paper from the small printer he was packing up. Bob looked at McVey's eyes and wondered how he had figured into Kevin's death and the upheaval in his family. He folded the sheets and put them in his coat pocket.

"Bob." Paul said as he finished tucking everything away in his bags. "Do you know Terry Kennedy?"

"Star Telegram right?" Bob answered. "I met him at a Hearst party last year."

"He ate, lived and slept McVey from the time the explosion occurred until the execution. He had the only jailhouse interview with McVey." Paul stopped to take a sip of coffee. "Bob you don't feed me enough."

Bob smiled as he bit the end of a sausage. "Fill your pockets, there's nothing but crackers on that jet.

Do you think you could call him and set up a meeting for tomorrow?"

"If he's in Texas, he'll be there." Paul seemed positive. "We go back a long way, and he likes to talk about his work." He took another bite of the Danish he was trying to eat. "Bob, what do you make of this?"

"I don't know Paul. This issue was pretty dead and I never paid much attention to him when he was news. I was in South America and had plenty to worry about there." He took a last sip of coffee he had in his cup and looked at the floor. "Paul, people are dead over this information." He tapped his coat pocket. "You and I are the only ones who know for sure what Kevin found out and I want to keep it that way…not a word to anyone!"

"I'm with you Boss." He said picking up his bags, let's get back to Texas."

Bob dialed Kathy's room. "Hello Honey, let's go."

He walked to the hall and told the officer they were ready to go to the airport. Kathy opened her door and Bob went inside to get her bags. The officer was busy on his radio. In a matter of seconds they were headed for the elevator and the waiting police cars downstairs.

As they exited the hotel she recognized the young officer with the Band-Aids on his face as the one whom had helped her the night before.

"I wondered how you made it out last night." She said. "Thank you."

"You're welcome, I'm glad you're both okay." Nelson said through bandaged lips. He closed the door and jumped into the passenger seat for the trip to the airport.

Bob was talking to the lead officer in the front seat. "Tell Mr. Bradley I appreciate his trust and help and that I'll be in touch."

"I'll do that Sir." The officer was looking in all directions to make sure there were no more surprises in the sunny afternoon. "We lost some good people last night Mr. Shroud."

As they drew near to the airport Bob thought about how smart it might be to travel with the only discs containing such important information. Bob tried to put the possibility of problems out of his mind and pulled his coat tighter around the discs and printouts.

The jet was warmed and waiting when they got to the hanger and Bob felt a sense of security to be airborne and moving away from Duluth and the cold weather.

Twenty minutes into the flight Paul hung up the in flight phone and walked back to Bob to tell him the meeting with Terry was set for 11:00 am tomorrow.

"For Worth is pretty dull these days. He's really curious."

Chapter 32

The flight to Addison's small airport was smooth and uneventful. The small jet touched down without so much as a bump and Bob was happy to see the familiar surroundings of Dallas.

Bob thanked the pilot and headed for his old Suburban in the parking lot with Kathy, Amy and Paul in tow.

"Could you drop me off at the house Bob?" Paul asked as they put the bags in the back of the car.

"Sure. I want to finish going over that material today." Kathy heard the urgency in her father's voice as she got in the back seat with Amy. He glanced around to them. "I have a car seat in the storage room. I'll get it out as soon as we get home."

"I'll just grab a shower, some fresh clothes and I'll be right over." Paul was watching traffic as Bob pulled out through the security gate. "Will you check in with the paper and let them know I haven't wandered off?"

"I'm going to call Mac as soon as I get home. He probably thinks we lost his jet." Bob smiled thinking of his old friend. They had worked together for twenty years and had been through a lot.

The traffic was light and it only took a few minutes to get to Paul's apartment from the toll road. As Bob pulled away from the complex Kathy mused. "It feels good to be back in Dallas." She leaned her head against the window and watched the scenery roll by.

"Did the discs tell you anything, Dad?"

He didn't want to lie to her but knew the fewer people with knowledge of Kevin's find the better. "Most of it was testing the surveillance cameras and links. He had quite an elaborate system of equipment up there." He stopped to watch traffic and negotiate a couple of turns to put him closer to his home.

"I don't know what to make of the problem getting in touch with Alan and the people at Barrett Security Systems."

"My husband is gone and they don't even answer their phones. Kevin was about to put that place on the map and now look at them." She was mad and hurt.

Bob's eyes fixed on hers and she caught his glance. "You okay?" He asked trying to console more than inquire.

"I'm fine. I just need some answers."

"We all do." He looked back at her. "Hopefully I'll have some for you tomorrow. Right now I want to get you two tucked in safely and let you get some real rest while I sort things out."

"Do you remember Tom and Mary Macnamara?"

"Your crazy neighbors?" Kathy smiled. "I remember them."

"They'll keep an eye on you and Amy if you need anything, they'll be close by."

Bob pulled up in front of his town house and felt safer than he had in the past three days. Things had really changed in the few days since he left for Orlando. His priorities had been altered so drastically. He hadn't worried so seriously about Kathy and Amy in so long.

Their lives and futures seemed to be secure and progressing well. What a difference a couple of days could make.

The inside of Bob's home was not the picture of neatness and Kathy smiled as she could imagine her father packing for a quick trip as he had so many times before.

The saddest times in her life were when he would leave and the happiest were when he would return, always with a gift for her and her mother. As she was growing up she could never figure out why anyone would want a job where they would have to travel.

They seemed to miss so much and her mother spent so many days and nights worrying about him.

She sat Amy down on the floor of the living room and headed to the guestroom to see if any old toys were there. "Dad, do you have anything Amy can play with?" She yelled as he disappeared up the stairs.

"Blocks." He replied "Big box of blocks in the closet."

She went to the closet and found some alphabet blocks to keep the baby busy. After scattering them around Amy she sat on the couch and scanned the room. She had not been to the house in a couple of years but nothing had really changed much since her dad had moved here from their old home.

She walked over to the bookshelf and looked at the pictures scattered among her father's awards. Her mother always looked so happy in the pictures. No one knew how sick she was till the end. She didn't want to worry her husband.

Amy was scrambling the blocks and laughing as Kathy headed for the kitchen and saw her dad's old typewriter on the counter. Bob didn't like computers and still did his work on an old Underwood manual typewriter. "Can you still buy ribbons for this old thing?" She asked as he came down the stairs.

"I bought a whole case of them. Found them a while back." He stopped to hit a key on the old machine. "I have enough to last till I croak." He seemed to think that last remark was funny but Kathy frowned at it.

"Don't talk like that." She said as she opened his refrigerator door.

"Dad this is quite a collection." She smiled over her shoulder. "Don't you ever look at the dates?" She gathered a number of cartons and jars to throw in the trash.

"Not very often, Honey." He said laughing. "How about pizza tonight? Paul and I will be working late." Bob heard Amy fussing and started into the living room to check on her. She had blocks everywhere when Bob picked her up and sent her into a case of the giggles. "What are you building girl?"

She shrieked with laughter and he put her back down with the blocks. "Kathy, I've got to call the paper and get them up to speed on this." He stopped for a moment. "Do you mind how I handle Kevin's information?"

"No Dad." She looked up from her spot on the floor in front of the refrigerator. "Use it whatever way you need to, to find out what happened. I don't care what you do with whatever you find." She threw another jar into the trash. "Nothing will bring Kevin back."

He patted her on the head as he passed by on his way to the den. He sat down behind his old cluttered desk to call his old friend and boss and catch him up on the events of the last two days.

Mac picked up on the first ring. "That you Bob?" He had seen the number on the caller screen.

"Damn." Bob laughed "You must have really been worried about that plane."

"Ass hole." His boss chuckled. "You know better than that. Are you and the kids okay?"

"Kathy's holding up pretty well, Amy's great. I'm just confused." He closed the door. "I don't know what we've uncovered but I feel we'll have a better handle on it tomorrow."

"I've had a few odd calls about what you and the paper had to do with the investigation in Canada and now Duluth. It seems like all hell broke loose up there."

"You might be putting it mildly." Bob settled into his chair. "It seems the Military might have been involved in both instances. I really don't know."

"Will this be a story?" Mac hesitated and then slowed. "You know I'm sorry about Kevin but there are a lot of people looking for a story."

Bob was studying the discs in his hand and wondering what else Kevin had discovered.

"Are you there, Bob?" Mac's voice was anxious.

"You'll have your story Mac. Give me a little time to get everything in place and you'll have a story."

"Do you need any help?"

"I'd appreciate it if you'd call one of your friends on the force and have their guys keep an eye on the neighborhood. Strangers and stuff, you know. I'm going to alert our security but just to be safe." He was thinking of Kathy and the baby.

"I'll call the chief right now. Don't worry, Bob." Mac's voice showed more concern for Bob and his family than the story but it was hard to keep the news hounds from coming out. "Keep in touch!"

Paul arrived with his workbags. Bob had cleared off part of his desk for Paul to set up his computer. "You have enough room?" He asked as Paul plugged in wires.

"Plenty Bob. I brought a bigger flat screen monitor so we'll get a better look at whatever he found." He continued. "This printer will give us a lot better clarity on any pictures."

Bob got a chair out of the kitchen. "We're going over the discs in a couple of minutes." He told Kathy who was still cleaning up.

"I ordered a couple of pizzas, they should be here in about twenty minutes."

"Good, I'm starving." He carried the chair back to the den. "Let's go." He said to Paul as he sat down.

Paul started skipping through the sequences leading up to the McVey identification. When that portion appeared Paul printed out the information and they continued to view. Bob took out the new print outs and checked the dates of reference on the data.

This information was fresh off the FBI databank. "Kevin must have been as surprised as you and I when he saw it."

Paul was watching the screen as Bob pulled the pictures out of his workbag. He held the pictures of the man on the snowmobile up beside the surveillance camera shot. "Definitely the same guy." He laid the two pictures down on either side of McVey's mug shot and the similarities were obvious. "The beard, mustache and hair color are the difference. Up to the time he was executed his look never changed. Every photo of him was always the same."

"Tell me about it." Paul chided. "Everybody in the country knew this guy." He pointed to the mug shot and then he held up the camera picture from the hockey match. "No one would think these two pictures were the same person especially when one of them has been confirmed as executed by the Federal Government."

Bob was watching the screen but his mind was on the story. If this was true they were on the verge of a Pulitzer, but what in the hell happened to Kevin?

Paul was back fast-forwarding the frames. "That's the end of this disc." He opened the tray and placed the second disc in the tray to start viewing it when they heard the knock on the door.

Bob called out to Kathy. "I'll get it," and went to his hall closet. He reached to the top shelf and brought down his old Colt 45. He chambered a shell and made sure the safety was off before tucking it into his back pocket and heading to the door.

He bent down to the peephole and was glad to see the red white and blue Dominos sign on the roof of the car outside. The pizza smelled good as he paid the driver and closed the door. He turned away but went back to set the deadbolt and chain. As he set the locks he thought about the frail latches that had kept the intruders from Kathy and Amy in the computer room.

"Pizzas here." He announced setting the boxes on the counter and heading back to the den. Kathy had the kitchen in order.

"Are you ready to eat Dad?" She asked knowing he had to be famished. She put some plates on the counter and went for Amy.

"We'll be there in a minute, Honey." He answered putting the pistol back in the closet. "Anything going on Paul?"

"Not much. It looks like he got a few more positive ID's, but nothing as spectacular as McVey. Most of these are immigration violations or provincial convictions, but the way Kevin's system interacts with the other agencies is great. I'm printing out all his positives in case you see something interesting."

"I'll bring you some pizza." Bob said starting to the kitchen. He went down the hall and was pleased to see Kathy had found her old highchair and had Amy busy eating pizza. He rubbed her head. "They don't make wooden ones anymore."

"I remember that thing. I used to love the teddy bears." She referred to the bears her mother had painted on the back.

"We're going to eat in there." Bob said loading a couple plates with pizza. "You find everything okay?"

"Sure Dad." She picked up some pizza Amy had launched off the tray.

Paul never took his eyes off the monitor as he ate his pizza. "It looks like he's shutting down for the night again, but he left the system on. This thing works on its own once he has it set so the unmanned application would be phenomenal. All it would take was checking when the computer signals a definite hit."

Bob sat down beside Paul and continued to watch as he clicked through the sequence shots. It was turning to night and the camera in front of the lodge showed vehicles coming and going. Little by little the parking lot emptied and the lodge emptied out except for the die hards that stuck around for a few late drinks. Paul sat upright as the Humvee pulled into the lot and turned to the spaces in front of Kevin's room. "Do you see that?" He asked Bob as the darkened figures headed to the front door and it gave way under their rush.

Paul switched the computer to the inside camera and could see the hooded figures enter the room. They watched in disbelief as Brady ran to the other room to struggle with Kevin.

Neither Bob nor Paul spoke or moved as the masked figure re-entered the room and began to scan the bank of monitors. When he pulled the hood off to better see what was going on the camera got a good frontal shot of his face. "You son of a bitch," Bob muttered.

Another figure was busy in the other room and Bob could see the bottles were missing from the dresser. The first figure was grabbing articles and putting them in his utility bag as the second sprayed the room with some kind of aerosol. The figure without the hood left the room as the second finished spraying and lit some kind of match. He tossed it on the bed where Kevin's motionless body laid and in seconds the room was in flames.

It was strange to see the flames start on the tables that held the computer and monitors, they grew larger and brighter and then the screen went blank.

Bob and Paul did not take a breath as they sat motionless staring at the blank screen. "Why did they do that?" Paul asked of no one, not believing what he and Bob had just witnessed. "He never had a chance. Those brutal bastards killed him for nothing. Those cold blooded bastards."

Bob put the pizza dish down and with a shaky hand picked up the picture of McVey on the snowmobile. "They must have had a good reason," He said tapping McVey's face. "I really wonder who in the hell they are." His chest was hurting as he took a deep breath. "I don't want Kathy to see this! Can you burn me a copy of these discs?"

"Sure," Paul said reaching into his bag for a box of blanks. "It'll only take a few minutes." He was busy for a minute. "How are you going to go after this?"

Bob watched Paul for a few seconds. "I don't think we're going to have to go after it. I feel it will be coming to us. I hope you weren't planning to go home tonight."

Paul smiled "I think you're right." He finished with the first disc and started to copy the second. "I Hope your couch is comfortable."

"I'm going to call my neighbor in case we need reinforcements." Bob picked up the phone to call his neighbor. "Hello Tom" He started when his neighbor picked up. "It was a long trip. A lot more miles than I figured." He paused a moment. "How about meeting me on the front porch for a few minutes." He hung up and headed for the front door, stopping to pick up the automatic on the way.

Tom Macnamara was a large red-faced individual. He had retired recently from Haliburton having spent a great many years overseas and in Central and South America developing oilfields.

"What's up Bob?" He smiled shaking his neighbor's hand. He noticed the gun in Bob's pocket. "Damn you're packing pretty heavy for the front porch, aren't ya?"

"Kathy had some problems up North and I don't know if they might have followed us home. If you hear me screaming I'd appreciate a hand." Bob didn't want to say any more and he knew Tom would understand.

Tom's smile turned serious "You call and I'll come running. Is she okay?"

"She and the baby are fine. Their worlds' been turned upside down but she seems to be coping with it. It's been a couple of real bad days."

"If you need anyone else I can call a few old roughnecks I know to cover all the bases, Bob, did you talk to security?"

"I called them when I got in."

"They're pretty good as long as you give them a heads up. Holler, if you need me." Tom turned and headed for his home.

"Thanks Tom, I hope I don't have to bother you."

"No bother" He said waving.

Kathy had cleaned up the few dishes and was taking Amy upstairs to go to bed when she stopped to give her dad a kiss good night. "I'll see you in the morning, we're exhausted."

He kissed the baby as she yawned heavily smelling of pizza. "I love ya! Good night." As she started back up the stairs he said, "Paul and I have a meeting tomorrow. If you need any help, call Tom and Mary."

"See you in the morning." She left the steps and closed the door of the guestroom behind her.

Bob pulled some pillows and blankets from the hall closet and dropped a few in the den for Paul, he took the rest to the living room. "Get some sleep Paul we've got a full day ahead."

Paul was spreading the covers on the sofa as Bob lay down on the living room couch. He pulled the gun from his pocket and held it in his hand under the blanket. He made sure he had an unobstructed view of the door so that he would be the first one to greet any unwanted company. He could not help think of Kevin falling asleep not knowing that his life would end so abruptly and violently.

Chapter 33

Morning came early and uneventfully. Bob had coffee making as Kathy came down the steps. "Good morning Honey." He said as she gave him a hug from behind.

"That coffee smells good" She reached into the cabinet for a can of creamer. "I slept like a rock. The baby is still out."

"Paul's in the shower, we have to be in Fort Worth this morning to interview someone." He poured her a cup. "We'll probably be gone all day, but I'll have my cell on."

"Did the discs tell you anything, Dad?" She asked pouring some cream into her cup.

"They told us plenty, honey. I think I know why Kevin died but we have to put a few things together before we can nail the people who did it." He didn't want to put her off but he didn't think it was good for her to know everything he and Paul had learned. "Honey, in case something happens to me and Paul." He went silent and showed her two discs that he put in the bottom of his large can of Maxwell House Coffee.

"You better not let anything happen to you!" She sounded stern. "You're all we've got."

Paul came out and Bob handed him a cup of coffee in a paper cup. "I suppose eggs and bacon are out of the question?" He asked with a smile.

"Your right" Bob said heading to the door. "We're late." He took Kathy by the hand and opened the pantry door to show her the pistol. "The safety is on. You remember how to use it?"

"Yes Dad." She suddenly realized how serious he was. "Be careful and call me!" She gave him a hug and they were out the door.

Chapter 34

The trip to Fort Worth was quick and Bob was impressed with the Star-Telegram offices. Terry Kennedy met them in the lobby. He was a tall young man with a big smile. "What in the world do two hot shots with the Dallas Evening News want with a good ole boy from Fort Worth?" He said shaking their hands.

"Help with spelling?" Paul said with a grin. "How have you been, Terry?"

"Great," Terry answered. "A little bored. This must be Mr. Shroud." He said turning his attention to Bob. "I've heard a lot about you and this is a pleasure."

"Thank you" Bob said modestly. "We met a couple of years ago."

"I remember, but you were surrounded with about twenty five people all talking at once and I never got to tell you how much I like your work."

"I appreciate that." The elevator opened and the three stepped in. "Terry, we need some help. Bob started matter of factly.

"I'm glad to help." He glanced at Paul. "What do you need?"

The elevator doors opened and Terry walked them over to a conference room. "Please, have a seat" Terry said. "How about some coffee?"

"I'll take some," said Paul settling into one of the overstuffed chairs.

Terry didn't wait for Bob. "Coffee for three," he said to a young man standing by the door. The young man dashed away and Terry closed the doors.

Bob got right to the point "Terry we want to pick your brain about Tim McVey." He didn't stop at Terry's surprised reaction. "We need to know everything you know about him."

Terry recovered from the initial question. "Well." He started "You came to the right place." He settled back in the chair and folded his hands in front of his face. "I was in Oklahoma City the day he blew up the Federal Building. I was four blocks away. The damn blast scared the shit out of me. I'd never heard anything bigger than a cherry bomb go off…I ran over to the burning building and pieces were still falling." He stopped for a couple of seconds. "I wasn't ready for that kind of carnage. I had one of those old mobile phones and was on the line to the paper and WBAP while the dust was still in the air."

"I remember your broadcasts" Bob injected.

"I just couldn't believe anything that bad could happen." He looked over at Paul "I had a mobile truck in Waco a year before when the Branch Dividian Compound went up in flames and I never thought a story would ever affect me like that again, but Oklahoma City knocked my dick in the dirt."

He shook his head remembering that day. "What do you need to know about McVey?"

"Everything." Bob replied.

"I was there from the time the building went down through his arrest and subsequent trial. I even had the only jailhouse interview with him after his sentencing."

"You attended the execution, didn't you?" Paul asked.

"Yeah I did." Terry paused and looked at Bob. "I wish I hadn't. I got to know McVey pretty well and he wasn't a real bad guy. I still have nightmares about his execution."

"You saw him die?" Bob asked.

"Yes." Terry answered. "Of course. I even have the only film of it."

"How could you have that?" Bob asked.

There was a knock on the door and the young man returned with a tray of coffee. "Thanks John." Terry said and the man disappeared through the doors. After Terry made sure the doors were closed, he walked over to his chair and leaned on its back. "You and I know the resources that are available to the Herst Corp." He was talking directly to Bob. "I was wearing a hidden camera and I recorded everything from the beginning to the end."

"What did you do with it?" Bob asked as Paul listened unbelievingly. "I never heard about it."

"It didn't come out. I was so shaken by the execution I never viewed it or showed it to anyone."

"Have you still got it?" Bob asked flatly.

"What in the hell are you guys after, Mr. Shroud?" His voice changed from that of information to caution.

"I've been doing all the talking." He paused. "It's your turn."

"We're off record right?" Bob began.

"Okay," Terry confirmed and sat down turning his chair towards Bob and leaning forward in a bullshit stance.

Bob looked at Paul and Paul nodded his agreement, not that Bob needed it, but he felt as though Paul was a major part of what had developed so far. "My son in law was murdered in Canada three days ago. My daughter and granddaughter were victims of a break in and an assault in their home in Minnesota two days ago, in which police officers were killed and wounded. It seems that information about McVey and his whereabouts may be the reason for all these events."

"His whereabouts?" Terry asked astounded. "What the hell are you talking about? I saw the man die!" Terry was on his feet now. He looked at Paul. "Is your boss crazy?" He glanced back at Bob and noticed how serious they both were. They were silent as Terry walked back and slumped in the chair. He rubbed his face and put his head in his hands. "I have to tell you something, honestly." He stopped again and raised his head to look at Bob's eyes. "When they executed him I had a terrible feeling they had fucked up royally. I don't know why but I felt like even after all the charges, trials, witnesses, yada yada——-they fucked up. I can't explain what I was feeling but that's the way I felt."

"I want to see that film." Bob said seriously.

"I sense a major story, Mr. Shroud. How are we going to handle this?" Terry paused. "We both seem to have parts of a puzzle and you know how that goes."

Bob leaned close to the much younger man. "Total honesty, I never settle for anything else, but nothing gets out until I can be assured that what's left of my family is safe from harm."

"I can appreciate that." Terry agreed "Let's get out of here. My home is in the country East of Alliance Airport." He started drawing on a piece of scratch paper. "It's about a thirty minute drive from here and we will not be disturbed."

Bob and Paul left the building and headed North on 35 west. "Can we trust him?" Bob asked.

"I think so. McVey was his life for six years." Paul watched the city of Fort Worth go by. "He was in the right place at the right time and McVey made him a name. He probably owes McVey everything that he is."

The traffic was light and it didn't take long to get to their exit off 35 west. "He has Ross Perot for a neighbor up here." Bob was joking.

"Really!" Paul agreed. "I think he owned this whole area."

Terry's house sat on a hill overlooking a small pond. The garage was on a lower level and he was standing by the doors to welcome Bob and Paul.

"This is beautiful" Bob said as they exited the Suburban.

"I call it the house that McVey built." Terry chuckled. "I ate, lived and breathed him for quite a while. I felt like we were related after a time." He looked at the pond. "Come on in." the place was huge. They went to a mid-level room with a large TV. There was a long sofa with a table in front of it. A couple of large boxes of videotapes and CD's were on the table.

"This is Tim McVey" Terry said pointing to the boxes. "Every still shot, tape, interview, location shot, is in this collection from the beginning 35mm and VCR and then we moved into the electronic age and digital saved a lot of space. You want something to drink?"

"I want to see the execution." Bob said flatly.

Terry looked at Bob and then at Paul. "Okay." He said quietly. He went to the bookcase beside the wide screen TV and touched a button that was hidden under a shelf. A door opened that was covered by a façade looking like law books. The door revealed a combination safe. He dialed the combination and the door opened. He reached inside and pulled out a mini-cassette without saying a word he went to the shelf housing all the electronics for his system and inserted the cassette. He walked over to the couch and sat down beside Bob. "Go for it." He said handing Bob the remote control.

Bob really didn't want to see someone die but he knew in his heart that it was necessary for him to view the information on the cassette. He touched his thumb to the play button.

Bob, Paul and Terry sat motionless as the TV lit up with the images of the inside of the death chamber. McVey was strapped to the gurney and the prison officials were busying themselves with the connections of the IV's and the respiratory monitoring devices. His face was stoic and he looked straight up at the bright light in the ceiling.

There was no sound on the recording so the images moving on the screen moving silently were even more eerie than in real life. There was a large clock on the back wall of the death chamber and as it clicked down to the top of the hour the chamber emptied out. At one minute before the hour McVey was alone inside. He was not moving on the flat gurney. He was not struggling. Just lying there, like he was relaxing. As the seconds ticked down to twelve up Terry must have sat up straighter and his view of the room improved.

Paul and Bob seemed to lean forward and Terry slumped back in the cushions of the couch not wanting to see what was about to happen.

Bob could hear himself breathing as the second hand hit twelve and you could see the solution move into the intravenous tubes connected to McVey. Bob expected him to jump or lunge straining at the straps but there was no movement. At thirty seconds there was a little twitching but nothing else. Bob watched McVey's chest move up and down in a regular rhythm. At forty-five seconds his hands twitched a bit and then his chest was still.

Nothing happened for a while. At one minute thirty seconds the prison officials walked in and started checking McVey.

"Back it up." Paul said. Making Bob and Terry jump.

"What?" Bob said.

"Back it up to thirty seconds after the hour." Paul was electric. He stood up and approached the TV as Terry began to watch him wondering what the hell was going on. Bob backed the tape up to thirty seconds after the hour and hit the play button. Paul stayed at the screen watching. As the seconds ticked away Paul stood poised. At forty-five seconds after the hour he pointed at McVey's right hand. "Watch this!" He said loudly and Bob and Terry sat up straighter on the couch.

McVey twitched a bit just before his chest stopped moving. "Did you see it?" Paul said jumping up and down.

"See what?" Terry exclaimed jumping up off the couch.

"Back it up, Bob" Paul said to Bob who was totally confused.

Bob pushed the buttons but Paul took the remote from his hands trying to contain his excitement. He rewound the tape and then played the same segment pointing to McVey's hand. "His right hand, watch this." Paul was shouting now.

Bob and Terry were standing now as Paul pointed to McVey's right hand strapped to the gurney. The tape played and McVey's hand twitched as the saline solution hit his vital organs. "Right there," Exclaimed Paul.

"What in the hell are you talking about?" Bob asked.

Paul rewound the tape and played it again. "Watch the fingers." He looked at Terry. "Is there any way to slow this down?"

Terry got up and went to the front of the TV. He took the control from Paul and hit a couple buttons. The sequence started over.

"I was in the Army for four years. For a year I was with the engineers and I had to make a parachute jump for the Communications Corps. They sent me to Columbus, Georgia to Fort Benning and I trained with some of the airborne guys."

"They're a crazy bunch and I kind of got adopted by a few of the Hispanics in their group."

Bob looked at Paul to see where this was going and Paul continued.

"These guys were telepathic. They worked in the dark, underwater, anywhere and they had codes and sign language no one else knew. I didn't get in on any of that shit but when they went drinking in town I went along a few times. When they had a few beers and they were out for broads they were crazy. The bitchier the better. The finest babes." He seemed to think back and smile.

"When one of them would score they celebrated." Paul looked at Bob's blank stare. He held up his right hand. "Thumb to first two fingers and then a fist meant mission accomplished. Now look at this!" Paul backed up and hit the play button.

Bob and Terry watched, as McVey's twitch became a deliberate and controlled signal "MISSION ACCOMPLISHED" Paul hit the pause button and collapsed onto the couch as they sat staring at the fist.

None of them knew how much time passed before someone spoke.

"Where's he buried?"

"His body was cremated the day after his execution." Terry answered. This caused Bob and Paul to glance excitedly at one another.

"What the hell is going on?" Terry asked again seeing them looking at each other.

"Sit down." Bob said as Paul started to hook his laptop up to Terry's equipment. Bob filled Terry in on what happened and why Kevin was in Canada.

He outlined Kevin's aspiration and connections and explained what had happened to Kathy and Army and the police in Duluth.

As Paul started the disc Bob watched as Terry took in the information from Canada. When the camera scanned McVey at the hockey rink Terry went stiff. As the mug shot and information came out on the screen Bob watched his face distort. "The son of a bitch is still alive!"

Bob signaled for Paul to stop the disc. He didn't want to have Terry view Kevin's demise. One thing at a time.

"Where do we go from here?" Bob asked an obviously shocked Terry Kennedy.

"I have no idea." Terry answered honestly. "You've got my library, Bob. Tell me what you need and I'll give you what I've got."

Bob thought for a minute and then looking from Terry to Paul. "They obviously stopped the legal trial with the cremation and the scattering of the ashes. We need to find if there was anyone he might have contacted after the fact. Were there any friends or family he might risk contacting?"

Terry answered quickly, "Nobody. This guy was a ghost. No friends, no matter what the other papers said about those assholes in Arizona and Missouri, he didn't keep in contact with any kind of family no matter what they said about Michigan. No girls, whores, no buds, no nothing. When he was in the service I only found one guy in his outfit that ever remembered him in Iraq."

"Who was that?" Bob asked quickly.

"A guy named Tray McGuiver." Terry thought for a few seconds. "I think he lives in Ennis Texas."

"Is he still there?" Paul asked Terry.

"We can ask Southwestern Bell." Terry said smiling. He picked up his phone and dialed 411.

After a few minutes with the operator he scribbled a few lines and hung up. "3166 Avenue A." He said to Bob who nodded approval.

"You want to come along?" Bob asked Terry.

"Hell yes!" Terry responded "I think I even have a map of Ennis."

They opted to use Bob's Suburban. As they traveled down 287 from Fort Worth everyone was thinking and no one was talking. Finally Bob broke the silence.

"Who paid for McVey's defense?" He asked.

"The American people." Terry answered. "He had a court appointed attorney. He had a lot of attorneys in the background." He thought for a minute "They did a hell of a good job. Everyone was watching them and one fuck up could have cause a mistrial. The public would not have put up with that."

As they neared Ennis Bob asked, "Did this guy serve in the artillery all the time McVey was in Iraq?"

"Not really." Terry responded. "It was as if McVey appeared and then disappeared. He was in an artillery battery and they figure that's where he learned about explosives but the Army never taught him anything about nitrate explosives. Uncle Sam doesn't make bombs out of fertilizer. They have commercial explosives. All he ever handled in the Army was 75mm and 105mm rounds. His MOS had nothing to do with covert missions or clandestine explosives.

Ennis is a small town and it took no time at all to find the address. The house was a run down structure surrounded with big wheel toys and broken bicycles. The old Dodge in the drive had quite obviously not run in a couple years and the word paint had not been used in the same sentence with the house that they were looking at for a lot longer.

Terry got out and looked around. Bob and Paul decided to stay in the car. "Tray." He shouted "Tray McGuiver." No one responded for a while.

"Who's looking for Tray?" A young woman asked looking out form a window with no screen.

"Tell him it's Terry Kennedy from the Fort Worth Star-Telegram." Terry strained to see if Tray was in the house.

A couple of minutes passed and a tall gaunt figure walked out of the house with a bottle of Budweiser in his hand. "That you Terry?" The man said taking a drink from the bottle.

"It's me Tray." Terry replied. "How've you been?"

"Pretty good Tray." Terry pointed to the Suburban. "I have a couple people I'd like to have you talk with."

"They cops?" Tray asked with the young woman looking out from behind him.

"No Tray, they're newspaper people who want to talk to you about Tim." Tray's eyebrow went up.

"No shit?" Tray laughed. "What the hell do they want to talk about a dead man for?"

Bob took his attitude as an okay to get out and he and Paul exited the Suburban and moved towards the house. Terry pointed to Bob. "This is Bob Shroud and his assistant Paul Martinez. Bob this is Tray McGuiver."

Tray nodded acknowledgement and tipped his beer bottle to Bob. "Tray, you were in Iraq with Tim during Desert Storm weren't you?"

"I was. He was a good artilleryman." He sipped the beer. "I told Terry that along time ago."

"Tray, did Tim have any connections with any organizations while he was in the service?"

"What are you asking Mr. Shroud?" Tray queried.

"I'm trying to find out if Tim was recruited by any other service agencies or organizations."

"Mr. Shroud, no one wanted Tim." Tray sent the girl for another beer and stepped out to sit on the steps. "You want a beer?"

"I sure would." Bob told him. "Paul would you go and get us a few cold ones?" He handed Paul a twenty. "The keys are in the car."

"Be right back," Paul said as he slid behind the wheel and started the Suburban.

"Two more." Tray yelled over his shoulder to the young girl. "Have a seat Mr. Shroud."

Bob took the beer the young woman offered and sat down on the steps facing the street. Things seemed awfully simple from Tray's perspective and for a moment he was reminded of his own youth in East Texas.

"What'd you think of Tim McVey?" Bob asked Tray directly.

"Tim was a good soldier, Mr. Shroud." Tray took a drink of his beer. He never asked anybody for anything or any favors. He did his job and never complained."

"Did he ever tell you what he wanted to do when he got out?"

"Na, they brought us back to Fort Reiley to muster us out and we lost track of one another there."

"What were his plans? Did you ever talk?"

"Not really. I was surprised when I heard he was a civilian." Tray finished a beer and the young woman left to go get him another one.

"He loved the Army, he was born for it. he wasn't looking forward to being a civilian again. The last time I saw him, he had volunteered for some kind of utility squad or something." He took a long drink of beer.

"What's a utility squad?" Bob asked.

"I don't really know. He left our barracks and moved to a different part of the Base. We always figured they were a Goon Squad." He looked at Paul as he put down the bag of beer. "No wetbacks, no blacks, just big white boys that followed orders."

"Are you saying it was some kind of racial or segregated group?" Terry asked. He was obviously hearing this for the first time.

"No, not really it's just that not everyone got picked or was offered the opportunity to join." He tipped the bottle, drained it and reached into the bag for another. "All I know is before they got a hold of him we were pretty tight, went through the Gulf War and all. He was like a brother, but that all changed, like that." He snapped his fingers. "How does a guy change like that overnight?"

"You never saw him again?" Bob asked.

"Nobody ever saw him again. It was like they took him off the face of the earth. There were thirty-four guys in our outfit, and you'd think he would've turned up somewhere. Mess hall, a movie, in town at a bar or at the supermarket." He paused to suck on the beer bottle again. "The next time I saw him they were walking him down the jailhouse steps and his picture was all over the newspapers."

Bob took a long sip of beer and realized that he and Paul had not eaten. "Tray, was Tim a political person?"

"What do you mean, Mr. Shroud?" Tray responded.

"Did he voice his opinions about the war in Iraq or maybe back home?"

"Not really, Mr. Shroud." Tray got serious. "Mostly we talked about fishing. Tim liked to fish. He used to talk about how he hated the desert and where we were based cause there was no water around." He reached into the bag for another beer. "There ain't no politics in fishing, just you and the fish." Bob smiled in agreement.

"What's this all about?" Tray asked Terry "Are they gonna investigate all this shit again?"

"We don't know." Terry replied as he got up off the steps to go.

"Tim didn't do all that crap they said he did and you can take that to the bank. I don't know how he got involved in that mess, but he would never hurt a kid." He finished the beer. "Uncle Sam killed the wrong man."

The three men headed back to the car. "Thanks for your time, Tray." Bob said as he opened the car door.

"Thanks for the beer," he said waving the bottle at them.

"Now there's a happy man" Paul said as Bob backed the car out of the littered drive and onto the street leading back towards Fort Worth.

Chapter 35

Kathy was changing Amy when she heard the knock on the door. she put Amy in her high chair and went to the closet to get her father's pistol. She had forgotten how heavy the weapon was.

As she peered through the peephole in the door, she was relieved to see the smiling face of Tom McNamara, her father's neighbor. She clicked the safety back on and opened the door.

"Good morning, Annie Oakley" Tom joked as he saw the large gun in her hands. "Everything okay?"

"Yes Tom" She said smiling as she relaxed and thought about how silly she probably looked with the big gun. "Come on in."

He followed her back to the kitchen and tickled Amy on the chair. "She's getting big, all I've seen are Bob's pictures, but this girl is growing up." Amy was laughing loudly.

"I'll be right back," Kathy said heading down the hall to put the gun up.

"Don't shoot yourself in the foot with that thing." Tom joked. His face changed as she returned. "I'm really sorry about Kevin, he was a good kid."

"Thanks Tom." She gave Amy a few more grapes from the bowl on the counter. "I've been on the phone with Canada for an hour trying to get his body released, but they are going to do an autopsy before they give him up."

"Your Dad probably knows someone at the paper who can put a little heat on them."

"I'm sure he does, but they've been real nice and I'm such a mess I guess if it takes a little longer it won't matter. The past few days have been a blur." She paused and her eyes moistened. "I miss him so much."

"I'm sorry kid." Tom reassured her again. "Call me or Mary if you need anything or you get scared. We're right next door." He started out "Lock up tight, you know how to use the alarm system, right?"

"Sure Tom, thanks for checking on us. Tell Mary I'll see her later." She dried her eyes and turned to get Amy more grapes.

Kathy turned her attention to the notepad and the telephone on the counter. She dialed the number for Kevin's employer again and was surprised to get a recording.

"Thank you for calling Barrett Security Systems" the recorded female voice started. "We're sorry but our office has been closed for renovations. If you need assistance please leave your name and number and someone will return your call."

Kathy left her father's home number and her name. She mentioned Alan's name and hung up hoping they would be prompt in returning her call.

She had just taken a seat on the couch and was looking at Kevin's picture in her day planner when the phone rang and startled her.

"Hello Honey." She was glad to hear her father's voice. "Everything okay?"

"Just fine Dad. How are you doing?"

"We're getting ready to drop Terry off and head back home."

"Did you find anything out?" She asked.

"Not really, but all the little pieces seem to be coming together. We'll see you later." He closed his cell phone as Paul steered the Suburban into Terry's drive. The three men got out of the car and looked at the clouds to the South. "Looks like we're gonna get wet on the way home, Paul."

Paul nodded as Terry spoke up. "What now Mr. Shroud?"

"I'm not too sure." He paused. "I need to talk with Reynolds in Canada to see if anything has turned up. I really don't know where to start looking."

Paul injected "Bob we probably know a lot more than any of the authorities at this point. The only lead they have to the perpetrators is the body of the man in Duluth."

"What body?" Terry asked puzzled, glancing back and forth to the two men.

"One of the people in the invasion and shoot-out in Duluth turns out to be a prisoner who should have been safely locked away in Leavenworth. God knows how he ended up in assault gear in Duluth, Minnesota."

"Damn." Terry mused. "You know Kansas was home to Tim before, during and finally after the whole Oklahoma City thing. There has to be some kind of connection. I'll dig out my old files and I'll check the Internet up dates to see if they have released any information on the dead man in Duluth."

"This card has all my numbers. If you hear anything or turn up anything give me a call." Terry took the card.

Bob started to get back in the Suburban and then hesitated. "Terry, we're dealing with some pretty serious people here. Be very careful who you talk to and please keep what we have between us until we decide to go public."

"Agreed Mr. Shroud." Terry turned and headed towards the house.

As Paul started the car and pulled it into gear he turned and glanced at Bob watching Terry disappear into the house. "Do you think we can trust him?"

"I hope so." He watched the scenery go by as they started the trip back to Dallas.

A few minutes into the trip his cell phone rang.

"Mr. Shroud, this is Captain Reynolds in Manitoba." The voice sounded very businesslike.

"Hello Captain. How is the investigation going?"

"Very confusing Mr. Shroud." The Mountie paused. "I had your son in laws body autopsied by two of our best investigative forensic people. The results confirm what you said about him was correct. His remains contained no sign of alcohol and they are conclusive the he was dead before the fire. They found traces of an accelerant on his body."

"Captain" Bob started, trying to decide how much he should or could disclose. "Have you had any success in locating the immigration official Kevin was working with?"

"Not really Mr. Shroud." The Mountie sounded irritated. "The Immigration Service has been less than helpful in that part of the investigation. It seems we have opened a Pandora's Box of embarrassment up here. No one wants to talk about what we were helping your son in law work on. The official that made arrangements for all the expenditures and manpower has taken a leave and cannot be reached."

"The higher ups in Quebec seem to have acquired lock jaw, which is really odd as they normally have plenty to say about everything." He stopped. "It seems that Kevin and his Canadian counterparts might have been treading on a patch of thin legal ice."

"Are you suggesting that Kevin was breaking the law?" Bob queried. Beginning to feel the Mountie was about to attack Kevin.

"Not at all Mr. Shroud" The Captain explained. "Kevin was here by invitation of the Canadian Government. All that he did, whatever it was, was sanctioned and supported by my Country." He took a deep breath. "It just seems that no one knew what was going on or wants to take responsibility for sanctioning his actions. I seem to be running into one wall after another. I feel someone is trying to cover up my investigation."

"Captain, it seems there is a very good possibility that the U.S. Government may be involved with what happened. We have looked into a few things and it seems that it would have been impossible for things to have occurred the way they have without the help of at least a few people in high places."

"Mr. Shroud, have you found anything out you can share with me?"

"Not yet, Captain, but when we get all the pieces together I promise you that you will know exactly what I know."

"Please don't take advantage of my trust and honesty, Mr. Shroud." The Captain's voice was stern, but still patient. "We'll talk again, goodbye!" and he was gone.

Bob looked back out the window at a group of horses grazing in the light rain. "How's the Captain doing?" Paul asked.

"He's getting impatient. They're stone walling him up there and no one wants to admit involvement with Kevin's project." Bob went silent again. "Swing by the office on the way home." He watched Paul nod an okay and relaxed back in the seat.

The trip to the Dallas Evening News office was quick. Traffic was building but everyone was heading out of Dallas as they were headed in on 114.

Paul parked the Suburban on the second floor of the parking garage in a space marked with Bob's name. "Where we going Boss?" He asked.

"I need to talk to a few people." Bob said. "How about we meet back here in an hour?"

"Sure Paul responded "I need to check my office and pick up supplies." He tapped his camera bag.

"Not a word." Bob continued placing his finger to his lips.

"Yes Sir." Paul answered turning to the stairs as Bob punched the elevator call button.

When the doors opened Bob stepped in and hit the forth floor button, but before the door closed he touched the bulge in his overcoat pocket and touched the stop button. He pulled the collapsible fishing pole out of his pocket and looked at it. "Let's see what you can tell us."

He touched the clear button and pressed the B2 button and the elevator started down.

When the doors opened on B2 Bob stepped out and started down the long hallway to his right. He stopped in front of a door marked Investigative Resources and slid his code ID card in the identification slot. The light turned green and Bob entered the room.

"Hi stranger." Piped a voice from the area behind the counter.

Bob smiled as a body emerged from the maze of shelving and machines. "Hello Joel. How have you been?"

"Great, Mr. Shroud." The thin young man put a pile of papers down on a desk and shook Bob's hand. "What can I do for you?"

Bob reached into his pocket and carefully pulled the fishing rod out, being sure to keep it wrapped in the handkerchief. I need you to check this for any kind of good fingerprints." Bob pulled the rod back as the young man reached for it. "I need you to keep this between us, understand?"

"No problem, Mr. Shroud." The young man answered. "Have you got a reference number?" He asked preparing to write something in a book on his desk.

"No reference number Joel. Just get me some good prints and I'll give you a reference number later."

"Sure thing Mr. Shroud." He carefully took the rod from Bob and started to the rear of the lab. "Do you want me to run them for you?" He asked to see if Bob wanted to have him cross reference the prints with the papers NCIC computer connections.

"No Joel." Bob answered starting for the door. "Just get me some good prints and call me in the office as soon as you have them done."

"Okay." Joel said disappearing into the world of gadgets and shelves of materials that composed the papers Investigative Resources Lab.

Bob left the lab and returned to the elevator and headed up to his office.

Joel put on a pair of latex gloves and started to unwrap the rod he had placed on his counter, he took a long thin probe from a drawer ad inserted it in the back portion of the rod handle. Picking the rod up by the probe he placed it horizontally in the vice on his worktable.

He worked quickly and took the small brush and spray powder from a shelf to his right. He sprayed the powder on the rod handle while slowly turning the probe. He pulled the magnifying glasses down from his forehead and slowly examined the rod. His attention centered on a section of the handle and he picked up the dusting brush. Very slowly and carefully be began to brush the area he was fixed on. His serious look slowly turned to a smile. "Bingo!" He said grinning from ear to ear.

He dusted the entire handle and scanned the other parts of the surface. Once finished he picked the piece up by the probe and headed over to a machine in the far corner. He opened the door and secured the probe-locking device and turned on the machine. Once the door was closed the ultraviolet light turned on and the fingerprints were clear and distinct. Joel continued to smile broadly.

As he exited the elevator and started down the hall to his office, Bob notice Mac nervously coming down the hall. His old friend reached out to shake his hand. "You alright?" He asked.

"Just fine. I thought I should stop by and see if I still had a job.

Mac smiled "That's one thing you never have to worry about. How are the girls?"

"Doing pretty well." Bob thought about his daughter. "They had quite a weekend."

"We're all real sorry about Kevin, Bob. If there is any thing they need or anything we can do please let me know." Mac was serious with his old friend.

"You've already done plenty. Thanks for the use of the plane and the pilot." Bob patted Mac on the back and started for his office. "I'm gonna earn my pay."

Mac watched as went down the hall and turned the corner. They had been friends for a long time.

Bob checked his mailbox and pulled out the large pile of letters and magazines. He entered his office and sat down behind the desk. He started sorting through the mail and reached over to sign on his computer. "You've got mail." The automated voice announced, and Bob started checking his messages.

It took about thirty minutes for him to clear the mailbox, printing and saving a few pieces and deleting most of the items. He saw an entry listed as Kevin B and clicked on it. The computer started to identify Kevin's message and then the screen went blank. Bob tried to back up the sequence but Kevin's identification and message were gone. Something was terribly wrong.

He went to the archive section of the newspapers web site and typed in Tim McVey. In moments he had a large list of choices. He selected arrest record. The computer whirred for a moment and soon pictures and choices flashed on the screen. The well-known picture of Tim being led down the steps by the police and marshals was the first in a series of pictures that the public knew all to well.

Bob clicked through the choices and stopped on Tim's identification sheet with his mug shots and fingerprints. Bob hit the print button and was waiting for his printer to spit out the information when the phone startled him. "Hello." He said to the speakerphone on the desk.

"Joel, Mr. Shroud" The young mans voice sounded excited. "You brought me an easy one. I got a full set of the right hand and the thumb and forefinger of the left."

"Great." Bob looked at the fingerprints sheet. "You're the best."

"I've got to drop some stuff off for other people on your floor. I'll drop this in your mailbox."

"No, Joel. I'm going to be in my office." Bob didn't want his link left lying around. "Just drop it off to me."

"Okay, Mr. Shroud, I'll be up in a minute."

Bob's heart was pounding while he continued to sort through his mail stack and waited for Joel.

Finding nothing interesting he threw most of the paper in the trash and scanned over McVey's record.

The knock on the door broke his viewing and he closed out the web before speaking. "Come in."

Joel was beaming when he walked in. He had two yellow envelopes in his hand. "They came out real pretty." He announced, handing the envelopes to Bob.

"Thanks for your help, Joel." Bob opened the envelope containing the fingerprint sheet. "Keep this between us, okay?"

"Sure thing, Mr. Shroud." The young man said turning back to the door. "Has this got something to do with your son in law?"

Bob was surprised by the question. "I don't know yet, Joel." Bob thought for a moment. "Is everyone aware of my son in laws death?"

"Pretty much Mr. Shroud." The young man said, "I hear Mac, I mean Mr. Macgruder put a lid on anything about the story."

"I appreciate that, and your help, Joel, but I really need for you to forget about this for a while." Bob said lifting the envelope with the rod inside.

"Yes Sir." Joel said obediently and left the room.

Bob's hand was trembling a little when he slid the finger print sheet out of the envelope. He walked to his scanner and placed the sheet inside. Returning to his computer he placed a clear sheet of Kodak plastic in the printer feed and began to type in commands. When he was finished he leaned back in the chair and listened to the printer start to work. Slowly the clear plastic eased through the printer. When the printer finished and ejected the sheet Bob slowly retrieved the plastic film and held it up to the light. It had copied the prints perfectly. He walked to the scanner and pulled out the print sheet Joel had created in his lab. He went back to his desk and sat down. He turned on the desk light for a bit more illumination. Bob placed the plastic over the sheet from the scanner and the copy on the plastic matched the print sheet correctly.

Bob removed the overlay sheet and reached for McVey's arrest sheet. He carefully placed the sheet over McVey's prints and tried matching the right hand thumbprint on the overlay with the arrest record from Oklahoma City. His heart skipped a beat as the intricate fingerprint lines matched perfectly.

Bob felt his chest tighten as he moved from print to print and the lines all matched exactly. "My God!" He said slumping back in his chair. "What in the hell is going on?"

The phone rang breaking his thoughts. "Are you ready to go home?" It was Paul's voice.

"Sure." Bob answered. "I'll meet you at the car, Paul."

Bob hung up and gathered up his paperwork. He went to the closet in his office and found a camera bag. He emptied the bag and put the envelope with the rod inside. He took the arrest report, overlay and Joel's print sheet and rolled them up. He had a small cardboard tube in his desk drawer. He inserted the rolled papers inside and put them in the camera bag. He straightened up his desk, put the bag over his shoulder and started to the parking lot, Paul, and home.

It didn't take long to reach his house and Paul parked the car handing Bob the keys. "I'm going to take my junk home. Take care."

Paul loaded his computer equipment in his car. "I'll see you in the morning, Bob."

"Take care, Paul. Call me about nine." Bob walked to his door and rang the bell. "Kathy it's me."

"Hi Grandpa." Kathy smiled as she opened the door with Amy in her arms. "How was your day?"

"Interesting." He said kissing the baby and taking her from Kathy's arms. "I just talked with Canada and no one seems to want to align themselves with Kevin's project."

"I have a bunch of papers and numbers in the apartment, but they're not doing us any good here." She closed the door. "I finally got an answer at Kevin's work, but it's a recording, and they never called me back."

Bob shook his head and hugged Amy tightly. "For a system everyone was excited about a few days ago, it sure seems odd no one wants to acknowledge involvement with its application now." He settled into a chair with the baby and the phone rang.

"Hello, yes, just a moment." He heard his daughter say as she brought him the phone and picked up the baby.

"Hello," he said relinquishing Amy, wanting to visit some more.

"Mr. Shroud?" The voice said.

"Yes, who is this?" Bob asked.

"My name is Fitzsimmons and I think its time we met."

"For what reason, Mr. Fitzsimmons?" Bob asked, puzzled.

"You are currently in an investigation concerning your son in laws death in Manitoba, and a subsequent intrusion in Minnesota." The voice was slow and direct. "I feel that if we meet I can save you a lot of time and effort."

Bob's heart was pounding as he asked, "Who are you?"

"I told you." The voice remained calm and cold. "My name in Fitzsimmons and I can help you."

"Where and when can we meet?" Bob asked.

"I know you are familiar with the field at Addison, I will have one of my people meet you at the information desk at nine in the morning."

"I'll be there." Bob hung up the phone, and tried to calm his pounding heart.

"Who was that?" Kathy asked as she tickled Amy who was reaching out for her Grandfather.

"Someone who seems to have information about Kevin and your visitors." He took the baby from her and started back to the sofa.

"And?" Kathy asked.

"I'm going to meet with him tomorrow." Bob saw her face go white.

"Where Dad?" She sat down beside him waiting for an answer.

"Addison Airport." He smiled at her. "Don't worry, I'll be okay."

"Are you going to take Paul or the police with you?"

"No." He patted her on the leg.

"Do you think this is smart?" She asked.

"Yes and no, but right now I have no leads. I don't know who we are up against and if this Fitzsimmons is able to make things easier, it's worth the risk."

Kathy didn't sound convinced. "I think you should call the police and let them know what's going on." She leaned over to his shoulder. "You're all we've got!"

He kissed her forehead and squeezed Amy a little harder. "Don't worry I'll be careful."

Bob kissed Amy and handed her back to Kathy. "I need to do a little work before bed. I'll see you in the morning." He kissed her forehead again and walked to his office.

He opened the drawer of the desk and took out a small recorder. He inserted a small cassette and started to speak. "This recording is to inform anyone, in the event of my death, about the events I have investigated and the information I have uncovered." Bob continued to record anything he thought might help fill in the blanks if anything happened to him.

When he finished he put the cassette in an envelope and put Kathy's name on it. After propping it up on his wife's picture, he went to the couch and tried to get some sleep.

Chapter 36

His night was filled with dreams of Kevin that caused him to sit up in a cold sweat. He thought of the phone call and the voice of the man he was to meet. It was plain to see he knew who Bob was and where he lived. He was worried for Kathy and Amy all over again and hoped this meeting could shed enough light on their situation to put an end to his fears.

He showered and dressed. As he looked in the mirror brushing his hair he noticed that he looked very old.

He put a fresh cassette in the recorder and slid it into his pocket. He opened the door to the hall and smelled the bacon Kathy had cooked. "Good morning, Dad. Sleep well?" She said, cracking some eggs into the skillet.

"A little." He answered, "how about you?" He moved across the kitchen to kiss Amy in her highchair. She was busy with a piece of toast.

"Like a rock. Amy never made a sound. That's the first good nights sleep I've had in a while."

Bob ate a quick breakfast and called Paul. "Good morning."

"Hey boss, what's the plan for today?" Paul answered.

"I have a meeting this morning." Bob thought for a moment. "Get with the paper in Duluth and see what they may have come up with that we didn't hear when we were there, I'll call you as soon as I'm free."

"Okay Bob, be careful." Paul said and hung up.

Bob appreciated the young mans concern. He liked working with Paul. "I'll call you later." He told Kathy, giving her a kiss and a hug. He unplugged his cell phone and made sure it was charged.

"You'll call me often." Her voice had a serious tone that went with the look on her face. "I'm going to worry about you all day."

"Don't worry." He said with a smile. "I have enough gray hairs for the both of us." He headed out to the Suburban.

Traffic wasn't too bad and the drive to the airport was short. He parked and headed into the small airport lobby. The security guard waved him through and into the structure. The lobby was nearly empty. Most of the people who used Addison were locals and a few corporate clients who knew the airport for its informal, personal service.

He walked toward the main desk and saw a man get up from one of the over stuffed chairs in the lobby. "Mr. Shroud?" The man asked, offering his hand.

"Yes," Bob answered, shaking the man's hand. "Who are you?"

"My name is Brady and I work for Mr. Fitzsimmons." Brady answered steering Bob to the exit door.

"Where is he?" Bob asked starting to worry. Brady was a powerful figure.

"A short distance away." Brady said, pointing to a small jet staged on the tarmac.

The men walked shoulder to shoulder towards the jet. Bob wondered if it would be a good idea to stop right now and try to control the meeting, but realized that Fitzsimmons was holding all the cards.

As they neared the jets extended stairway, Bob noted the numbers and the size, slightly larger than the one owned by the Dallas Evening News he had just used. He ascended into the body and was met by the pilot. "Good morning Mr. Shroud." He was holding a wand like the ones used by airport security. He motioned for Bob to extend his arms for a check. "If you would please?"

Bob held his arms out and the pilot searched his body with the wand. The pilot pulled bob's phone from his belt and removed the recorder from his pocket. "I'll give these back later Sir," he said, by way of explaining.

"Have a seat Mr. Shroud." Brady said "Would you like some coffee or a drink Sir?"

"I'll take a coffee if you have some." Bob said settling into one of the luxurious leather seats in the business jet.

Brady went to the galley and returned in a moment, handing Bob a cup of coffee. He placed it on the table between the seats and pulled out a server with cream and sugar. "Our flight will be short. If you need anything, please use the call button." He pointed to a control by Bob's chair and turned to the cockpit.

"What's the in flight movie?" Bob asked jokingly.

"No movie." Brady responded flatly and moved into the cockpit. The engines started to whine as he took his co-pilot seat and the jet started to roll. Brady reached back and closed the door and Bob was alone in the luxurious cabin of the jet.

He noticed the expensive fixtures and appointments. 'Fitzsimmons does pretty well for himself he mused as he sipped the coffee. The jet started to move and Bob reached over to open the shade pulled over the window by his side to see where he was going. The shade would not budge. He leaned over to the other side of the cabin to try to open one on the opposite window but that one would not move either.

"Please sit back and fasten your seatbelt, Mr. Shroud. We are about to take off." Bob was startled, but looked up to see the small camera that had been watching his every move from the rear of the cabin. He settled back in the seat and fastened his belt.

He took a sip of coffee and noted the time on his watch. 9:10 the engines noise increased as the jet accelerated down the runway and they were quickly airborne. Bob knew they had taken off from South to North and he waited to see which way they would turn. In a few seconds the craft started a turn to the East and held that track for a while, but he felt the turn lessen and the course seemed to be steady to the East.

His mind was racing as he thought about his position. He had not only put himself in the hands of strangers, but he was a potential prisoner in a jet going to a destination he was not supposed to know. As he took a sip of the coffee and put it back on the table he noticed the level of the liquid in the cup. They were making a gradual turn to the left, North. They were trying to make sure he didn't know where they were headed. He sat back and tried to relax, all the time feeling the eye of the camera on his back.

His watch read 9:42 when he felt the jet start to descend. It was 9:55 when the craft touched down and his mind was calculating approximately forty-five minutes of flying in the jet. He knew the paper's jet traveled at about three hundred to three hundred fifty miles per hour. He was envisioning a circle with Dallas as the center. He wondered if he was still in Texas or Louisiana, Arkansas, Oklahoma.

Owing to the Eastern turn at the start of the flight he could even find himself in Missouri or Kansas. He was still wondering when Brady emerged from the cockpit.

"Did you enjoy the flight, Mr. Shroud?" He asked.

"Very smooth, and the coffee was great." Bob replied trying to act casual. He watched Brady release the door latch and it was opened from the outside.

"Watch you step Sir." Brady said stepping back from the entryway and pointing the way out for Bob.

"Thank you." Bob said. "Don't go away, I have to be back for lunch." He smiled at Brady as he started out the door. Even bent over in the low ceiling of the cabin Brady looked big.

Bob watched his step on the way out and was quite shocked to see where he was. He had been imagining a flight to an isolated field in the middle of nowhere. The jet had landed on an obviously well maintained private strip in the middle of a golf course. A very beautiful golf course with lush green grass that was struggling back from the winter cold, but that had been very well cared for.

He noticed all the evergreen trees and foliage. In scanning the horizon he could see no high structures or landmarks to give him an idea where he was. No phone towers or power lines met his view. Just this beautiful golf course and the well-groomed man sitting on the fancy golf cart staring at him. He got off the cart and walked towards Bob removing his glove.

"Mr. Shroud." Bob recognized the voice.

"Mr. Fitzsimmons." Bob responded shaking his hand.

"It's a pleasure to meet you, Mr. Shroud." Fitzsimmons began nodding to Brady and the young man that had opened the jet door. Bob noted mentally how they seemed to relax as he dismissed them. Not a word was spoken as they, along with the pilot walked behind the plane and seemed to disappear into the foliage of the golf course. "I'm sorry we have to meet under such circumstances, but things are as they are and we must accept them and move on."

"What exactly do you mean?" Asked Bob.

Fitzsimmons hesitated for a moment looking directly at Bob. "Mr. Shroud, are you in a hurry?"

"I quit being in a hurry in my mid thirties." Bob said staring straight back at his host. "Every time I hurry I make mistakes." He noted the smile on Fitzsimmons face. "I'm not perfect but I'm a lot better if I proceed slowly."

"I can appreciate that and I hope you will allow me enough of your time to explain a few things to try and make you understand the events of the past few days."

"That's going to take quite a bit of explaining." Bob said, his mood changing to a serious one. "My son in law is dead, my daughter and granddaughter were attacked. Policemen were killed," He paused to take a breath. "Believe me that is going to take a lot of explaining." He stared at Fitzsimmons waiting for a response to his verbal assault.

"Hop in." Fitzsimmons said pointing to the cart. He took a seat behind the wheel and motioned to the hesitant Bob. "Come on. I promise if you give me enough time all your questions will be answered." He waited for Bob to slowly take a seat and then pressed his foot on the accelerator pedal to send the cart forward and away from the jet.

The fresh cool air felt good on Bob's face as they crossed the course. He searched the perimeter of the course for some type of landmark, but the place seemed enormous. No homes or buildings were visible. "Where's the clubhouse?" Bob asked.

Fitzsimmons grinned. "I haven't finished building it yet, and there will be a total of three." He pointed to a spot a small distance away, where Bob could make out a series of small grade flags. "There will also be a dozen hospitality bars and courtesy stops."

"Thirty six holes?" Bob asked.

"Good guess, Mr. Shroud." Fitzsimmons seemed to beam. "Championship caliber, all the fundamentals. In three years it will be available to join the tours."

Bob watched as they neared the first tee. "You're going to play the first game on a brand new course." Fitzsimmons braked the cart and got out, he went to the rear of the cart and pulled the cover of one of the beautiful bags in the bracketed frame. He noticed Bob did not move from his seat. "Please join me, Mr. Shroud, its not often you will be able to play such a peaceful game." He paused and noted Bob's incredulous stare.

"You're a lefty, right?" Bob started to move from the seat thinking there was not much sense in defying his host after coming this far. Fitzsimmons pulled the cover off the second bag. "I ordered these Calloways for you when I was sure you'd be here today. I think you'll be surprised with their fit."

Bob approached the custom bag of clubs and was visibly impressed with the craftsmanship. Fitzsimmons motioned to the box of balls on the back seat, selected a driver and headed for the tee, leaving Bob alone by the cart.

Bob selected a club and picked up a ball from the box and the gloves from the side of the bag and followed Fitzsimmons. His host was placing his ball and stretching as Bob approached. From the elevated tee Bob could see a few pieces of construction and excavation equipment nearly a half-mile off, but nothing else.

"Out here in the middle of nowhere, aren't we Mr. Fitzsimmons?" Bob asked watching his host address the ball and look down to the hole at the end of a long fairway.

"Not for long, Mr. Shroud." Fitzsimmons started a powerful drive that hit the ball solidly and straight down in the direction of the first hole. "Before long," he started, obviously happy with his first shot. "This will be surrounded with nearly eight hundred luxury custom homes, private airfield, thirty six hole championship golf course, one large mall, three or four shopping centers, convenience stores, gas stations, you name it. An entire community carved out of nothing in the middle of nowhere. We even have the bids out on three schools and a couple of churches."

"Baptist or Catholic?" Bob asked driving his ball in much the same direction and nearly the same distance as the player before him. "Damn this is a beautiful set of clubs!" He took a closer look at the driver he used and picked up his tee.

"Nice shot." Fitzsimmons commented. "Probably one of each to start with." He turned and started to the cart with Bob behind.

"What do you do, Mr. Fitzsimmons?" Bob asked as they replaced the clubs and sat down on the cart.

"This mainly." He started. "Build and develop. I started with houses and apartments. Small stores and strip centers. Then malls and intrastructure and now I do the whole works." He seemed very proud and sure of himself as the cart started down the course. "Everything from the water-sewer, electrical, cable, Internet, telephone, you name it and I develop it."

"You sound like a very busy man." Bob noted the way the sun had moved in the sky and determined the landing strip was northwest to southeast. A little more time would confirm his guess.

"Very busy. This is a near impossible luxury. A beautiful morning, a new course, fresh grass and good competition." He paused and slowed the cart as they neared their balls on the new grass. "What more could a man ask for?"

"I'd like a bit more information about my son in law." Bob said watching Fitzsimmons face.

"In due time Mr. Shroud. Please let me develop my presentation at my own speed." He was out of the cart again.

"I've done a lot of work and investigation on developers and I've never seen or heard of your name before." Bob selected a club and moved to his ball.

"I've read some of your work, Mr. Shroud. You're a good reporter. I have a great deal of respect for a man who has a reputation for being honest in your profession. I'm happy you never heard of me. You investigated some of the biggest crooks in the nation in Arizona. They scammed retiree, investors, the tax payers, even the crooked politicians they were working with." He took his shot and Bob watched as the ball fell short of the green by about twenty yards.

"You got a few of them, but I can tell you that far more of them never got a scratch and last year alone they probably cleared thirty or forty billion dollars. They just changed the names on the signs and the contracts, went home, had dinner and a good nights sleep and came back in the next day and started all over again."

Bob's feelings weren't hurt by his statements. He was only stating facts. He hit the ball and was even further away on his lay when it stopped.

"It looked like you pulled your shot a little, Mr. Shroud." Fitzsimmons said. "You're not trying to let me win are you?"

"Not at all." Bob said replacing the club. "Just getting used to the clubs." Bob got back in the cart and as they traveled to the green he saw a folder with his name on it slide into view in the dash of the cart. "Who do you work for, Mr. Fitzsimmons, or are you the boss?" His host turned to look directly at Bob. "I'm the boss, but I work for a lot of people." He got out and picked another club. "Were you in the military, Mr. Shroud?"

Bob smiled as he walked towards their balls in the lush grass. "You tell me, Mr. Fitzsimmons. From the thickness of that file with my name on it I would say you probably know more about me than I do." Bob pointed to the file on the cart. "Why so much interest?"

"Navy, I believe. Enlisted during Vietnam War. Served four years and went home, right?"

"You hit it right on the head." Bob answered, watching Fitzsimmons chip the ball onto the green and wincing as it came very close to rolling into the cup.

"Why just four years?"

"It wasn't for me." Bob reflected "I hated Vietnam. I spent most of the time on ship and didn't have to go through the crap that the grunts did, but I still hated it." He made his shot and watched it roll ten feet past the cup. "I came home and went back to school, fell in love, got a job and I'm sure you know the rest."

"Sounds like the perfect life." Fitzsimmons said as they walked up on the green and Bob pulled the flag.

"It really has been. I might change a few things if I could." Bob said thinking of the loss of his wife. "But up till last week I've been pretty blessed."

"You're a lucky man, Mr. Shroud." He tapped the ball in the cup with no problem, retrieved it and took the flag from Bob to let him shoot. "What do you think of the military?"

"You mean the Navy or the military in general?" Bob leaned on his club staring at Fitzsimmons, his curiosity buzzing.

"The military. The whole military community in general." Fitzsimmons made a large circle in the air with his hands.

"I enjoyed the Navy. I just hated where I was at, and I knew it was not the thing for me. I served my tour, got out and moved on with me life." Bob putted the ball and it stopped three inches short. He walked up and tapped the ball in. "Where's this going?" He asked as they started back to the cart.

"Do you know many twenty year men or lifers?"

"Not too many." Bob thought "I've interviewed a few over the years, but the military is not really my beat."

"Have you ever looked into the military as a whole, about opportunities, benefits and retirement possibilities?" Fitzsimmons asked.

"Not really, Mr. Fitzsimmons." Bob could see his host was beginning a new track and figured he should listen for a while.

"Did you know that Military families suffer a higher number of divorces, suicides and bankruptcies than any other occupation?" He went on without letting Bob answer. "The longer the career the worse it gets. Families are always moving and wives are normally left alone for long periods of time. Kids grow up not knowing their Fathers or Mothers, what with the increase in female military enlistees."

"Finances get all screwed up and most don't buy a house until the last eight years of their career. Military budgets have been cut for the last ten years." He hesitated and his face got a dark red. "That damn Bill Clinton might as well spit in the face of every man and woman in uniform. He and the congress decimated the budgets of our fighting forces in a way that was near criminal. The Veterans Administration is well past being bankrupt and is fast becoming second rate to welfare." He paused and put the putter back in the bag. "Hell some of our Vets would probably be better off on welfare."

"Do you know how long a person has to wait to get service at a VA Hospital? By the way eight have been closed in the past administration. Five to seven hours. God help you if you need hospitalization. The waiting list is three weeks in some areas. Men and women who have served their country are dying while they wait for procedures that welfare patients receive daily."

Fitzsimmons took a deep breath and the two men started to the next tee. "If an enlisted man spends thirty years in the service and comes out a sergeant, his retirement is sixteen hundred dollars a month. A teamster gets twenty seven hundred, an electrician gets thirty eight hundred, and a plumber gets forty five hundred. Every facet of the military mans existence has been cut. All benefits have been cut. Most allotments have been curtailed and Vets have to fight for what was promised by the politicians of years gone by and done away with by those bastards and their pork belly projects in Washington, DC."

"CEO's of small companies make one to three hundred thousand per year, with options, bonuses and perks that would choke a horse, but a General with fifty thousand men to command and protect and thirty years of loyal service gets less than a plumber and believe me if a plumber screws up he gets up the next day and goes back to work, but let a commanding officer or one of his subordinates screw up and he's history."

"Alcoholism and drug abuse is rampant in our retired ranks, counseling and psychiatric help is disappearing every day. The dollars are not at the VA Hospitals. They are in the private sector and there go the doctors."

"VA hospitals are old and falling apart. There's no new money. We have a shortage of everything from nurses to bedpans and there's no help in sight." He shook his head as he got out of the cart.

As they reached the rear of the cart he looked straight into Bob's eyes. "That's who I work for, Mr. Shroud. I work for those Vets. I work for every slob that the Government of the United States promised to take care of, if they took care of the country and its people for twenty or thirty years. I work for every individual who put his or her faith in the word of their commander and chief and loyally obeyed and served their commanding officers, trusting that everything would be okay when they got old and were no longer able and needed. Those are my employers, Mr. Shroud."

Bob quietly followed Fitzsimmons across the grass not knowing if he should speak or let the man continue. He decided listening would be prudent.

Fitzsimmons teed up the ball and then turned to Bob. "From this point on, Mr. Shroud, I need your word that our conversation will be off the record.

Bob thought for a moment "I need to know why, Mr. Fitzsimmons."

"I'm going to be completely honest and candid with you about some things that very few people know and could or very well would hurt a great many thousands of innocent and helpless people."

"You mean like members of my family, Mr. Fitzsimmons?" Bob asked seriously.

"Touché, Mr. Shroud, but I must insist on your word in order to spell out the rest of this and then you can ask your questions." He stopped and waited for Bob.

Bob looked hard at the man's unwavering eyes. "Proceed, Mr. Fitzsimmons."

Fitzsimmons motioned Bob over to an umbrella-covered table with a small cooler by its side. "Soft drink or beer Mr. Shroud?"

"I think I'll take a beer." Bob said reaching out to take a cold Budweiser from the man's hand.

"Good choice." Fitzsimmons said taking one also.

Both men took a long drink and the beer felt good on Bob's dry throat as Fitzsimmons started to speak.

"I retired from the Air Force in 1984. I spent the last three years in the Pentagon. Prior to that I was all over the world. In twenty-six years I had eighteen duty stations. I loved the Air Force and the Military. I never lost touch with the enlisted man on my way up through the ranks."

"My MOS before returning stateside was, I guess you'd call it, Human Resources. That's about as close as I can equate to a civilian business position. Every day was a challenge no matter what base I was at. I have a good wife and she had a teaching degree, so she was able to go right to work wherever we were transferred, and we didn't have the money problems a lot of my fellow officers had, because of that second income and a few lucky moves we made with our money."

"I recognized the plight of our retired people and the future problems that faced the Veterans Administration early on. Military people are like the Fire Department, when your house is on fire you want to know they'll be there, but the rest of the time you'd rather not see them. The difference is that the Police and the Firemen have a union that guarantees them the best in wages, insurance, benefits, retirement and cost of living increases that are constantly keeping pace with the economy."

"The Military has to depend on the money budgeted to the Veterans Administration and that has been constantly cut and attacked since 1982. The money budgeted to Military retirees and beneficiaries hasn't gone up a penny since then and hospital and medical costs alone have gone up 100%. Hell, even more than that."

"Injured Vets and by injured Vets I don't mean someone who got a rash on his butt in Iraq in 1991 or someone who got a sunburn in Grenada or Haiti in the 80's, but some poor slob who has shrapnel moving around from a 60mm in his body from Vietnam or his reoccurring infection problems from frostbite's suffered in Korea, or the few remaining World War II Vets that are dropping like flies because of old age and long lines at the VA Hospitals waiting to get treated for simple things that develop into serious problems because of the length of time it takes to get treatment."

"Hell 15% of the diseases and infections occur or are picked up when they come into the hospitals to get checked for something else." He took a long drink. "It's a damn disgrace."

"Anyway, I saw the problem getting worse and when I finally came back stateside and got to the Pentagon I couldn't believe how bad it really was and how bad the projections were looking. It was hard to believe, when your working in DC, The City with Golden Streets, that a lot of Vets were living in one room, eating very little, getting sicker and sicker waiting for that little green check every month to live on for the next thirty days."

"Most Military people don't make too many sound financial decisions. When you're young you drink too much. You smoke too much. You don't save much money if any and family life is always a mess. As you grow older you end up paying the price for bad, early decisions, physically, mentally or financially. Personal problems lead to divorce and broken families and then things just constantly go down hill."

"It doesn't remain a problem only for one level of the ranks, it runs from Airmen or Privates, all the way up the ladder. A man can be a brilliant field commander, but if you put him in front of the big board on the NASDAQ, nine times out of ten he'll make the wrong move and loose a lot of money."

"You kind of loose touch with reality being stationed in DC, those bastards up there waste so much tax payer's money. I was assigned to procurement and finance department. They bought and allotted payment for everything the Air Force used, from toilet tissue to C5A Galaxies. Everyday I'd see over two or three hundred million pass over my desk. I had a good friend who retired in 1982 and went to work as an advisor to the VA as a civilian contractor. Civilians run the VA. Most of them are ex military, making three or four times what they made in the service as civilian contractors. You can go into that quagmire with all the best intentions, but after you have enough money thrown at you and attend a few dozen DC parties you kind of forget who you are supposed to be taking care of, and what control you have over the life of the little guy. While you're sucking down $200.00 a bottle glasses of champagne and chomping on lobster puffs the caterers are charging $150.00 a plate for, some of these Vets are eating Alpo tacos.

"It was a coincidence that a few of us met one evening in Alexandria, Virginia at a memorial service for a general that had just passed on. After the service we decided to go downtown and have a few drinks together. One of the men knew the manager of a place in Georgetown that had a private room and we called to reserve it."

"As the booze started to flow we started on old times, as most of us had served together under the man we had just memorialized. Old times turned to current events and current events turned to thoughts of the future and retirement plans of some of us. When we started comparing notes about our future I questioned my friend and his colleagues from the VA and they started to give up some of the news, most of it bad, about the future of the VA."

"About half of the group weren't too worried, but the other half expressed real concern about their future if they didn't continue working. All were concerned about the problems at the VA and the way the military was being reduced and funding was disappearing."

"Everyone was concerned with the plight of the Vet who had to depend on the VA for help, be it medical, financial or personal."

Fitzsimmons pulled another beer out and handed it to Bob and got one for him. "I can't remember who initiated the conversation but we started discussing the possibility of starting an investment group to benefit the people who needed help but were not getting it and who were totally ignorant about how much worse it was going to get."

Bob could not listen anymore without a couple of questions for clarity. "Do you mean separate from the Veterans Administration?"

"No, Mr. Shroud, not at all." Fitzsimmons smiled. "I mean a parallel support group that would pump much needed funds, equipment and human resources into the VA and the retired military community."

"Sometimes it could mean needed supplies which are in demand. It eventually led to jobs, income, workshops, counseling, therapy, you name it."

"You're talking about a lot of money and a lot of people, Mr. Fitzsimmons." Bob said thinking of the huge scope of what his host was suggesting.

"That's not the way it started out." He relaxed back in the chair and took another sip of beer. "There were only eight of us there that night. As we talked I could see we already had the basics to put together the start of the finances."

"What about the bosses?" Bob asked.

"We were the bosses." Fitzsimmons chuckled. "The Generals don't run the machine in peace time, Colonels do." He paused, "The Generals are busy with politics and meetings and dinners and functions and handshakes. While they are taking care of all that, the Colonels are running the machine. We controlled the money, the lines of supply, logistics, transportations, news and information, hell we even signed their pay allocations."

"Where did the money come from?" Bob asked, probably knowing the answer.

"Mr. Shroud, I know you have been on bases here in the States and seen all the construction that goes on."

"Yes sir." Bob answered.

"It's on going. Billions of dollars in construction that never ends and is not taken out of the military budget."

"How can that be?"

"It's a dirty little secret. That way the major contractors can obtain the bids, start the work that never seems to end. Costs overrun triple or even quadruple the original costs and bids. The contractor continues to get rich and if anyone complains they spread a little cash their way."

"Who pays the bills for all that construction?" Bob queried.

"The great black hole. The General Services Administration, they have the deepest pockets in DC, most importantly, they control the auditing process for everyone else." Fitzsimmons smiled again. "Two of our original eight worked at the GSA."

"Washington, DC is a strange city. It's actually a different world. There is so much money there for the taking. The stupid people loose sight of normality, fall for the bait, get caught and get kicked out. The smart ones learn the system. Research the system. Play the system using the systems weaknesses and go on forever."

"We started by forming a corporation in Delaware, 55 miles away. A minority owned corporation."

"Were any of you minority?" Bob asked.

"No, we just filled out the papers, filed and formed the corporation."

"No one ever checked you out?" Bob asked.

"Never once." Fitzsimmons seemed proud. "We rented a small office in a strip center in Wilmington, got a post office box and opened for business."

"All requests or requisitions go through the GSA, but first they go through the individual branch of the military that requests the service. We simply looked at the local requests and picked a few we thought we could handle. Please keep in mind, Mr. Shroud that the military is like a child when it is on a base. It must be fed, clothed, cleaned, laundered, given a place to sleep, it needs gas for its cars, and it needs diesel for its trucks. It needs toilet paper, soap. Its grass must be mowed its edges must be trimmed. Buildings must be painted. Light bulbs changed and every other little thing that it takes to run a home, office, school, and small town times ten. It all works on a bid system."

"When bids are submitted a number of things come under consideration, price, reputation, past performance and at the bottom of the sheet, minority owned? That seemed to rule out all the others during the 80's. We could basically pick the jobs we wanted or the supplies we wanted to get involved in and give ourselves the bids."

"Our first real contract was a new parking lot at Dover Airbase. We got a copy of the base newspaper and found a retired airman that did a little concrete work. He became our first job foreman. We leased equipment, hired local labor, brought in another retired airman to do the electrical work, utilized some surplus GSA light poles and parking barriers, ordered the concrete and steel and went to work. It was amazing the job was done in a week, we paid everyone very, very well and made over $250,000.00 in profit. The base commander and administrator of the base hospital couldn't believe it. They figured their traffic would be screwed up for six months.

"Where did you get the funds to get started?" Bob asked.

"That's the great part." Fitzsimmons smiled, "when you get the bid you can draw thirty five percent of the total bid to operate on, it was amazing. The original check hadn't cleared the Government Bank and we were already submitting the final bill."

"We couldn't believe what we had generated in such a short period of time. The opportunities were baffling. The base at Fort Belvoir, Va. Used 52,000 gallons of regular gas every month for its base vehicles. We checked out the current supplier and found they were marking the gas up .40 per gallon over what they were paying their supplier. We cut the mark up to .25 and took the contract away. All this was paper profit. No expense, just mark up and billing."

"Didn't you think you were breaking the rules a bit?" Bob asked.

"Not really." He leaned forward. "We were saving the military and the tax payer's money by cutting the prices. We were much more efficient and I dare say that our work was just as good if not better than the inefficient greedy contractors we were replacing. It was a win-win situation for all concerned. We didn't go after the big construction jobs, at least not at first and most of the competition was fat cats who were paperwork organizations just like we had created. We simply streamlined the process."

"Things started to grow and more people came under our umbrella. In less than a year we were nearly seven hundred, not counting the casuals and some of the contract labor we used."

"It sounds like you simply created another bureaucracy within a bureaucracy." Bob injected. "You have basically explained how every Government contractor started."

"Not quite, Mr. Shroud. We all had jobs to do that we were getting paid well for. As the computer age advanced there was a bit less paperwork and a bit more free time in our schedules and we used our free time, be it one or two hours a day to build our organization and share the responsibilities."

"The main thing was what we did with the profits. About twenty percent was set aside for growth and compensation, but eighty percent went back into the VA directly. Slowly our corporation started to become one of the largest corporate benefactors of the VA and their hospital systems. It took several forms. It may have been one hundred hospital beds in one location replacing old rusted pieces of junk that were fifteen or twenty years old."

"Possibly a new centrifuge for the lab or a new blood analyzer. New computers and software, money for alcohol and drug programs. Job counseling sessions that actually put thousands of possible future human resources in our files for future projects."

"That sounds like a pretty noble venture." Bob was really impressed with what Fitzsimmons was outlining.

"Mr. Shroud, the problem with the system up until the time we started was that everything and everybody was taking from the system and no one was trying to put anything back. It's been that way since the first government contractor. They get the work they do the job and they send the bill. Most times the bill is for a hell of a lot more than the original bid award but the bill gets paid and if anyone complains they grease him a little and go on to the next bid."

"We were working with guaranteed fixed honest bids and bills. The profit that would normally disappear into the private sector was being funneled, through the back door, to the VA system."

Fitzsimmons was happy to see Bob was taking a real interest in his story, knowing that would make the afternoon a bit easier.

"Slowly but surely the people in the Senate and The House continued to cut away at the VA's budgets. Every other thing in the Country was receiving more and more money but the military, and the VA in particular, was being reduced. The more they cut the worse it got. The worse it got the more we bid on and grew. The more we grew the more we were able to stop the bleeding. Hell, the food in the VA Hospital was even getting to the point it tasted pretty good."

"My time to retire came up in a hurry and it was decided I should head up this outfit. We continued to spread out and began to do a little developing in the private sector."

"It sounds like you were doing pretty well for yourself Mr. Fitzsimmons." Bob didn't mean for it to sound sarcastic, but he knew it came out that way.

Fitzsimmons looked hurt. He thought for a moment. "Did you know that sixty five percent of the fighting men in the Second World War and the Korean conflict smoked?" He didn't wait for an answer. "In the Vietnam era fifty percent smoked. In the 80's seventy five percent of the veterans hospitalized in the Veterans Administration facilities were suffering from throat, heart and lung disease, most of it cancer or cancer related, but the VA had no way to treat them." He shook his head. "By 1986 we had built three state of the art Radiation Therapy Centers and had them giving the vets the first chance to get out of bed and not have to lay there and rot waiting to die. I'm proud to say that now we have twenty including several overseas, that service local and international patients, in addition to serving our vets. If a hospital wants to buy a Varian system they have to wait one year and pay three million dollars. We can get one in three months for half that and have it treating patients in a new center before six months go by."

"I guess that you can say that I've done pretty well for myself but I've never missed a days work. Our little idea to date has donated and maintained over eight hundred billion dollars worth of equipment and service to the Veterans Administration. We're directly responsible for creating about six hundred thousand jobs a year currently and because of our honest competition, realistic bids costs have seen a twelve percent decrease and new laws have been written to stop the overrun scams that contractors have been perpetrating on the American taxpayers for years."

"We hold the highest approval rating of any government contractor. We're the go-to guys when Uncle Sam wants something done, done right, done on time and within the parameters of the bid."

"We hold the contracts for the cafeterias in all the VA hospitals and annex's. Since we took it over ten years ago portions have increased by forty percent, menu items have increased three fold.

Selected diet and individual meal programs have been introduced and cost to the VA has decreased by thirty five percent. We are learning and earning to do more with less."

"We pay for all the hospice work relating to veterans and have been responsible for the building and donation of no less than thirty safe haven houses for families to stay in when they visit vets in the VA hospitals, all these services are free to the vets and their families."

He looked Bob straight in the eyes. "Mr. Shroud, I guess you could say I've done all right for myself, but if you knew the full story and I can assure you that you've only had time enough to hear a minuscule synopsis of what we've been able to accomplish in plowing back into the system a small portion of the trillions of dollars that are being drained out of the wallets and pocket books of the tax payers, you might feel differently." Fitzsimmons slumped back in the chair looking fairly exhausted from all he had outlined to Bob.

"Mr. Fitzsimmons, I'm amazed and proud of what you and your people have been able to do and I can see the benefits in your actions as I do know a lot of veterans. I've seen the change in the Veterans Hospitals and noticed the difference in the services and support available. I really wondered how they were doing it with the way Bill Clinton treated the military." Bob paused.

"Fuck Bill Clinton. He did more to decimate our Armed Forces than the German Army did in World War II." Fitzsimmons voice was terribly bitter. "You don't turn your back on your Veterans. You don't sell your Armed Forces down the river. When a man or woman puts their life on the line to fight for freedom and democracy, whatever the cost, they shouldn't have to find out they've been lied to or forgotten. The commitment they make for us should not be more than the commitment we guarantee them."

"I think you're right, Mr. Fitzsimmons." Bob started. "I can't agree with you more. Our fighting men deserve our respect and the support they were promised." Bob noted the look on Fitzsimmons face. May I ask you some questions now?" He stopped and waited for an answer.

"Yes Sir, ask away. But I must insist on one thing."

"Go ahead," Bob prompted him.

"If you ask me a question I will answer you with complete honesty, but I must be allowed time to explain all the things and surrounding events that may have brought about events that I know you'll be asking about."

"Agreed," Bob could see Fitzsimmons bracing for his first question. "Could I have another one of those Budweisers?"

Fitzsimmons smiled and relaxed. He really liked Bob and hoped that what was coming next would not make them the enemies that it could. "Of course." He said reaching into the cooler.

"I'm going to get it right out." Bob said opening the beer. "Are you responsible for the death of my son in law?"

Fitzsimmons eyes never left Bob's "Yes Mr. Shroud I am. Those were my people and while I never meant for any harm to come to anyone I was directly responsible for their being there."

"It was your people in Duluth the other night that broke into my daughter's apartment and had the confrontation with the police." Bob was leaning forward as if interrogating a prisoner.

"Yes it was. I have to assume full responsibility for their presence and actions.

"Bob's heart was pounding at the direct answers and the fact that he basically had Kevin's killer sitting at the table with him. A lot of things were running through his mind. He leaned back in his chair to give Fitzsimmons some room. "Is Timothy McVey alive?"

Fitzsimmons knew the question might come up but he was expecting Bob to pursue other lines first. He thought for a moment and then gripped the arms of his chair. "Yes, Tim is alive."

Bob tried to look relaxed but he wanted to jump up and stomp the crap out of his golf partner. He couldn't believe the audacity of this man. He sat silently for a bit trying to regain his demeanor while trying to cope with the information that had just been thrust upon him.

"Before we go any further I want to sincerely apologize to you and your family for the loss of Kevin."

Fitzsimmons was very serious. "My people were looking for information and things got terribly out of hand."

"That seems to happen to you people a lot!" Bob snapped.

"Unfortunately, I can't justify or apologize enough for the fiasco that both incidents turned out to be. We had bad information in both incidents and the actions of one of my people were stupid and thoroughly uncalled for. I' m glad your daughter and granddaughter were not harmed."

"Thank you, but they have been harmed. They lost Kevin and your people nearly scared them to death in Duluth. To say nothing about a chase with guns going off and cars crashing."

"I know that and I'm sorry. I have been trying to make things right after that. As we sit here your son in laws body is arriving in Dallas and being cared for. I had some of our people arrange that through the Canadian Government. I hope that will save your daughter a lot of time and paperwork."

Bob was shocked. Through all that had happened he hadn't forgotten about Kevin but he had not really given much thought to getting his body back. "Thank you." He said, taking a long drink of the beer. "How the hell does Tim McVey figure in all this?"

"Tim was one of my people, he was living in Canada under a new identity and your son in law got him on a scanning camera that was on a new identification system. Kevin was on an open link with the Canadian Immigration and the Canadian FBI equivalent. His computer got into US Computer Security Systems through an unknown back door and compromised Tim's security."

"Why the hell should he have any kind of security and what the hell was he doing working for you in lieu of all the good things you say you're doing? This man was a monster." Bob relaxed and shut his mouth trying to regain his composure. He decided to let Fitzsimmons speak.

"Mr. Shroud." He began very slowly. "How long have you lived in Texas?"

"A long time, since the sixties." Bob replied.

"You were there when the state was in the middle of the oil boom in the seventies, correct?"

"Yes," Bob said thinking of the crazy times when the state went nuts.

"Mr. Shroud, in the fifties, and sixties oil was six dollars a barrel and Texas had a lot of millionaires." Fitzsimmons leaned forward and started slowly. "In the seventies oil prices were allowed to be artificially inflated to forty dollars a barrel. The Government stood by and let the public be screwed by the oil companies, blaming it on OPEC-South America-Mexico, everyone but the greedy bastards here getting rich. At forty dollars a barrel everybody was a millionaire. Between 1973 and 1982, Texas and Oklahoma were booming, oil was king and the sky was the limit."

"In 1982 things started to turn around and by 1986 Texas and Oklahoma were disaster areas. The oil boom was over, the public knew it had been had. Ten years of lies and bullshit were coming public and as oil went down, so went the economy of both the States that had been riding so high. All these overnight millionaires who never thought the good times would end, came to the realization that the party was over, and slowly watched themselves go broke. Banks failed, the savings and loan organizations went belly up."

"Property values plummeted. Businesses closed. Jobs disappeared, people lost their homes, cars, futures. Everything went to shit. Oklahoma and the Oklahoma City area were especially hard hit."

"In 1989 the economy in Oklahoma had hit what we decided was the bottom. The state's economic quotient was terrible. Jobs had never come back, but owing to the situation in the Mid-East we decided that Oklahoma and particularly the Oklahoma City area was ready for investment planning on a comeback."

"We started investing quite a bit of money, in the Oklahoma City area. We started quietly buying large amounts of property all over Central Oklahoma. We were centering a major part of our efforts all around the undeveloped areas near Tinker Air force Base and the surrounding area to the north and east were our target areas."

"All this was prime land for homes and businesses as Tinker grew. The Air force had some inside information that made this a no loose situation for us and we learned it early on. Land was so cheap because nearly everyone had gone bust. The RTC was controlling so many parcels of junk land and business property and had no buyers. The S&L scandals were getting worse and worse and the Federal Government was giving the land away to get out from under all the scrutiny."

Fitzsimmons smiled and Bob caught himself smiling back, when he remembered all the crooks that got caught.

"In the S&L predicament. The fortunes that were lost were unbelievable. Savings and Loans had so much paper money available but when oil went down it didn't take long for the roof to cave it, and Uncle Sam was left holding the bag."

"We were able to buy land two miles out of downtown Oklahoma City for twelve dollars an acre, a lot of it. The fall was terrible for Oklahoma."

"Texas was hit pretty hard too." Bob stated.

"But not like Oklahoma, the state basically died except for Oral Roberts, and I think he was threatening to jump out of his tower, if people didn't send more money."

Bob had to grin remembering when God almost took old Oral home.

"Everything was for sale back then and there were very few buyers. We once bought a complete oil drilling jackknife rig complete for twenty thousand dollars; the damn thing was worth about two million when it was new. If we'd have waited three months I could have got it for ten thousand dollars. The place was like a wasteland." He stopped, took a breath and looked around the course. "And then it started to change."

"The late eighties began the rebirth of Texas and Oklahoma and we were in the perfect place. The Government was continuing to cut military budget, so we were looking for work in the private sector to replace the work we were losing because of the base closings. The Congress decided to close a total of thirty-six bases in the late eighties with more to come in the nineties. Reduction in military needs and consolidation of services mandated it."

"We had won the Cold War. Russia was whipped. We were not really ready to concentrate on rebuilding at home. We as a group decided to concentrate a number of our efforts in mid America. When we started to develop our interests around the Central Oklahoma area our investment was massive. Besides the initial real estate investment we started to move major portions of our staff and infrastructure there and that's when we started this sort of thing on a small scale." He pointed to the golf course.

"We brought businesses in and that meant jobs and jobs meant workers who needed homes and we were already clearing land for them. We started the wheels in motion in Oklahoma and soon the economy in the area, along with the Texas economy, began to turn around drastically. Things were right on track and working just as we planned."

"Are we getting to Tim, Mr. Fitzsimmons?" Bob asked. He was interested in the story but he remembered the economics of the eighties and wanted to get to the story on McVey.

"Yes we are Mr. Shroud. Tim was the victim of a real estate deal gone bad." Fitzsimmons waited for the statement to sink in with Bob.

"We had an unbelievable amount of money and resources invested in the Oklahoma City area and things were working well when someone threw a monkey wrench in the gears."

"We had been assured by people close in with the base reduction closing committee that Tinker Airbase was safe from closings. We were assured Kelly Air force Base in San Antonio, Texas was going to go."

"A major part of the decisions was the C5A Galaxy Maintenance. This was being done in Sacramento, California, San Antonio, Texas and Oklahoma City, Oklahoma."

"Real estate in California was going sky high and the big boys out there were agreeable with the closure because they wanted to cut up the base property and sell it off for the billions it was worth and would be worth to the area around it."

"San Antonio had a pretty good Military buffer during the crash in Texas, with Kelly Air force Base, Randolph Airbase, Lackland Airbase, Brooks Airbase, Fort Sam Houston Army Base, Brooks Army Medical center, and Camp Bullis. The politicians figured closing Kelly would be the least painful impact on the local economy because so many jobs could be shifted to some of the other bases."

"Tinker was most of what Oklahoma had and most of the city economy revolved around the base and its surrounding businesses. We felt we were okay, and that there was not a problem, but then the Mexicans started whining and Bill Clinton was elected."

"Clinton promised the minorities the world to get elected and when they put him in he had to pay back the favors. He put Henry Cisneros in as the head of HUD and Henry Cisneros home town was San Antonio, Texas."

"We had major problems." Fitzsimmons scratched his head as he remembered the struggle.

"The really stupid thing was that Kelly was a joke. Most of the work done there was substandard and had to be redone. The pilots used to joke about it. When they'd go through their check lists on the ground they'd say that they hoped they could make it to Tinker to have the plane fixed correctly."

"Seventy percent of the people working at Kelly were minority and the place was a joke. The San Antonio locals had a joke they used to tell. "Hey man does your dad have a job? No man he works at Kelly." Both men smiled. Everything took twice the time at Kelly and their performance rating sucked but no one wanted to incur the wrath of the minority vote. Politicians are flaky."

"The parade went on. The officials would go to San Antonio and the locals would feed them tacos. They would come to Oklahoma and we'd feed them barbecue."

"Tinker was by far a more efficient base in every way but the minority thing kept coming back up. No one wanted to make the move so they kept dragging things out. Money wise it took less than half the money to keep Tinker operating, but everyone was worrying about the loss of jobs in San Antonio."

"We were looking at a possible four billion immediate hit if they closed Tinker and we were in a panic. It had finally come down to a see saw type situation and we were looking for something to tip the scales in favor of Oklahoma City and Tinker Field."

Fitzsimmons could see that Bob was hanging on his every word. He took a deep breath and began. "I remember the meeting where we were discussing the situation and some suggested that everyone was feeling sorry for San Antonio and the possible loss of jobs, but no one was feeling sorry for Oklahoma City because of the resurgence in their economy."

"San Antonio didn't take the hit from oil that Dallas and Houston did. The town has always been built on tourism-military bases and agriculture. The town is run by old money. Smart money. A lot of Air Force money is in the right place down there and we had to be very careful."

"I suggested we find some way to sway public opinion in Oklahoma City's favor. Get some local sympathy or a reason for the politicians to tell the minority interests to back off and preserve Tinker." He took a breath. "We adjourned and left it at that."

Bob slumped back in his chair, realizing what was coming next.

"About a week later one of my people came up with the Federal Building idea." He paused. "Actually they had two targets, City Hall and the Federal Building, but a final decision was made to target the Federal Building. Some of the DEA agents at the Federal office building had been involved in the Waco mess a year before and we felt the one year anniversary was a good time and reason to pull this off. We planned to leak information to the press and blame it on sympathizers of Koresch."

"You son of a bitch." Bob said flatly, "you gave the order to blow up the nursery?"

"I had no idea there was a nursery in that building and believe me we never intended to cause the devastation that occurred."

"My people didn't want to use military explosives. Believe it or not they gave up that idea because they thought it would be too powerful. They decided to go with the fertilizer bomb to make it look unprofessional."

"We had an Army engineer in our group. He was in charge of selecting and designing the explosives. All we wanted to do was blow out a few windows. Tear up a few cars in the parking lot. Make a lot of noise. I had no idea it would create so much chaos and destruction. To that point, in all the years I had been on this earth I had never inflicted so much as a scratch on another human being."

He looked out into the horizon. "From the time we started this endeavor all we wanted to do was make things better for people. We created, we built, and we bettered the situations for Vets and a lot of other people. We never ever did anything to hurt or destroy anything and what I thought we were doing was going to sway public opinion to the side of Oklahoma City and Tinker."

"Well," Bob said, "You certainly did that." He stopped. "Where did McVey come into all this, and you mentioned Army personnel. I thought your boys were all Air Force?"

"Mr. Shroud, just as we help all Veterans we employ and are made up of all branches of the military. Our resources are spread evenly throughout the services. It started out all Air Force, but quickly spread, veterans don't just were blue uniforms."

"As for Tim," Fitzsimmons took a moment to look at Bob. "Tim was a soldier, doing his job. He followed his orders and he was apprehended before he got back to his base."

Bob sat up. "You said he was a soldier. Tim was out of the Army. What are you saying?"

"Tim worked for us. We recruited him when he was active and he took a job with us after he mustered out.

He's a good kid and a good soldier. All he was, was a delivery boy in this situation. He rented the truck, helped load it and parked it where he was told."

"Are you telling me he didn't do this to protest the killing of Koresch and his followers in Waco?" Bob asked.

"Absolutely. That story came out of our meeting, it was all a part of the plan. Tim is not a political person. He had no idea what was going to happen when that bomb exploded."

"He was in the artillery! He knew explosives! He had to know what that much material might do!" Bob argued.

"Tim loaded a field gun. He was no explosives expert. His job in the military was to shove a round in a chamber and another guy closed the breech so a third person could fire the gun. The press made the rest up."

"The press can't just make things like that up." Bob stated flatly.

"They can and do if they're Terry Kennedy." Fitzsimmons snapped back.

Bob's mouth dropped open in surprise. "What?"

"Shocking isn't it? He was the first on the scene." Fitzsimmons wanted to make the most of this surprising news. "When I realized what a mess we created I sent everyone over to help out. I had people working in that building and I wanted to help in any way I could."

"Kennedy, who, by the way contacted us ten minutes after you dropped him off yesterday to blackmail us was the first reporter we gave information to. He was in the right place at the right time and we fed him enough to keep control of a very bad situation."

"He's a good reporter but we opened a lot of doors for him personally and arranged for him to get to Tim on several occasions to get the story we wanted, out." Fitzsimmons took a breath. "He was very useful, but very predictable."

Bob was still in shock and was trying to get his thoughts together. "You said Tim was trying to get back to his base. He was headed north. Where was he going?"

"Kansas, Fort Riley. We have a facility there and he was headed home when that over eager cop stopped him. He shouldn't have been on that road but he made a bad decision after he dropped off the truck."

"What about the friends in Arizona and the relatives in Michigan?" Bob asked. "They were implicated."

"Not at all, just bullshit to build the story that Tim was retaliating for Waco."

Bob thought for a moment. "It really worked didn't it?"

"What's that?" Fitzsimmons asked for clarity.

"The Tinker-Kelly thing." Bob replied.

"Yes it did." Fitzsimmons said looking down obviously happy with the results, but trying to make sure Bob knew he was rocked with remorse for the way the Federal Building incident worked out. "It took about a week for the decision to start to leak. But from what we heard, it was made the day after the original pictures came out of Oklahoma City."

Fitzsimmons watched Bob thinking for a few seconds and decided to add. "Mr. Shroud, I want you to know that our idea was a bad one and we had no idea the damage would be anything remotely like what occurred." Bob didn't look convinced. "Since the incident we have had an office full of people extending resources and aid to anyone affected by our actions."

"What do you mean, Mr. Fitzsimmons?" Bob asked.

"We can't bring anyone back. I wish we could!" He stopped and stood up stretching his legs. "Since the incident I have had people working on each family. In the background mind you. To offer and insure aid and support whether it be money, jobs, scholarships, counseling, you name it and we have been there for anyone who needed it."

"They wouldn't have needed it if you hadn't blown the hell out of them." Bob was furious.

"I know that, Mr. Shroud. It was a terrible mistake and we have been trying to help to rebuild Oklahoma City and those effected families. It's an on going work in progress. We're not going to forget them. We'll always be there for them.

"I would imagine your investment was safe, Mr. Fitzsimmons?"

"Very safe." Fitzsimmons replied. "As safe as Oklahoma City's economy of which we have been a great part. We've donated and supplied more to the city and the surrounding area than any other entity and our investment in the city has been second only to the Federal Government. In most cases we have done more than the Feds." He paused. "At any rate, Mr. Shroud, that would have happened with or without the devastation. It would have taken a little more time but the out come would have been the same."

"Even without Tinker?"

"Even without Tinker." Fitzsimmons replied.

"We had plans, if the based closed, to push for the City to move Will Rodgers Airport facilities to the Tinker Field properties. The new Oklahoma City International Airport would have been able to make use of the finest runways in the world and land jumbo jets. With the central positioning of Oklahoma a trade zone would have been established and Oklahoma would have taken advantage of the NAFTA agreements that we knew were coming.

"There will probably be at least two automobile manufacturing or assembly plants built here by 2008, so you see, Mr. Shroud, we did our homework and when we benefit, everyone benefits." He stopped and put his hands in his pockets.

"What about Tim?" Bob asked. Getting back to his first question.

"We assured Tim that, if he followed orders, he would be set for life." Fitzsimmons stopped, thinking about Tim. "He's a good soldier. He did exactly what he was ordered to do. He kept his mouth shut. He said what we told him to say. He acted the way we told him to act. He went through the trial and the abuse and never said a word."

"What did he have to look forward to? Why would he trust you people?" Bob asked confused.

"Tim was a very private, simple boy who liked to fish and hunt. He didn't like crowds. He didn't like the war in Iraq. He didn't like noise. I promised Tim that if he continued following orders he could live wherever he wanted and never need to worry about money for the rest of his life."

"And he bought it?" Bob asked.

Fitzsimmons was very serious and his eyes turned dark. "At anytime from the point when the Oklahoma cop stopped him to the time the needle went into his vein he could have opened his mouth and brought all this down around our ears." He paused to let the words sink in. "He chose to obey orders and trust in the promise of his superiors to keep their word and secure his future." He stopped again, "that's what I do, Mr. Shroud, and believe me my word and my promise to that boy, that soldier, is more important than anything else in my world."

Bob took in the man's powerful words slowly. He got up and walked around thinking, feeling Fitzsimmon's eyes on his back. "How'd you pull off the execution?"

"Stage play." Everybody knew what they came there for. We just gave them the show they needed." He paused. "It was our theater, a closed chamber, our executioner, our doctor, our ambulance, our crematorium, and our hand picked audience. The rest just took a little rehearsal."

"Did you know about the tape Terry had of the execution?" Bob asked.

"Not till yesterday morning." Fitzsimmons replied.

"How did you think you were going to be able to hide this guy?"

Fitzsimmons thought a moment. "Describe Tim McVey to me."

"Tall, then, white, crew cut, big nose." Bob had to smile.

"He never changed that image. You could ask anyone in the USA and they would give you the same exact description." He paused. "Let that hair grow and make it darker. Add a mustache and a beard and something other than those prison khakis and no one would ever know that Tim and the man you saw on that disc, were the same person."

"No one but Kevin." Bob said.

"No one but Kevin." Fitzsimmons agreed. "The best laid plans."

"What about Kevin?" Bob asked.

"When my people entered Kevin's motel room they had no idea they were going to confront an American Software Engineer, we were under the impression the Canadians had pulled a fast one on the FBI and had gained access to computer information they would use to create an international incident that could devastate our organization."

"They didn't think anyone was in the room and when Kevin woke up startled a struggle ensued, one of our people reacted badly and Kevin died." Fitzsimmons face was white.

"These people had US Military equipment, helicopter, big helicopters." Bob raised his voice. "How can you gain access to his kind of equipment?"

"We were the Military." Fitzsimmons started slowly. "We are still very close to the military and they share our views and actions for the common good. If we need something we borrow it."

"The FAA had no record or radar contact of the craft leaving Duluth, how did you pull that off?"

"New stealth systems and flying low to avoid specialty radar, Mr. Shroud." Fitzsimmons answered.

"What about Duluth?" Bob started, "what about my daughter's apartment?"

"We had no idea you daughter and granddaughter were in the apartment. We were told they were staying with a friend. When they heard noises in the hall things got out of hand in the heat of the moment and again one of my people reacted badly."

"It seems your people have a habit of reacting badly."

"Just one of them, but he died in the altercation with the Duluth Police." Fitzsimmons apologized.

"Was he the one who killed Kevin?" Bob asked.

"Yes he was." Said Fitzsimmons matter of factly, lying to protect Brady.

"Very convenient." Bob snapped, not really believing his host.

"Mr. Shroud, I know your upset with me about the events of the past weekend and I don't blame you, but I am trying to handle this situation in such a way that you and I can be friends and not enemies." Fitzsimmons paused and moved closer to Bob. "I'm a very busy man who has cleared his schedule to be completely honest with you in this situation. There is no way I can turn back time and rebuild the damage we have caused. All I can do is appeal to you for your discretion in this matter, while we try to make things right."

"You mean, make it go away?" Bob asked.

"Exactly." Fitzsimmons answered.

Bob walked around a bit. "What's to keep me from going back to Dallas and writing this story? Tomorrow morning McVey's face would be all over the USA. His new face." He looked to Fitzsimmons for his response.

"I don't think you'd break your word to me. If I didn't think you were honest and trustworthy, we'd have never met. There would have been no need. I could have handled all damage control from right here and you would have never been aware of my existence. I chose to take you into my confidence and explain the whole situation."

"You seem pretty sure of yourself." Bob assessed Fitzsimmons cool attitude and decided to test him a bit. "There are other people who know about this."

"Not anymore, Mr. Shroud. At least not any who will support your assertions."

"What do you mean by that?" Bob asked.

"Well." Fitzsimmons began slowly. "The Canadian Government is thoroughly embarrassed. Kevin's surveillance technology has been judged in violation of personal privacy laws. They are all running around pointing the finger at one another."

"The fact that he was able to bypass security barriers in the United States most secret information bases by using Canadian Immigration Systems access has really given them a black eye. No one wants to take responsibility for his actions up there so they were planning to make him look like a rogue hacker."

"That's absurd." Bob snapped. "Kevin was up there at the request of the Government, his boss can testify to that." Bob was infuriated at the possibility that Kevin would be made the bad guy in all of this.

"Don't get upset, Mr. Shroud." He tried to calm Bob down. "The good thing about bureaucrats is that no one wants to throw the first stone. Things have a habit of backfiring on the one who does."

"While they were upset with our incursion into their Country they didn't want to complain to loudly because they thought it may have been the US Military trying to slam the door on the assault on their computer systems and information bases."

"What a situation!" Bob said think of all the people north of the border trying to protect their jobs.

"We contacted a few people we work with in the Canadian Government and pulled a few strings." He stopped and waited for Bob to take his seat. "The immigration official has been reassigned. He's scared to death of being dismissed and will never discuss this event again. The technicians were removed, separated, transferred to other Provinces. The equipment was removed by new crews and since the lodge was under insured the Provincial Government is pitching in to fund the rebuilding of the motel units."

"One of your crews?" Bob asked.

"Quite possibly." Fitzsimmons answered, matter a factly.

"What about the RCMP investigation?" Bob asked.

"I think you mean Captain Reynolds." Fitzsimmons answered. "The Mounties are a very small, very busy organization. Canada is a very big country. The investigation has been taken out of his hands and he has moved on to other cases."

"What about Kevin's vehicle and equipment, it leads right back to his company in Duluth and Minneapolis?"

"Not anymore, Mr. Shroud. We bought that company and their Duluth offices out Monday morning. We control all their materials, employees and technology."

Bob was shocked. "Well I'll be damned. Alan sold him out."

"Don't blame them, Mr. Shroud." Fitzsimmons tried to smooth things over. "They were looking at the loss of a number of large clients and the wrath of the US and Canadian Governments, through no fault of their own, they took the money and the easy way out."

"What about Duluth?" Bob asked.

Fitzsimmons shook his head. "Duluth is going to take a while. That was a very unfortunate situation, we will be working on that until we can reach a comfortable settlement."

"You seem to have left quite a few loose ends hanging, Mr. Fitzsimmons."

"How so, Mr. Shroud?" Fitzsimmons asked patiently.

"There are other people involved." Bob said, not wanting to mention names in case his host was not aware of their roles.

"If you mean Terry Kennedy he will no longer be a threat." Fitzsimmons voice was hateful.

"Sounds like he might be dead!" Bob said looking at Fitzsimmons face for a reaction.

"I told you. I don't hurt people. There's no future in it, for us or for them. I deal in resources." He stopped and leaned forward on the table. "Terry Kennedy is a fool. We made him who he is. At any moment in the Oklahoma City event we could have pulled his plug and cut him out, but we kept him in the loop. He owes us his career and he called to hold us up yesterday."

"What did you do to him?" Bob asked.

"We paid him, we paid him a lot. All you can do with a blackmailer is pay him and hope he'll go away and never bother you again." Fitzsimmons dusted his hands off like he was trying to get rid of some dirt.

"Do you think he'll come back?" Bob asked.

"Of course. He's a leech. But he'll be surprised when he does."

"Why is that?" Bob asked.

Fitzsimmons looked at his watch. "As we are speaking the moving van is pulling away from Mr. Kennedy's house. We paid him." He paused. "We paid him a lot, but we don't deal with bags of cash in the middle of the night. We bought him out. Bought his house, bought his land. One of the conditions was that he quit his job, which he did yesterday afternoon. Another condition was that he take a position with one of our contractors about six thousand miles away as a media consultant."

"How do you know he'll turn over everything that he has?"

"We've had people on him since you called him Monday morning. We've covered his every move. When the moving company leaves his house it will go to our warehouse in Fort Worth and unload, everything will be searched. By the time he gets to his new location we will have search and scanned everything he owns."

"When he boards a jet at DFW in about twenty minutes." Fitzsimmons said. "We'll relieve him of his laptop and replace it with another. We'll switch his carry on and search every piece of his luggage. When he goes through the x-ray scanner we'll be sure and have him triple checked and if he has a disc up his ass we'll retrieve it."

Bob had to smile thinking of Terry being strip-searched. "Pretty thorough, Mr. Fitzsimmons." He complimented his host. "Anyone else?" Bob was waiting to see what Fitzsimmons might give up.

Fitzsimmons started slowly figuring Bob would have a bad reaction to his next statements. "Your assistant Paul has accepted a position with one of our advertising contractors." He saw Bob slump back in his chair with shock. He paused and then started again. "Don't be upset with Paul. He's a very loyal young man, but we put together a package that will insure his financial and occupational future that was impossible for him to turn down."

"Money." Bob said with disgust.

"It makes the world go around, Mr. Shroud." Fitzsimmons was trying to console his shocked guest.

"I suppose you got the discs Paul had?" Bob asked.

"I believe we have all but one set." Fitzsimmons stated.

Bob was happy with Fitzsimmons smugness. He was in possession of an ace in the hole.

"Mr. Shroud, you don't have much of a poker face." He started "We already have the discs from your home and I'm happy to see you like Maxwell House. It's my favorite also."

"You son of a bitch!" Bob snapped "You've been in my house." He stood up and pointed a finger at Fitzsimmons. "If you hurt my family at all I'll never stop until I take you down."

"I believe you, Mr. Shroud. That's why you're here today. Please relax, my people will never again do anything remotely close to hurting you and certainly not your family." He was showing a great deal of remorse in his voice. "We've done too much damage already." He stopped. "That's not what we want to do."

"Collateral damage." Bob said in a low voice. "Isn't that what Tim called it?"

"A poor choice of words." Fitzsimmons replied to the statement. "But given the situation and what we were trying to put forth to the press, very appropriate."

Bob reached in the cooler and took out a couple beers, handing one to Fitzsimmons. He noticed how the sun was starting down in the sky, affirming his guess on the direction of the runway. "What now, Mr. Fitzsimmons?" He said taking a drink.

"That's up to you, Mr. Shroud." Fitzsimmons took a drink and looked hard at Bob's eyes. "You're in the drivers seat. All I can do is sit back and clean up the damage that you might decide to create."

"You're serious about that?" Bob asked.

"Absolutely." Fitzsimmons stood up and looked at Bob. "Are you ready to start home, Mr. Shroud?"

Bob felt quite relieved. "Yes sir. I am." He got up from the chair and the two men started across the grass. As they sat down on the golf cart Fitzsimmons placed the beer in the holder and started to drive the cart back towards the runway area. "What about the last discs" Bob asked.

"Funny you should be asking me about them, Mr. Shroud." Fitzsimmons smiled. "I'm sure you left them in your car in the lot at Addison Field. My people have probably searched that vehicle and one way or the other I'll know if we have them after you take off. At any rate the ball is in your court. I met with you today to tell our side of the story and sincerely apologize for the agony and pain we have inadvertently caused your family."

The cart slowed at the side of the jet and Brady, the pilot and the ground man were waiting by the stairs.

Fitzsimmons got out first and crossed in front of the cart offering his hand. "Mr. Shroud, if we never meet again, I want you to know that it has been a pleasure and I wish it could have been under more agreeable circumstances. Please believe me when I say that you're the kind of person I like to have on my side."

The men shook hands strongly. "It has been interesting, Mr. Fitzsimmons." He started up the stairs and turned around "Thanks for the golf and the beer. You've got a good swing." With that Bob entered the cabin and sat down as the engines started to warm up.

In moments they were airborne and Bob sat back in the chair trying to sort out what he had learned in the past hours. His head was a buzz with the decisions he had to make and the information that he had absorbed. First, he thought, he had to get home safely and check on the girls.

He felt terribly violated that someone had been in his home and retrieved the two copied discs. He wondered who might have been inside his house and how they got in. The fact that they found the discs in the coffee can, was incredulous, they would have had to search the entire house to have found them.

He thought about Paul and felt bad that the young man had chosen to take the offer they made him. Bob thought back to his youth and what he might have done if financial security was dangled in front of him. He might not have had to make all the sacrifices he had, like the time he lost with his family and the events in his daughter's life he had missed.

He thought with anger about how people up North had deserted his son in laws memory and were planning to make him a scape goat in this situation. He thought about Fitzsimmon's intervention and his obvious help and he was torn.

The flight was quick. There was no deception turns just a straight flight path-south to Addison.

The landing was a smooth one. Bob barely felt the wheels touching the ground and in moments they were back to the spot on the tarmac where they had departed from that morning.

Brady emerged from the cockpit and opened the exit way. "Take care, Mr. Shroud, it was a pleasure meeting you." Brady sounded sincere. He handed Bob his phone and recorder.

"Thank you, have a safe flight home." Bob said.

"Thank you sir." Brady said giving him a brief salute as he pulled the door shut watching Bob start to the airport building.

Bob watched the jet turn to the taxiway and when he was sure they were headed out on the runway wrote the aircraft identification number on a small piece of paper from his pocket.

He dialed his home number knowing Kathy would probably be frantic. "Hi Dad." She answered carefully. He was surprised "How'd it go?" He couldn't believe, knowing Kathy, that she wasn't wracked with worry.

"Pretty well Honey. I'm sorry I didn't call." He apologized.

"Not to worry Dad, Mr. Fitzsimmons's office called twice to let me know your meeting was running long, did you find out anything?"

Bob was in shock. He didn't know whether to be mad or relieved that they had taken the time to call her so she wouldn't be worried. "How's Amy?" He said glad to be back in Addison.

"She's fine and we've got some great news for Grandpa." Kathy said bubbling over.

"What's going on?" Bob asked.

"Just get home. I have a roast in the oven and it's just about ready to dig into."

"I'll be right there." Bob said. "I love you." And he hung up. He turned to watch the jet leave the ground and climb very quickly to the north.

Bob headed into the airport lobby and turned down the hall to the flight controller's office. Inside the small office was a man in a crisp white uniform and a nametag identifying him as the flight director. "Mr.Shaffer?" Bob asked looking at the name on the badge.

"Yes sir." The man answered. "How can I help you?"

"I took a flight on this jet this morning." He showed the paper with identification number. "I'd like to know what destination they listed on their flight plan."

"Sure." The man looked oddly at Bob, probably wondering if he forgot where he went. He searched the book on the desk in front of him. He checked the number again and then ran down the series of numbers on the day's log.

"Not today sir." He said handing Bob the piece of paper.

"What do you mean not today?" Bob asked the man.

"I mean that aircraft didn't fly out of this field today, sir." The flight director stated flatly.

"That's not correct, Mr. Schaffer." Bob couldn't believe his ears. "I just stepped off that jet and watched it take off again before I walked in here."

"You must be mistaken sir." The director responded. "But let me check." He turned to a computer on the desk and typed in a command and the identification number. "Nothing here sir." He pointed to the screen. "No record of one or two flights from here. That number doesn't show up on any logs from this field all month."

"It just cleared your runway lights." Bob was trying to keep from shouting at the man.

"Let me check the tower." The director said. Bob waited and a couple of pilots came to file flight plans.

The director got on the radio and asked the control tower about the jet and gave the ID number. "Negative." Was the answer.

"Sorry sir, you must be mistaken." The director said. The two pilots were looking curiously at Bob.

"Thank you." He said, "Thanks for checking." He shook his head and started out the door. When he reached the lobby he started towards the front exit, but just short of the front doors he turned to the door marked baggage check. The young woman answered the bell and Bob gave her the stub he had written the ID number on. She left the door and returned with the small camera case Bob had handed to her that morning. He gave her a ten-dollar bill, took his bag and stub and walked out to the nearly empty lot with the camera case under his coat.

As he approached the Suburban he looked around the lot to see if he was being watched. The car looked okay. Everything seemed to be as he had left it. He started the motor and was happy when the thing didn't blow up in his face. He smiled when he thought about his apprehensiveness. He had worked cases when conspiracies were alleged or asserted. He had seen people fall apart, afraid to leave their homes over worry about being killed or attacked.

He decided to relax. If they wanted him dead they could have done it at anytime today and no one would have been the wiser. According to Addison the jet was never here. He shook his head in disbelief.

The trip home was quick and when Kathy opened the door she was smiling and gave him a big hug. "Hi Honey." He said. Amy was in the living room and when she heard his voice she came crawling out from under the coffee table at a high rate of speed.

"Hi, big girl." He said handing Kathy the camera case and reaching down to pick up Amy. He hugged the squirming child tightly and kissed her all over her face.

"We got some great news today." Kathy said, putting her arms around her dad.

"What's going on?" Bob asked, moving over to the couch.

"You're going to need to sit down." Kathy said, she ran to the kitchen and returned with a beer for her father.

"The Canadian Government called this morning. They released Kevin's body and made arrangements to have him brought down here to Dallas." She stopped and waited for her dad to speak.

"That's great Honey, I'm glad we've got him home." He hugged his granddaughter tightly and leaned over to kiss his daughter on the forehead.

"That's not all Dad." She continued "Mac called and we talked about Kevin and the paper is taking care of all the arrangements and setting up the service. I told Mac it would be okay to take Kevin to the same place that took care of Mom. "Dad, did you know Kevin wanted to be cremated?"

"No Honey, I didn't." He couldn't believe Mac had gotten involved. He was a good friend and he really appreciated his helping Kathy.

"He mentioned it a few times. But I never thought it was something I would have to worry about so quickly." Her voice started to quiver talking about her late husband.

Bob put his arm around his daughter's shoulder and gave her a tight hug while trying to hold on tight to Amy. "It'll be okay Honey." He tried to console her "Don't worry, it'll be okay."

"I know Dad." She straightened up and got up from the couch. "I want you to read something."

She went to the kitchen and got a handful of papers off the counter. "This came today." She said holding up two letters with registered mail seals on the envelopes. She pulled one letter out of the envelope, unfolded it and handed it to her father, she reached down and picked up Amy. "Come on Baby." She said, "Lets get you something to eat while Grandpa reads the letters." The baby didn't like the idea, but Kathy headed to the kitchen with her to put her in the highchair, Bob watched as she strapped her in and gave her a piece of something to eat and then turned his attention to the letter she had given him.

The letter was from a well-known Life Insurance Company and was notifying Kathy she was beneficiary of an insurance policy with a double indemnity accidental death clause for her husband Kevin. The policy amount was for one million dollars. The letter went on to explain how to file and what kind of papers and certificates to include with her filing, "My God." Was all Bob could say.

"Did you know Kevin had this policy?" He asked his daughter.

"No way Dad." She answered. "We were having a hard time paying the bill on the hospitalization and medical policy he had at work." She stopped for a minute. "The crazy thing is, it has your address on it, we just got here Monday."

"That is strange." Bob said, but then continued. "Kathy, if this is on the level and it certainly looks as though it is. You and Amy are set for life. Kevin really made sure you were going to be okay."

"I don't know how I didn't know about it." She paused "Why didn't he tell me about it?"

"You know, the company may have paid for the policy, what with the importance of the work Kevin was doing." Bob started to get up.

"No-No" She said, pushing him back. "You stay right there and read this one." She handed him the other letter and headed back to the kitchen to check on Amy.

The letter was from Kevin's boss at the company that Fitzsimmons had told Bob earlier that day he had purchased. In the letter Alan was trying to console Kathy on the loss of her husband and telling her what a great guy he was. "That sorry bastard." Bob said under his breath. As Bob got to the bottom of the first page, Alan started to explain the buy out of the company and their technology including the software Kevin was working on. The second page of the letter went on to explain how, the board of directors, credited the software Kevin had developed with the interest sparked by their new parent company. In keeping with the research and development clause Kevin's contract, they valued his software applications, which, after development, became their property at two million dollars. The third page was a simple fill in the blank page with space for signatures and a notary certification.

The fourth page was instructions for filling out the third page so that Kathy could get her check for two million dollars. He went on to say that if there was anything he could do to help, for her to call and if she needed anything how to get a hold of the new directors of the corporation.

Bob put the letter down and stared at his daughter leaning on the kitchen wall. Neither one said a word for a long time. He slowly picked up the beer and finished it without taking a breath. "Damn!" He said as he put the bottle down.

"Hard to believe, huh, Dad?" Kathy finally spoke.

"Not really." Bob said, thinking of Fitzsimmons.

"What do you mean, Dad?" Kathy looked puzzled.

"Let's eat." Bob said, hearing Amy starting to fuss. "The boss is calling and I'll tell you what I mean later."

They went to the kitchen and Bob noticed the great smells coming from the oven. Kathy pulled the roaster out and placed it on top of the stove. It reminded him of her mother. Bob's wife was a great cook and he missed the great food she was able to create.

"I love roast." He said lifting the lid and smelling the aroma coming from the meat and vegetables. He started to put the lid back on the large pan when he saw the Maxwell House coffee can against the wall. He reached for the can and opened it shaking the coffee around. The discs were definitely gone. "Was anyone here yesterday? In the apartment I mean, besides us?"

Kathy thought for a moment "Only Tom from next-door." She started to serve the plates. "Why Dad?"

"Did you tell anyone about those discs?"

"No Dad, of course not." She watched puzzled as he stood in front of the stove and scanned the kitchen and the living room.

Bob walked back into the living room and went to the far wall scanning every square inch of the room. He went over to the fireplace on the wall his home shared with Tom's home. After going over the wall thoroughly he bent down by the hearth of the fireplace and stared into the darkness. Something caught his eye. He reached into the shaded darkness and grabbed the small camera that was nearly invisible far back in the fireplace. He jerked on the wire and it tore loose from whatever bracket it was fastened to above the fireplace. Bob quickly walked out to the front door and his front yard. He turned to look back at the two chimneys that rose from his home and Tom's. He could see the wire coming from his and going back down into Tom's. "Damn" He said out loud. "Damn, damn, damn." He started back into the house.

He walked back into the kitchen and hugged his confused daughter. "Get the baby's stuff." He whispered into her ear "We're going to the lake."

Kathy didn't question her father and went straight upstairs to get Amy's diaper bag and small overnight bag. Bob got a large Tupperware bowl and put the roast and some vegetables in closing the lid tightly and checked to make sure the burners were turned off.

Bob put his camera bag over his shoulder and stood by the door to wait for Kathy. She came down the stairs quickly and in minutes they were through strapping Amy in the car seat and were headed for Lake Texoma.

The trip would normally take about thirty minutes but Bob kept doubling back to see if anyone was following them. When he got close to the lake he stopped on the narrow approach road to see what cars, if any, were following behind them.

It seemed to be safe so Bob drove on to the lake house, Kathy was glad to see the place. It had been a couple of years since she had been here and was glad to see it was as beautiful as ever.

Kathy had been quite on the trip but when they pulled up in the drive she spoke. "Dad, do you want to tell me what's going on."

"Let's get inside and eat." Bob said with a smile knowing Kathy was probably thinking he had lost his mind.

Bob went up the stairs with the Tupperware and the camera case. He unlocked the door and pushed it open. The air was a little musty. It had been three months since Bob had been up at the lake. He put the Tupperware down in the kitchen and went to the other side of the house to open tall drapes that exposed the porch and the lake.

"My God it's beautiful" Kathy said walking to the windows with Amy. She slid the door back and Bob opened the cover on the fireplace.

"I'll get some heat going. Don't take Amy's coat off yet."

Amy was pointing to the lights around the lake and gibbering at her mother, when Bob walked out on the deck. "It hasn't changed much has it?"

"A few more homes but the lake looks great." She rocked Amy back and forth. "I always wanted to spend my whole life here."

"The summers were great, weren't they?" Bob asked remembering his daughter, her friends and the fun they used to have when they spent so many sunny days at this home away from home!

"The best." Kathy beamed.

"It ought to start to warm up, if you want to go in and I'll dig some plates out." Bob suggested.

The girls went in and Bob locked the glass doors. The fire was roaring and the main room was warming up nicely as they sat down to eat. Bob had brought the car seat in and Kathy had rigged it to be a highchair for the baby. She was having a ball with the food Kathy had cut up for her.

Bob watched his family as he ate. This was it. He had no other brothers or sisters. Kathy and Amy were all that he had.

Since his wife passed on he had done nothing but work. He tried to keep as busy as he could but he was burning out slow but sure. He missed the girls and for the life of him could not explain why he hadn't seen more of them. He didn't want to be a pain in the ass, was the excuse he used, but he knew the kids liked having him around.

"Kathy," Bob began "What would you think about staying here. I mean, you and Amy could live here. I can go to Duluth and pack you up. You can move anything you don't want out to the storage shed and move your things in here."

"I'd love to Dad" Kathy was smiling "Are you serious?"

"I sure am. The schools here are pretty good and the bus will pick her up right out front when she's old enough to go."

"Slow down Dad, she's not even out of diapers yet." Kathy smiled and moved her food around with her fork. "How's the roast?"

"Better than your mothers!" Bob smiled.

"What's going on Dad?" Kathy asked.

"It's not very often I get to have dinner with a couple of good looking millionaires." Bob smiled. He was avoiding the question.

"I can't believe it." Kathy answered. "Do you think its true?"

"I'm sure it is." Bob thought for a moment. He could imagine Fitzsimmons waiting to see if he accepted what was obviously a peace offering for his silence.

Bob watched his daughter and granddaughter eating the meal and thought over the events of the last few days. His life had been turned upside down and his family had suffered a great loss. He was sitting on top of what had to be the story of the year, but he had given his word that everything he had learned was off the record.

He was torn between the reporter and the father. On the one side he wanted to blow the story wide open and help the authorities go after the brazen individuals that had wronged his family so badly and caused all the chaos in Duluth. But when he thought about all that the money would buy for Amy and Kathy, he hesitated.

He had mixed feelings about Fitzsimmons. He could see the good he and his organization were doing, but the devastation in Oklahoma was inexcusable.

Bob didn't really give a damn about Tim McVey one way or another, but he was the trigger that set the events of the last few days off.

His son in law was about to be made the bad guy in this situation by the Canadian and U.S. Governments, but Fitzsimmons had stepped in to smooth things over and protect Kathy from the pain and embarrassment that would have followed from the scandal.

He didn't condone Fitzsimmons methods, but the result of his efforts in propping up the VA, were obvious. His group was doing a lot more good than bad, but all the good in the world wouldn't bring Kevin back.

"What are you thinking about, Dad?" Kathy asked, "You seem miles away."

"Sorry Honey, I'm just trying to put a few things together." He smiled at her and Amy who had eaten all her food except for the portion she was wearing.

"The service for Kevin is tomorrow at 7PM." She looked at her plate and pushed her food around, obviously not hungry any longer. "I'm not going to call anyone, I want it to be private. Kevin would have wanted it that way."

"Bob put his hand over Kathys. "I'll be there with you, Honey." Bob watched his daughters eyes fill with tears and fought back the lump in his throat.

"Were you serious about us moving down here?" She asked, wiping her eyes with her napkin.

"Absolutely." He squeezed her hand "I'll make some calls and fly to Duluth later this week to pack you up."

"I don't want to go back to that apartment Dad." She wiped Amy's face. "I don't think I could handle that."

"Not to worry. Let me take care of all that." He reassured her. The fire had warmed the house and he felt good to have his family together. "You two have nothing to worry about."

"Thanks Dad." She smiled at him. "It's good to be home."

"I'll run into town to get us some breakfast in the morning and we'll call the grocer later to fill the shelves."

"You use the big bedroom, I'm going to sleep down here on the couch." He started to pick up the dinner dishes.

"Still worried?" She asked.

"I always worry Honey." He said. "The TV works if you want to watch while you try to sleep."

She picked the baby up and started towards the stairs, pausing to kiss her Dad goodnight. "We won't have any trouble falling asleep. I always felt safe in this house."

"Good night girls." Bob said kissing them both. "See you in the morning." He headed for the sink with the dirty dishes.

As he rinsed off the dishes he thought about all he had to do tomorrow. His thoughts were on Kevin's memorial service and how his daughter would handle the stress.

He put the last dish in the drainer and got a beer from the refrigerator. He pulled on a windbreaker from the clothes tree by the lakeside doors and walked out to the crisp night air. He leaned on the rail looking out over the empty lake and the houses on the opposite shore line and wondered if anyone was looking back at him. "First things first." He thought pulling his cell phone from his pocket.

He dialed a number and placed the phone to his ear. Bob's face turned dark and agitated as the voice answered.

"Hello." Tom Macnamara said.

"Tom, you son of a bitch." Bob started. "I want every piece of camera or surveillance equipment you put in my house gone tonight, or I go to the police in the morning."

"Bob." Tom started. "I'm sorry. I"——

"Don't give me any shit Tom. Just get it done and don't ever cross my path again." Bob was deadly serious and Tom didn't interrupt. "I'm going to have a security company sweep the place at noon."

"Okay Bob." And with that Bob hung up.

He leaned back on the rail and looked up to see the light turn off in Kathy's bedroom. Taking a drink of the beer he wondered how many more people were involved in this situation.

The air was getting colder and he headed inside. He sat down on the couch facing the fire, put the beer

W.W. Hill

on the end table and in moments the warmth of the fire
put him to sleep.

Chapter 37

The sunrise was bright in his eyes as day broke over the lake. He had forgotten to close the drapes on the large glass windows. He stood up and stretched. The coffee maker on the counter was a little dusty so he washed things off before starting a pot.

While the smell of fresh Maxwell House filled the room he threw some water on his face and brushed his teeth. He put on his jacket and poured a quick cup of coffee, and started out the front door.

The trip to McDonalds didn't take long and he had just received the bag from the drive in window when his phone rang. "Hello." He said.

"Mr. Shroud?" The voice said cheerfully. "This is Administrator Bradley from Duluth."

"Yes sir, how are you doing?" Bob asked, surprised at the man's call and trying to think what to say to the questions that were probably to come.

"I'm fine." Bradley began. "I just called to thank you for the donations. They just arrived yesterday and believe my they are really appreciated."

Bob was completely surprised. "I beg your pardon, I'm not sure what you mean."

"The donations from your paper. In your name, for the families of the officers who were hurt the other night? That was one hell of a great gesture and I wanted to let you know my department really appreciates your support."

Bob couldn't believe it. "Well" he started "You're very welcome. I'm glad we could help."

"And help you did. At least the families of those downed officers won't have to worry about money." Bradley paused. "The apartment managers have repaired your daughter's door, so everything is secure there. I'm leaving the tape up, but I'm pulling the officer off the premises, if that's okay? I'll have people keep an eye on the building and keep it on a priority respond."

"That will be fine, Mr. Bradley, thank you." Bob answered.

"No, Mr. Shroud, thank you." And with that he hung up, not a word about the investigation, no questions.

"It's all about the money." Bob thought aloud, as he drove back to the lake house with breakfast for the girls.

"Good morning." Kathy said when he walked in balancing the tray of juices and the bag of food.

"Did you sleep well?" He asked putting the food down out of Amy's reach.

"Great Dad. I found some of Mom's old sweats in the closet." She said holding her arms out as if to model the outfit.

"Looks comfortable. She used to love those things." He responded. "Mickey Mack okay?" He asked unpacking the fast food items he brought home.

"It smells great Dad." She said handing Amy a potato patty and pouring some juice in her bottle. "Amy likes it too." The baby was tearing into the potato.

"What's the plan for today?" She asked.

"We'll go back to town this afternoon and get changed for the service. I think we'll come back out here again tonight, if that's okay?" He looked at her for her answer.

"That's fine, Dad. I'm going to need a few days of peace and quiet after tonight. I think I'll take you up on your offer to live here." She sipped her juice.

"I'm glad." He said reaching over and pretending to try and take the snack away from Amy who turned away to protect her breakfast.

Chapter 38

That afternoon Bob and his family drove back to Dallas. When he parked in front of his home he noticed Tom and Mary's cars were gone from their usual spaces.

As he stepped from the car he saw the wire was gone from the top of the chimney. He wondered if there were any other bugs or cameras as he opened the door for the girls.

When he entered the house he went from room to room looking for anything that looked out of place or irregular. He checked in the fireplace with a flashlight, but found nothing. After a quick sweep of the downstairs rooms he went up and checked the bedrooms. He could not find anything that looked suspicious so he went back down to Kathy who was curiously watching him.

"What's up, Dad?" She asked.

"Just checking, Honey." He replied smiling. "Trying to see if we had any visitors while we were out."

"I know there are some things you want to talk to me about." She was looking straight at her dad. "When are we going to sit down and talk turkey?"

"Pretty soon, Honey." He reassured her. "There are a lot of things, hunches, leads, you know, things that I'm not sure of yet. When we sit down I want to be able to speak of sure things, and right now nothing is carved in stone." He paused. "I don't want you worrying about anything. You concentrate on you and Amy and let me take care of everything else."

"Thanks Dad." She gave him a big hug. "I'm going to take a long bath and start getting the baby ready. What time do you want to leave?"

"Let's shoot for six. That'll give you some time to settle when we get there." He thought about his daughter and how she would be at the memorial. The casket was to be closed and he knew Kevin's body was nothing that she should see. He watched her take the baby upstairs and hoped he could be strong enough to get all three of them through the evening.

The phone rang and it was Mac. "Hi stranger. Are you and the kids okay?"

"Yes Mac. How's things at the paper?" Bob asked, thinking it was funny Mac called ten minutes after they walked in. Bob looked out through the front windows to see if there were any strange cars parked around the house or street. Everything looked clear.

"Great Bob. How's Kathy holding up?"

"Pretty well. I think tonight will be rough though. Thanks for asking." He paused. "I want to thank you for taking care of this memorial. Kathy has a lot on her mind and she didn't need this to worry about too."

"Glad to help, Bob, you need anything else?"

"As a matter of fact, I got a call from Bradley in Duluth about a donation the paper made in my name." Bob waited for Mac to answer.

"Oh, we thought we'd help out." Mac seemed to be stumbling over his words. "They took pretty good care of Kathy."

Bells went off in Bob's head. Fitzsimmons said that they were told Kathy and Amy would not be home that night in Duluth. He searched through his memory to see if he had told anyone that Kathy and Amy were not going to be at Margaret's home from the time they had heard about Kevin's death. He was the only one who knew the apartment would be empty that night.

"Are you still there, Bob?" Mac asked. Puzzled by Bob's silence.

"Yea Mac" Bob said steadily piecing things together in his mind. "I need to run a few things by you for a story I'm thinking of writing."

"I'll be at the service tonight, maybe we can step out for a few minutes." Mac's voice had changed.

"Sure thing" said Bob. "I'll see you tonight and I'll lay out some of the evidence I've accumulated." He hung up mad at an old friend and employer.

Bob got out his note pad and went back through some of his notes. Mac was the only one who could have told Fitzsimmons Kathy would not be home. He had known Bobs every move since the pilot had to be in contact with the office every few hours.

Paul had been with him through every step of the last few days. Paul reported to Mac and Mac was reporting to Fitzsimmons. "Damn." Bob's hands were shaking when he hung up the phone. He walked into the living room and sank into the couch.

The feeling of complete betrayal was eating into Bob like nothing he had ever felt before. He and Mac had worked together for nearly two decades and he trusted him more than anyone on earth. They had been through a lot together. He remembered him being there at Kathy's Baptism and Marriage, he thought about the support he had provided when Bob's wife passed on. He stood beside Bob at the funeral and was his best friend through the years.

It didn't seem possible Mac would do something like this. Bob started across the living room to a picture on the mantle. It showed Bob, his wife and Mac in front of the house the day they had moved in.

He shook his head as he thought about what they had shared and experienced. "Why Mac?" He thought out loud. A few moments later he reached over and picked up the camera bag. He opened the top and pulled out the envelope with the rod inside. He slowly opened the envelope and pulled the rod out. It was wrapped in a plastic baggy to protect the fingerprints. Bob stared at the rod and finally put it back in the envelope. He pulled the tube out with the print sheets and carefully pulled them out and unrolled them.

He scanned the papers and again placed the plastic over the print sheet Joel had made for him. He wondered if Joel had contacted Mac to let him know about the prints on the rod. He wasn't sure but he thought Paul had seen him put the rod in his pocket at the boathouse.

Slowly he rolled the sheets up and replaced everything in the camera bag. He took his notebook and placed it in the camera bag. Everything he knew about Kevin's death and the past few days was in that bag. He picked out the envelope with the letter to Kathy and opened it, the discs slid out into his palm and he thought about what had happened because of them and what they contained. He thought about what could happen, if what they contained would become public.

Bob didn't give a damn about Fitzsimmons and his group of thugs dressed up like businessmen, but he did respect what they were doing for the VA and the servicemen it served.

He could see how he was tangled in their web of cover up, but without their help Kevin could have really been smeared and branded a hacker. The truth would clear Kevin but it would be damned impossible to get the truth out owing to the resources and connections of the Fitzsimmons Group.

Finally, his word, Bob had spent his life building a reputation as an honest, accurate reporter and individual people talked to him openly because they knew they could trust him. He wasn't a Terry Kennedy. He had scratched his way to his position in the news community. He had had a few lucky breaks, but mostly it had been hard work and good investigation that moved him up in the ranks of the thousands of individuals trying to make a name in the newspaper business.

He thought about Kathy and Amy and the security of the money Fitzsimmons obviously had arranged for them. it would not replace Kevin, but it would certainly secure their future. Bob didn't want to think of the money as pay off, but as money owed to the girls for Kevin's death and inventiveness.

He was wracked with the natural wish for revenge and the realization that the situation required patience and caution.

He got up from the couch and went to the den and opened the closet. He pulled out a black suit and removed the plastic cover from the dry cleaner. "I hate black." He said heading for the bathroom.

Chapter 39

The drive to the service was a quiet one. Kathy stared out the window most of the way and Bob didn't say much. Amy was tired and had not taken a nap before they left so she was looking like she wanted to fall asleep.

The place was a somber building that smelled like flowers. There were a few funeral sprays around the closed casket. The room was small and dimly lit. Bob walked down the isle carrying Amy and the diaper bag. Kathy was trembling as she walked beside him. They went to the front row of seats and sat down. Kathy was starting to cry and Bob was having a hard time swallowing as his heart tightened thinking of Kevin laying dead and burned in the casket. His anger was turning to hate.

He held Amy tighter and kissed her cheek as she watched her mother cry. Kathy patted her Dad's leg and got up. She walked to the casket and kneeled on the cushioned brace beside the cold looking box. As she knelt to pray, Bob felt more helpless than he ever had in his life. He always worried about her living away from Dallas and if they were okay. He was always offering any type of help he could to try and make the kid's life easier. But in this situation all he could do was sit and grieve along with her.

After a few moments she got up and turned to return to her seat. Her face was red and streaked with tears. She took the handkerchief Bob offered and wiped her eyes. She reached for Amy who hugged her mother tightly as if she knew what was happening. Bob felt the tears fill his eyes as he watched his family hurt.

He got up and walked to the casket and knelt down. "Don't worry Kevin." He said, hoping his son in law could in some way hear him. "I'll take care of them."

After a few moments he stood up and patted the top of the casket in a good bye gesture. He turned to walk back to Kathy. In the middle of the rows of seats behind where he had been sitting he saw Mac looking very somber. The place was nearly empty, but he saw two people sitting in the rear of the seats. One of the people was the man who had met him at Addison Airport, Brady. Bob started to shake. "These people have no shame." Bob thought.

He sat down beside Kathy and offered to take Amy, who was fussing quite a bit as she was probably getting tired and sensed something was wrong with her Mother.

"No Dad. I'm going to take her to the ladies room." She managed a slight grin. "I think she needs a dry diaper." She got up and took the diaper bag with her as she headed to the ladies room. She reached out and touched Mac's hand as she passed him. "Thanks for your help Mac." She said, not knowing he was partially responsible for her situation.

After she left the room Bob turned and stared at Brady and the man he was with. He stood up and walked back to Mac. Mac rose to meet him and started to speak, but Bob cut him off.

"You're paying for this, but I wish you hadn't invited them." He said gesturing to Brady. "Does Fitzsimmons own you too?"

"You know better than that Bob." Mac responded. He was beginning to sweat nervously.

"No, I don't Mac." Bob started "You're in this up to your neck." He noted Mac wince like he had been slapped. "You sent those people to Kathy's apartment. You're the only one who knew where she was and Fitzsimmons told me someone assured him she was away. You bastard, I could be here looking at three boxes." Bob didn't let him respond. "These people are killers. What the hell were you thinking?" He glared at Brady and then back to Mac.

"Bob." Mac broke in. "I'm sorry. Things got out of hand, but we're handling this and no one ever meant to hurt the girls."

Bob grabbed Mac by the lapels and turned him towards the casket. "And what about Kevin, Mac, did things get out of hand then too?" He shook his old friend. "What about Kevin?"

Mac slumped back into his chair when Bob let go of his lapels. "We can't change that. We're trying to make it up to the girls. I know that money will never take the place of Kevin, but it'll make their lives a little easier."

"Money." Bob snapped. "That's all this is about, isn't it?" He pointed at the casket. He looked hard at

Mac. "I have a story that could cost you all a lot more than money."

"Bob we need to talk about that." Mac said straightening his suit and trying to take control of the conversation. "You need to let go of that story, you need to forget what you know, I want you to give me all that you have on this story and give it up."

Bob glared at Mac. "Like hell I will."

"Bob this story will never go to press." Mac paused. "It's a dead matter. It's been squashed and the evidence you have will only prove to be a nuisance that can't be proven."

Bob knew Mac was right about suppressing the story. The people who owned most of the newspapers and media in the US were probably as involved as Mac was. Bob felt more helpless than when he was staring at Kevin's casket.

He turned away from Mac and was starting back. "I quit Mac, I'll send you my resignation from home."

"Bob, don't do that. We've been together too long and we can work this out." Mac wanted to say more but Bob had turned away as he heard Kathy and Amy coming back into the room.

Kathy walked in with Amy asleep over her shoulder. The baby was so peaceful and Bob was glad that she would probably never know what actually happened to her Dad. Once the girls were seated the director appeared from the side of the room.

"Are we ready?" He asked very quietly of Bob and Kathy.

Bob looked at Amy and Kathy and said, "Yes." Nodding his head.

The man motioned and his assistant entered from the back of the room and pulled back the heavy curtains uncovering the large metal doors to the crematorium.

They quietly rolled Kevin's casket over to position it in front of the doors. Kathy started to cry and hold Amy tighter. Bob held his daughter's shoulder as she sobbed. His mind was racing with the things that had transpired while she was out of the room.

The director nodded to his assistant, who opened the doors and the room filled with the faint smell of the blackened chamber. The two men centered the cart with the casket on the doors and the assistant clamped the bracket that would hold the cart in place.

Bob held his breath as the director raised the rollers on the cart to allow the men to slide the casket into the cremation chamber. They both moved to the end of the casket and prepared to slide it forward.

"Just a moment." Bob said standing up.

Kathy looked at her father through her tears, wondering what he was going to do.

"Trust me," he said squeezing her hand.

She nodded, still puzzled at her father's actions.

Bob reached down and picked up the diaper bag. He placed it on his chair and unzipped the top. He pulled the camera bag out and made a slight gesture to Mac as he walked towards the casket.

Kathy didn't see Brady and the other man get up or watch Mac stop them with a wave of his hand, she only watched her father.

Bob walked to the casket and spoke to the director. "Open it up." He said.

The director was taken by surprise. "That's quite irregular, sir." He said, in a low quiet voice.

"Don't argue. Open it up." Bob repeated looking hard into the man's eyes.

The director responded releasing the latch on the end of the casket.

Once the lid was opened a few inches Bob pulled it up to a 45-degree angle and placed the camera bag in the charred arms of his dead son in law. "Take care boy." He said closing the casket and looking back at the director. "Go ahead, do it."

The director looked at Bob angrily, but did as he was told. He and his assistant slid the casket into the cremation chamber and closed the doors. The latch closing on the doors sounded terribly loud and Bob could feel the heat on his face as he sat back down with his daughter and held her tightly.

He could hear the sound of the gas as the fire began to roar behind the doors. Kathy continued to cry as he looked back over his shoulder to glare at Mac and was surprised, but relieved to see his chair and the chairs occupied by Brady and his associate empty.

Chapter 40

The afternoon sun was warm on his face as he sipped a beer on the deck. The lake was full of boats. The weekends were always busy when the weather was as beautiful as this.

He heard a noise inside the house and Amy's voice. "Grandpa, Grandpa." She was running full speed as she came on the deck and into his arms.

"Hey, he kidded, "you'd better slow down, you'll run right into the lake." He picked her up and gave her a big hug.

"Can we go on the boat?" She asked excitedly.

"Sure we can." He answered as Kathy appeared in the doorway.

"Hi Dad, did you find your lunch?" She asked kissing him on the cheek.

"I sure did, thanks Honey." He put Amy down. "I'll get my shoes on and we'll go sailing in about fifteen minutes." He told Amy who ran off laughing and headed down to the dock.

"Don't go out until Grandpa gets there, Amy." Kathy called after her. She looked back at her dad. "That's all she talks about anymore, you and sailing."

"Hell, that's all I talk about anymore." He said heading inside the house. "Did you have a busy morning?"

"We sure did." Kathy answered "How about you?"

"Slept till nine," bob winked. "This retirement is really easy to get used to."

"Back to work!" Kathy laughed as they heard Amy yelling for Grandpa!

He headed down and out on the dock with his granddaughter holding his hand. Kathy leaned on the deck rail as she watched them climb into the little sailboat they both loved so much. She felt so secure here at the lake.

She watched as Amy and her father pushed off and the wind caught the sails as they unfurled them. Four years had gone by so quickly.

Chapter 41

Bob was sitting on the deck with Amy asleep, leaning on his shoulder. The sail and the swim after had worn her out.

Kathy finished the dinner dishes and stuck her head out the door, "Want me to take her to bed, Dad?"

"No. This feels pretty good." Bob answered.

"How about a beer?"

"Maybe one more." He answered looking at his watch.

"When she returned with the beer he took a sip and picked up his address book. He scanned the numbers and picked up his cell phone to dial, he punched in the international code and a long set of numbers.

It took a while for the call to go through. "Hello," said a woman with a quiet voice.

"Hello," Bob answered "Mildred this is Bob Shroud. How are you?"

"I'm fine, Bob, how have you been?" The woman's voice perked up.

"Enjoying retirement, Mildred, I wish I had done it five years earlier." Bob answered "Is Rupert there?"

"He sure is, Bob, let me transfer you up to the ivory tower." She started pushing some buttons and then added, "come see us!"

"I will, take care."

"Yes." Snapped a man's voice.

"Di ya think a man could get a Fosters on credit?" Bob kidded.

"Well, I'll be damned." The voice answered with a heavy Australian accent. "I thought you were dead." He laughed "Are you looking for honest work?"

"If I was looking for honest work I wouldn't be calling you, you old plagiarist." Bob answered.

The man on the other end laughed loudly. "How're you doing Bob? Coming for a visit, are you?"

"No." Bob answered, "I think I'm gonna write a book, and I'm looking for an unscrupulous publisher who doesn't care what he puts in print."

"You just wrote my résumé." The man laughed again. "Are you serious, are you really going to write a book?"

"Yes." Bob thought for a minute and looked down at his sleeping granddaughter. "I'm going to write one but it might get you sued."

"Hah." The voice joked. "You write it I'll print it. I've been sued before. I've got plenty of lawyers. What's it going to be about?" The man thought for a moment. "Hell I don't give a damn what it's about. Just send it to me and I'll have it off the press and in hard cover in a week."

"Are you sure Rupe?" Bob asked "You're probably going to piss off a lot of people in the publishing and media business up here."

"The more the merrier. There's nothing I like better than mucking up the American Press. When can I get my hands on it?"

"I wanted to talk to you before I got started." Bob got serious. "I'm going to use a pen name and I want all the proceeds that would go to me donated in your name to the U.S. Veterans Administration Hospital Systems.

"That can be arranged. Is this going to be a true story?" The voice was serious. "Are you writing some kind of expose?"

Bob looked at his granddaughter sleeping peacefully. "Let's just call it a piece of fiction that I have evidence to prove."

"I love it, Bob" The man said. "Get it over to me and call me a week later for the first copy."

"Thanks Rupe." Bob thought about his old friend. "Thanks for your help."

"Not help my friend." The man replied. "I have owed you a lot of favors for a very long time. Come see me and Mildred."

Bob hung up the phone and picked up Amy. She was getting so tall. He walked into the house and carried her up to her room. As he passed through the living room, Kathy smiled at them. "Out like a light, huh, Dad?"

"She had a busy day." He answered.

"Just put her in her bed, I'll be up in a while. Are you going to bed?" She asked.

"Not just yet." He answered "I think I'm going to write a little. I'll be in my study."

She watched him go up the stairs. He hadn't mentioned writing since Kevin died and she knew what a big part of her father's life it had been. "You did say you're going to write, didn't you?"

He looked down and smiled at his daughter. He reached the top of the stairs and turned to Amy's room. Bob gently laid the child down on her bed and covered her with a light cover and leaned down to give her a tender goodnight kiss on her forehead.

When he left the room he walked to his study door. It had been a while since he was in the room and it was a little dusty. Kathy bypassed this room at her father's request. He sat down at his desk and wiped off the keys of his old Underwood typewriter.

Thoughts of the many stories he had hammered out on the old machine before being forced to use a computer slowly filled his head. He reached over and opened a drawer on his roll top desk. The paper was waiting to be filled as Bob took a sheet and scrolled it into the old Underwood. He could feel his mind coming alive as he slid his chair closer to the desk end and his old mechanical friend.

He looked over at the articles on his desk and began to type. He centered the spacer bar. He began to type. "Bluebird, by W.W. Hill"

This is a work of fiction and any resemblance to any person or persons living or dead is purely coincidental.

As he continued to type he could imagine McVey sitting on the bank of a river or lake fishing. His fingers were humming over the keys of the old Underwood, stopping only long enough to slide the carriage back to start the next line. He smiled as he hammered away and looked over the sun setting outside his window. The sun reflected off the chrome trim on the handle of the collapsible fishing rod he had taken from the boat house. He smiled more broadly as he looked at the fingerprint sheets in the tube sticking out of the camera bag and the small stack of computer discs lying by the bag.

He thought about Fitzsimmons words. "Stage play. Everybody knew what they came there for. We just gave them the show they needed. It was our theater, a closed chamber, our crematorium, and our hand picked audience. The rest just took a little rehearsal."

He smiled and laughed a bit as he slid the carriage back to the left and realized how good his life really was.

THE END

About the Author

Ward Hill is a person who chooses to take the time to investigate events behind & below what is put forth in the modern press.

This work of fiction presents another side of what could be. Some times the cake is sweeter than the icing!

Printed in the United States
28321LVS00005B/12

9 781420 822205